continued . . .

What Looks Like Crazy

Hot Shot

"A tough-talking, in-your-face heroine . . . romantic comedy at its best."
> —Janet Evanovich, *New York Times* bestselling author

"One of the best books of the year . . . every wonderful character created by Charlotte Hughes is outstanding."
> —*Affaire de Coeur* (five stars)

"A delightful read with very real characters readers can relate to and root for."
> —*Romantic Times*

A New Attitude

"An appealing romance filled with charm and snappy dialogue."
> —*Booklist*

"With well-crafted characters and delightful banter, this is just plain fun!"
> —*Romantic Times*

Valley of the Shadow

"Hughes's snappy dialogue and strong writing aptly describe the small Southern town and its attitude toward a girl corrupted by the big city . . . An entertaining and fast-paced murder mystery."
> —*Publishers Weekly*

And After That, the Dark

"One of the Southern thrillers that never lets up and makes you unable to put it down. It's exciting enough to even give terror a good name. Charlotte Hughes is the real thing."
> —Pat Conroy, *New York Times* bestselling author

"This story and its characters will remain with you long after you've turned the last page."
> —Janet Evanovich, *New York Times* bestselling author

Jove titles by Charlotte Hughes

WHAT LOOKS LIKE CRAZY
NUTCASE
HIGH ANXIETY

HIGH ANXIETY

Charlotte Hughes

JOVE BOOKS, NEW YORK

THE BERKLEY PUBLISHING GROUP
Published by the Penguin Group
Penguin Group (USA) Inc.
375 Hudson Street, New York, New York 10014, USA
Penguin Group (Canada), 90 Eglinton Avenue East, Suite 700, Toronto, Ontario M4P 2Y3, Canada
(a division of Pearson Penguin Canada Inc.)
Penguin Books Ltd., 80 Strand, London WC2R 0RL, England
Penguin Group Ireland, 25 St. Stephen's Green, Dublin 2, Ireland (a division of Penguin Books Ltd.)
Penguin Group (Australia), 250 Camberwell Road, Camberwell, Victoria 3124, Australia
(a division of Pearson Australia Group Pty. Ltd.)
Penguin Books India Pvt. Ltd., 11 Community Centre, Panchsheel Park, New Delhi—110 017, India
Penguin Group (NZ), 67 Apollo Drive, Rosedale, North Shore 0632, New Zealand
(a division of Pearson New Zealand Ltd.)
Penguin Books (South Africa) (Pty.) Ltd., 24 Sturdee Avenue, Rosebank, Johannesburg 2196,
South Africa

Penguin Books Ltd., Registered Offices: 80 Strand, London WC2R 0RL, England

This is a work of fiction. Names, characters, places, and incidents either are the product of the author's imagination or are used fictitiously, and any resemblance to actual persons, living or dead, business establishments, events, or locales is entirely coincidental. The publisher does not have any control over and does not assume any responsibility for author or third-party websites or their content.

HIGH ANXIETY

A Jove Book / published by arrangement with the author

PRINTING HISTORY
Jove mass-market edition / January 2010

Copyright © 2010 by Charlotte Hughes.
Cover art by S. Miroque.
Cover design by Rita Frangie.

ISBN: 978-0-515-14740-7

JOVE®
Jove Books are published by The Berkley Publishing Group,
a division of Penguin Group (USA) Inc.,
375 Hudson Street, New York, New York 10014.
JOVE® is a registered trademark of Penguin Group (USA) Inc.
The "J" design is a trademark of Penguin Group (USA) Inc.

PRINTED IN THE UNITED STATES OF AMERICA

10 9 8 7 6 5 4 3 2 1

HIGH
ANXIETY

chapter 1

....

My name is Kate Holly. I'm a clinical psychologist. My patients think I'm normal. If I've told them once, I've told them a thousand times: There is *no such thing* as normal.

For example: I'm obsessive-compulsive. It started when I was ten years old, shortly after the death of my father, a fireman who never made it out of a burning building. To keep from thinking about it, I began counting things because I was really good at counting. While riding in the car I counted telephone poles and the yellow dashes in the center of the road. I also did multiplication tables in my head, taught to me by my grandfather, who was a math teacher.

So I discovered early on that numbers were safer than words, because there are some words a person should never have to hear.

I'm thirty-two years old now, and I still count things. Lately, I've caught myself washing my hands more than I should. I have tried to stop, but so far I can't quiet the urge. I'm hoping it's just a stage I'm going through.

My patients don't know that I can be as neurotic as they are. Case in point: Despite losing my father to the Fire Gods, I did what I swore I'd never do: I married a firefighter. The only excuse I have is that I fell so hard and fast for the man that I completely lost my head.

Jay Rush is and will always be the love of my life, but the three years we lived together as man and wife weren't easy. Because I'm OCD, I practically lived on the Internet, where I was able to keep up with how many firemen were injured, maimed, or killed in the U.S. every year. I set up Google Alerts so I would receive updates. I drove myself up the wall and took Jay with me. I pleaded and begged for him to give up firefighting, but I may as well have been talking to a deaf warthog for all the good it did. So the first time he became injured, I packed my bags and left.

We are now trying to work things out. I think I've come a long way. I did not freak out when he received another injury six weeks ago. I nursed him back to health. We were supposed to celebrate his full recovery that very night because he was returning to work the following morning. We'd planned dinner at our favorite restaurant, followed by lots of hot sex at my place. Only, I'd gotten sidetracked at the last minute by agreeing to sit in on an anger management group session for a colleague. And on a Sunday, to boot!

My best friend and receptionist, Mona Epps, had insisted on coming with me when I'd called to bitch and moan about it. She and her much younger boyfriend had broken up, and Mona did not like spending evenings alone. We were presently parked across the street from St. Francis Catholic Church in midtown Atlanta, where the session was to be held. The neighborhood was lower-income. Christmas and New Year's had come and gone, but some of the residents hadn't bothered to take down their lights. Mona's custom Jaguar didn't exactly blend in. She was probably the only receptionist in Atlanta who owned a Jag, not to mention a limo and a mansion with more square feet than a Walmart Supercenter, thanks to her much older late husband, Henry Epps, who'd been filthy rich.

Mona had her high-powered binoculars trained on the parking lot of St. Francis, where the members of the anger management group were arriving.

"Those people look dangerous," she said, breaking into my thoughts.

"They're not dangerous," I told her. "They just have problems expressing their anger in a healthy manner."

"If it were me, I'd pull a no-show."

"I can't do that. I promised Ruth." Ruth Melvin was the colleague who'd called from the airport. Her mother had suffered a light stroke, and Ruth was flying home. I couldn't say no. "I'm curious," I said. "Why do you keep binoculars in your car?"

She looked at me. "Don't ask."

I shrugged. I was too caught up in my own thoughts at the moment. My plan was to cut the meeting short, meet Jay for a quick dinner, and still have time for a roll in the hay afterward. I gave a little shiver of pleasure at the thought.

"I need to get over there," I said. "The meeting starts at six thirty. I plan to be out by seven fifteen."

Mona lowered her binoculars and turned to me. "You know, I'm thinking this class might be just what you need after all. You've been angry for a long time."

"I'm not angry," I said.

"This is me you're talking to, Kate. I can tell when you're angry."

"I'm not angry!" I said angrily. "If anybody has been angry, it's *you*."

"Why on earth would *I* be angry?" she asked.

"How about the fact that your love life is in the toilet right now," I said.

"I'm managing just fine."

"If you say so." To be honest, Mona and I had both been a little testy lately. We'd snapped at each other a couple of times, something we'd never done before.

Mona started the Jag and put it in gear. A moment later, we pulled beside a pickup truck with a gun rack in the back. "Uh-oh," Mona said.

I gave a huge sigh and reached for the door handle. "Let's just get this over with." We got out of the car and headed toward the church.

Ruth had told me to enter the building through a heavy wooden door at the back, pass through the dining room, and take the stairs to the basement. Mona followed me inside. The dining room held a dozen six-foot-long tables, each bearing a vase of artificial flowers. A blackboard announced an upcoming potluck dinner.

I found the stairs easily enough. "Be careful," I warned Mona as we started down the steep, narrow flight of badly scuffed steps. Naked lightbulbs dangled above our heads, casting an eerie glow against the stone walls and making me think of a dungeon. It was an old church. We reached the basement, where the paint on the concrete floor had long since faded.

Eight people—five men and three women—had arranged

their chairs in a circle. On the wall behind them hung a clock as well as a large painting of Jesus holding a lamb.

The group gave Mona and me an odd look.

"Who are you?" asked an older man with a grizzled beard. His head was completely bald and as shiny as a new appliance.

I forced a smile. "Hello," I said. "My name is Kate Holly, and this is my, um, assistant, Mona Epps. Ruth Melvin had a family emergency and asked me to take over the meeting tonight."

They looked from me to Mona and back at me as if sizing us up. I wondered if they were making comparisons, weighing Mona's blond hair and size three Versace suit against my dark hair and larger-sized Jaclyn Smith outfit. Mona ordered her clothes from New York; I bought mine straight off the racks at Kmart. Mona's footwear was designed by Prada, Jimmy Choo, and Manolo Blahnik. I wore whatever was on sale at Discount Shoes. I had long ago decided it must be fun being Mona, even on bad days.

A middle-aged man in a business suit got up and retrieved two chairs from a number of folded ones leaning against the wall. The group widened the circle as he unfolded them, making room for Mona and me. We thanked him and sat down.

"You're late," another man said, holding up one arm and tapping his wristwatch. He wore dark slacks and a blue work shirt with the logo "Hal's Tires" stitched above his left pocket. He was staring at my legs.

"Shut up, Hal," an elderly woman said. Her voice reminded me of my aunt Lou's, who smoked unfiltered cigarettes and whose vocal cords sounded as rough as burlap. A walker sat beside her, within arm's reach. An oversized purse had been tied to the handrail with a lime green scarf.

Mona and I placed our handbags beneath our chairs. I noted the time on the wall clock. Six forty. I usually asked people to introduce themselves before starting a meeting, but that would take additional time. I looked around the group. "If there is anything you'd like to share, feel free."

Dead silence. I watched the minute hand on the wall clock make a full rotation.

"You first," Hal said, leaning back in his chair, arms crossed.

I blinked. "Excuse me?"

"You come in here expecting us to spill our guts," he said. "We don't even know you. Besides," he added, "you don't seem so happy yourself."

Mona looked at me. "See? I told you. This would be a perfect opportunity to unload all your pent-up hostility."

"I don't feel hostile," I said.

Mona shrugged. "Okay, stay in denial."

My face burned. I shot her a dark look. Mona had been watching *Dr. Phil* for years—she recorded all his shows—and had become an armchair psychologist. She took careful notes, not only so she could advise my patients behind my back but because she dreamed that one day I, too, would have a TV show—called *Dr. Kate*.

"You *both* look pretty hostile to me," Hal said.

"You're wrong, Hal," Mona said. "I'm just trying to help Dr. Holly come to terms with her anger. I, personally, have no reason to be unhappy. I'm rich, and I wear a size three."

My irritation flared. I *so* wanted to tell the group that Mona had broken up with her boyfriend because of their age difference and the fact that she'd grown tired of Botox injections. "I suppose I *have* been a little irritable these past few weeks," I finally admitted. "Not to mention frustrated. But I'm feeling much better now."

"So what got your panties in a wad in the first place?" Hal asked.

I hesitated. I had not planned to slide my own dysfunctional life beneath the lens of a microscope for all to see; but, unlike Mona, who genuinely cared about me, Hal was apparently getting off on my discomfort. I refused to add to his pleasure by letting him see me squirm.

"Well, Hal," I said calmly, "my husband is a firefighter, and he recently was injured, so I've been acting as his nurse." I decided not to mention that Jay and I were actually divorced, since I *had* intended to stop the proceedings the day we were to go to court, but I'd ended up in the ER instead. Too complicated. Sort of like everything else in my life.

"You're pissed off because you had to take care of him?" Hal asked.

I read the looks of disapproval from the group. "I'm *not* pissed off," I said sharply.

"You sure as hell sound like it to me," the elderly lady said.

"All right already!" I said. "I *was* angry. And do you want to know *why* I was angry?" I didn't wait for a response. "I had hoped my husband and I could spend quality time together. I hadn't counted on all the firemen within a twenty-five-mile radius dropping by unannounced after their shifts. Who do you think got stuck picking up all those beer cans and peanut shells? Me, that's who! My husband and I barely had five minutes alone at Thanksgiving and Christmas because 'the guys' kept stopping by. So, there you have it."

Dead silence. My face flamed.

One by one, the members began to nod and clap, all of them except for the old lady with the walker. Mona threw her arms around me. "I'm so proud of you, Kate!"

I just sat there, not knowing what to say or do. But I had to admit, I felt better. "Thank you for listening," I told the group, trying to regain my composure.

A woman who appeared to be in her mid- to late forties slid forward on her chair and raised her hand haltingly. Her long red hair had been braided, and she wore a gingham dress. She looked nervous. "I would appreciate it if we didn't use foul language," she said. "After all, we're in the Lord's house."

"I completely understand," I said, then smiled. "Would you like to share?"

She hesitated. "Well, um, okay. My name is Sarah-Margaret," she said, her voice trembling. "I attend St. Francis, and I heard our church was offering this group, so I signed up. As everybody knows, my husband left me for another woman. I was devastated. And angry," she added.

She pulled a tissue from her purse and dabbed at her eyes. "But I finally realized, like Ruth said, I've only been hurting myself, so I'm trying to let go of it." She shrugged. "That's all I have to say."

"Thank you, Sarah-Margaret," I said gently. I looked at the man sitting next to her. He was casually dressed with thick salt-and-pepper-colored hair.

"I'm Ben." He gave a small wave. "Also going through a divorce. There seems to be a lot of that going around," he added with a rueful smile, "but I've pretty much come to terms with it. I don't really have anything more to share."

Then it was Hal's turn. "Hal Horton," he said and pointed to the patch over his pocket. "I own a tire company. Some of my customers can be a real pain in the ass. It's like you can't please 'em, no matter what. I had it out with one of them and—"

"He broke the man's nose," Ben said.

Hal frowned at him. "I was getting to that part. How about you mind your own damn business and let me tell my story?"

"Please," Sarah-Margaret said. "I don't feel comfortable around people who use bad language."

Hal tossed her a dark look.

I glanced at the wall clock.

"I punched the guy in the nose," Hal said. "He pressed charges. My wife told me to do something about my temper, or she was going to walk." He paused and shrugged. "Anyway, Ruth said we needed to keep a journal and write down what triggers our anger," he added.

"Did you find that helpful?" I asked.

"Yeah," Hal said with a grin. "My trigger is bitchy customers." Several people laughed.

I wondered if Hal was serious about the class or merely taking it because his wife had threatened to leave him.

"I guess I'm most likely to get angry if I'm stressed or hungry," he finally admitted.

Sarah-Margaret raised her hand. "I suggested to Hal that he keep protein bars in his desk for those days he is too busy to take a lunch break. As for me, I've started walking an hour every day. Exercise raises your endorphins. My stress level has dropped dramatically."

Hal gave a grunt. "Sarah-Margaret is our star pupil," he said, his voice edged with sarcasm. "Which is why I wonder how come she keeps attending," he added. "If you ask me, I think she and Ben are boinking each other. I think they're raising each other's endorphins, if you know what I mean."

Sarah-Margaret gasped, and her face turned the color of beets.

Ben glowered. "You know what, Hal? You're a jerk and a pig."

Hal flipped him off.

"Oh, that's real mature," Ben said. "You want to take this outside?"

"I got no problem with that," Hal replied, standing.

"Nobody is going anywhere!" I said authoritatively, deciding it was time to step in. It was clear to me by now that Hal was a bully. If it were my own group, I might have tried to work with him, but I had to admit to myself that I was just trying to get finished in time to get to dinner.

Surprisingly, Hal sat without comment.

The older woman with the smoker's voice and the walker raised her hand. Her face was mottled with age spots, and her gray hair fell to her shoulders in no particular style. She wore a denim dress and tattered white sneakers. "My name is Bea," she said, "and I'm here because my daughter-in-law is a bitch." She indicated the professionally dressed young woman beside her.

The woman's head snapped up. "I resent that remark!" she said.

Bea shrugged. "You can resent it all you like, Sandra, but you're still a bitch."

Sarah-Margaret raised her hand. "Language, please!"

"Quit your whining," Bea said to her and then looked my way. "I moved in with Sandra and my son six months ago, because I've been having trouble getting around," she said, indicating the walker. "Bad knees," she added. "But Sandra makes my life miserable."

Sandra made a sound of disgust. "We both know you were miserable long before you moved in with us. The only reason we put up with you is because your other children didn't want you."

"That's a lie!" Bea said, grabbing her walker and pulling herself to her feet. "All my kids adore me. The only reason I agreed to live with you and Brandon is because you have the biggest house, and I don't have to climb stairs."

"Brandon is the poor sucker who lives with them," Hal said. "He made them come here because they were driving him up the wall."

Bea ignored Hal. "My son is working himself into an early grave trying to pay for a fancy house, because my daughter-in-law is selfish and materialistic."

"You are the most ungrateful person I've ever met," Sandra said, "not to mention a troublemaker. You're constantly trying to drive Brandon and me apart."

Bea scoffed. "My son deserves better. You're not good enough for him."

Sandra bolted to her feet as well and planted her hands on her hips. "Listen here, you old lady," she began.

"You'd better watch your mouth," Bea said. "I am *not* old!"

"Hold it!" I said, cutting off Sandra's response. Things were quickly getting out of hand. These two had anger down to a T. It was the management part they lacked. Time for me to reel them in. "Perhaps it would be a good idea if we all calmed down and took some deep breaths."

Sandra ignored me as she focused her attention on her mother-in-law. "All you do is watch game shows while Brandon and I support you," she went on. "You're eating us out of house and home. Your room is a pigsty, and you don't even bathe on a regular basis. I'm surprised Brandon turned out so well, considering his mother lives like white trash."

"Who are you calling trash?"

Sandra looked at me. "She smokes in the house when we're at work, even though we've asked her not to. She even keeps a gun under her pillow. Brandon and I certainly do *not* approve of weapons!"

"Deep breath," I said loudly.

"Maybe it's time I let you have a good look at my gun!" Bea said, snatching a pistol from her pocketbook and aiming it at her daughter-in-law.

Fear hit me like a brick. "No!" I yelled, jumping up as everybody in the group, including Sandra, ducked. I made a mad dive toward Bea, trying to wrestle the gun from her hand. Hal grasped her from behind, and I pulled the pistol free. Somehow, my finger accidentally hit the trigger, and a deafening shot rang out, followed by the sound of screams and splintering glass.

Sandra disappeared up the stairs.

Bea swung her walker hard, and its legs slammed against Hal's shins. He yowled. Ben joined in the scuffle, trying to contain the woman, who was obviously not as frail as she appeared.

"Oh, my God!" Sarah-Margaret screamed at me. "You shot Jesus!"

I glanced over my shoulder. The large picture of Jesus holding the lamb lay shattered on the floor.

I didn't have time to think about it, even as Sarah-Margaret staggered toward it, wailing.

"Somebody call nine-one-one!" I shouted. I sank onto my chair, put the gun on the floor at my feet, and waited. I suspected I was going to miss dinner after all.

chapter 2

....

Two policemen arrived within minutes, their weapons drawn. "Everybody on the floor!" one of them shouted, his voice ricocheting off the walls. His name tag read Benton. "Facedown, hands behind your heads!"

The other officer kicked Bea's pistol aside. "On the floor!" he echoed loudly. "Now!"

We hit the floor. Everyone but Bea, who claimed she was too old.

Sarah-Margaret lay prostrate on the concrete, still sobbing. "You don't understand!" she cried. "She shot Jeeee-sus."

Instinct told me that managing her anger was the least of Sarah-Margaret's problems. The woman obviously had a loose screw.

Beside me, Mona gave a huge sigh. "This could only happen to us."

A lone reporter who had followed the police inside began snapping pictures.

I raised my hand as Benton glanced my way. "I can explain," I said.

He regarded me. "This better be good."

I told him my name and why I was there. "The lady with the walker tried to shoot her daughter-in-law," I said.

Bea scowled at me. "Rat fink."

"It's true," Ben said. "Dr. Holly risked her life grabbing the gun from the old lady, but it accidentally went off in the process." The other members nodded in agreement.

"She's a hero," the businessman added.

The reporter snapped my picture.

"Everybody stay put," Benton said as his partner frisked Bea.

She glared at him. "Pervert! I'll bet you get off feeling up senior citizens."

"You're under arrest," he said, cuffing her and spouting her Miranda rights.

"You can't arrest me!" she said. "I'm too old to go to jail."

"You should have thought of that before you tried to shoot somebody," he said.

Benton bagged the pistol. "Everybody can get up and take your seats now," he said, "but nobody leaves the room until we get a full report from every one of you."

We reclaimed our chairs. Sarah-Margaret had stopped wailing, but it had given her a bad case of hiccups. She sank onto her chair, holding the framed picture of Jesus, minus the glass. Two more officers arrived; Bea cursed mightily as they all but carried her up the stairs.

"Is it okay if I make a call?" I asked Benton, who nodded. I called Jay and gave him a brief rundown of events, skipping the part where I'd actually rushed Bea and caused the gun to go off. Jay had been known to criticize me in the past for getting mixed up with crazies; I didn't want to give him any ammunition.

"Damn, Katie, are you okay?" he asked. "Should I come and get you?"

"There's no need. Mona will drop me off at the shopping center where I left my car. Unfortunately, I can't leave until I give some kind of statement. I probably won't be finished in time to meet you for dinner," I ended on a sigh.

"There's always tomorrow night, babe," he said. "I just want you to be safe."

I hung up and waited for my turn to answer questions. Thankfully, Mona and I were among the first to finish. Still, it was after eight thirty by the time we were allowed to leave. Mona was not happy.

"My brand-new outfit is filthy from lying on the floor, and I scuffed the toe of my Jimmy Choo!" she said. "And would you look at this?" She held up her thumb. "My nail is broken, and I just had them done yesterday!"

I felt bad. Not only did Mona spend a fortune on her clothes and shoes, she took pride in her nails. I couldn't blame her for being annoyed. Trouble seemed to follow me wherever I went. I drew the disturbed, the deranged, and the dangerous like a magnet. If I were a cat, I would have already used up about half of my nine lives.

Mona and I were quiet on the drive back to my car. We mumbled a quick good night to each other as I climbed out of her Jag. She drove away before I had a chance to unlock the door to my car and climb in. That was unlike her. Like me, she always waited to make certain I was safely locked inside my vehicle with the motor running before she went on.

Traffic was light, and I made it home in record time. Jay and my dog, Mike, met me at the car. Mike wagged her tail frantically as Jay pulled me into his arms, enveloping me in his warmth and the scent of his aftershave.

"I'm glad you're okay," he said.

I wasn't *really* okay, but I decided to fake it. In her excitement, Mike began spinning in circles like a top. Finally, I reached down and petted her. I had bathed and brushed her the night before, but she was still the same wiry-haired stray who would never win a beauty contest. I'd let her inside during a thunderstorm some months back, thinking at the time that she was a he. She'd proved me wrong by delivering five puppies in my laundry room. Nevertheless, we'd bonded, and I often wondered what I would do without her. I could whine and even throw myself a pity party now and then, and it would remain our secret.

"How about I whip up a couple of omelets?" Jay suggested, once we went inside the house.

"That sounds great," I said, hoping I could hold food down. I dropped my purse on top of the TV, which was tuned to CNN. A reporter was covering a wildfire that had struck the drought-ridden Apalachicola National Forest in Tallahassee, Florida, the week before. So far, more than fifty thousand acres had burned. It was all people could talk about. They still remembered the monster fire in 2007 that lasted for months and had burned more than 500,000 acres in southern Georgia and northern Florida. It had devastated the Okefenokee Swamp and destroyed hundreds of homes.

Jay had been among the firefighters who'd worked the fire.

"Reinforcements have been called in from neighboring states," he said.

"Have they managed to contain any of the blaze?" I asked.

He shook his head. "High winds are whipping it all over the place. What they need is rain, and lots of it."

"Has the weather forecast changed at all?"

"Nope. Doesn't look like we can count on even a drizzle."

I felt awful for the people whose lives were being affected by the fire, knowing many would probably lose their homes, but I was too frazzled at the moment to think about it and start feeling worse. I headed straight to the bathroom and washed my hands twice. I'd heard an expert on TV tell viewers that the only sure way to free your hands from germs was to use antibacterial soap and scrub long enough to sing "Happy Birthday" twice. I preferred to run through a set of multiplication tables.

I went into the kitchen and grabbed a chair at the table. Mike exited through her doggie door, obviously needing to do her business. Jay poured me a glass of wine. "This might help you relax," he said, leaning over to kiss me on the top of my head.

"Thanks," I said and gave him my best smile. I wondered if Mona was okay.

Mike returned after a few minutes and plopped down beside me, resting her head on my foot as though sensing I was troubled.

Jay shoved the sleeves of his sweater to his elbows and pulled an onion, some fresh jalapeño peppers, a large tomato, and chopped pieces of ham from my refrigerator. He kept my refrigerator stocked these days; it had come about after he'd tasted one of the frozen dinners I often dined on.

I watched him move about my kitchen easily, rinsing, chopping, sautéing. Jay had learned to cook after becoming a firefighter. They made their own meals at the station, and most of the guys were pretty decent at the stove. Unfortunately, they seldom finished eating the meal before the bell sounded and off they went.

I continued to watch Jay as he cooked. I loved watching him. Although he had healed remarkably well from his injuries, I knew there was still some soreness because I saw him wince now and then when he moved a certain way. He never complained, though.

"Hey," I said, suddenly feeling nostalgic. "Do you remember the first time we saw each other?"

He glanced at me, wearing a half grin. "Yeah, you were the scrawniest eight-year-old kid I'd ever laid eyes on. And I was thirteen and already fighting the girls off with a stick."

"Not *that* time," I said, remembering the incident, a picnic where dozens of firefighters had congregated with their families. Jay's father had worked at the same engine company as mine. As with most companies, there was a strong sense of camaraderie, a bond among the men. They and their families celebrated birthdays, graduations, weddings, holidays, and summer cookouts together. I'd developed a schoolgirl crush on Jay early on.

"I'm talking about when we ran into each other at that alehouse. As adults," I added. I had finished grad school and was working at the mental health center at the time. I'd been so naïve, thinking I could make a monumental difference in the lives of those who needed the most help. Unfortunately, I'd spent more time filling out paperwork and attending meetings than I had seeing patients.

"Oh, yeah, Paddy's Alehouse," Jay said after a moment, "the premier hangout for off-duty firefighters."

"All of you were celebrating your promotion to captain that night," I reminded him.

"Uh-huh. Only, once I laid eyes on you, I sort of forgot about everything else."

I remembered how our gazes had met in the crowded bar where I'd gone with coworkers to celebrate a supervisor's retirement. I'd felt a shiver along my spine as Jay's lips had curved into the sexiest smile I'd ever seen on a man. The next thing I knew, he was standing next to me.

"Little Katie Holly," he'd said. "All grown up."

I couldn't believe he had recognized me.

"Did you know then that we were going to end up together?" I asked.

"Sure did," he said. "It was just a matter of time."

"Really?"

"Yup. I knew that night, as a matter of fact."

"How did you know?"

Jay gave me a look. "Babe, come on. It was meant to be."

He was right. For me, it was the closest thing to love at first sight. "Do you remember our first date?"

"Sure do. We ate barbecue. You wore a yellow dress with tiny blue flowers on it." He glanced at me. "You didn't think I would remember that, did you?" He didn't wait for me to answer. "You shared a stick of gum with me later. When I kissed you, you tasted like Juicy Fruit."

I smiled. I vaguely remembered him commenting on it. That kiss had knocked me off my feet.

"When did you know you were in love with me?" I asked.

"After I dropped you off at the end of the evening," he said. "I drove around for a couple of hours afterward. Couldn't get you off my mind," he added. "Couldn't wait to ask you out again."

He'd called me at six a.m. the following morning and invited me to a shrimp boil that the guys from work had planned the following weekend, and I was immediately embraced by his friends and colleagues. We agreed to date exclusively. I was smitten. A month later, we spent the weekend in Savannah, where we'd made love for the first time. It had sealed the deal for me. We still visited Savannah from time to time for long weekends just to recapture the magic we'd shared the first time.

It wasn't until after our wedding, a Caribbean honeymoon, and my move into his loft that the full impact of what I'd done hit me. I had sworn I would never marry a firefighter and risk going through what my mother and I had gone through when my father died. But that's just what I had done. And *that's* when the problems between Jay and me began.

Before long, the room was filled with mouthwatering smells. I finished my wine and carried the glass to the sink as Jay placed the omelets on the table, along with a short stack of toast. "Dig in," he said, joining me. Mike got up and went into the laundry room, where she began eating her own dinner from a bowl with the word *Diva* painted on it.

"Thank you for going to all the trouble," I told Jay.

"It's the least I can do for my favorite gal." He smiled.

His blue sweater was the same color as his eyes, which was why I'd chosen it as one of his Christmas gifts. It enhanced his dark hair and olive complexion. I sometimes wondered what our children would look like. I wondered what it would be like to carry Jay's baby. The mere thought warmed my belly and gave me goose bumps.

While we ate, Jay gave me the latest on *General Hospital*. He'd become a fan during his convalescence, as had the guys who'd visited during that hour. Word spread. Half the engine houses in Atlanta had the TVs turned to *General Hospital* come three p.m., and the firefighters complained bitterly if they got a call before it ended. They'd counted on Jay to fill them in.

The wine had settled my stomach. "This is delicious," I said. "I didn't realize how hungry I was."

"I'll bet you skipped breakfast and lunch."

"Nope. I chose a healthy snack from one of the vending machines."

"Hmm. I didn't know the words *healthy* and *vending machine* could be used in the same sentence." He sat back in his chair. "So, do you want to talk about it?"

I knew he wasn't referring to vending machines. "The woman with the pistol was old and on a walker," I said. "Can you believe it?"

"Nothing surprises me these days."

"She wanted to take out her daughter-in-law. Fortunately, the young woman escaped."

"How?"

"Um, well, the bullet missed her. It hit a picture on the wall instead. It all happened so fast, you know? Like a movie played on fast-forward. Everyone reached for their cell phones and dialed nine-one-one. The police arrived within minutes. They arrested the old lady, thank goodness. She could use a little jail time. I hope they throw away the key. Of course, Mona got a scratch on her shoe and broke a nail, so she's not happy with me right now.

I'll bet a good shoe repairman could do something about that scratch, though."

I suddenly noticed Jay was looking at me oddly, and I realized I was babbling. If people babble, you know they're not giving you all the facts.

"Thank God nobody was hurt," Jay said, covering my hand.

We finished our dinner. I stood and began to clear the table.

"I'm pulling kitchen duty tonight," Jay said, taking my hand. "You've spent enough time taking care of other people, including me." He led me upstairs and into the bathroom, where he turned on the water in the tub and added my favorite lavender bath salts.

"You really know how to spoil a girl," I said. My voice shook, and the backs of my eyes burned. My emotions were raw.

"Oh, Katie," he said, gathering me close.

"I guess I'm suffering aftershocks." I tried to laugh it off but did a poor job.

Jay continued to hold me as the tub filled with water. I prayed it would stay hot, because hot water in my house was a miracle akin to the parting of the Red Sea. Then, slowly and tenderly, he undressed me, kissing my bare shoulders, the hollow of my throat, my breasts. He helped me into the tub, and I gave a sigh of pleasure as the water enveloped me.

I thanked Mad Ethel, the name I'd given my house, for the hot water. I had named my house Mad Ethel after experiencing her mood swings. If she was having a good day, she gave me hot water and other things I've learned not to take for granted. On a bad day, fuses blew, the air and heat went MIA, pipes leaked, and there was barely enough hot water to brush my teeth. But my rent was cheap by Atlanta's standards, so I kept my mouth shut when my landlord came around.

"I'll be back as soon as I straighten the kitchen and set up the coffeemaker for morning," Jay said as he headed out of the bathroom.

I leaned back in the tub and closed my eyes. I thought of Mona again, and I suspected she'd driven straight to the mall. Mona dealt with stress by shopping. I knew her decision to break things off with her boyfriend, the med student, had been difficult, but she had not wanted to arrange her life around a doctor's schedule. Plus, she didn't enjoy hearing about perforated organs at the dinner table, and perforations of all kinds seemed to play a big role in the life of a physician.

Jay returned and slipped off his clothes. He slid into the tub behind me and pulled me onto his lap, and we fit together like human puzzle pieces. He picked up what he called my girl soap and fat sponge and worked up a thick lather. He washed my back, my neck, and my arms before reaching around to my breasts.

Despite being weary with fatigue, my body responded. My belly warmed. Jay dropped the soap and sponge into the tub and slipped one hand between my thighs. All my nerve endings did happy dances when he touched me, and the hairs on the back of my neck stood like flagpoles when he pressed his lips at the base of my head. He stroked me. He found what he called my magic button, and his fingertips played it like an instrument. From behind my closed eyelids, I imagined the music filling me and the tempo building, vibrating, pulsing. I felt the crash of cymbals, and my song was so rich and sweet and perfect that it brought hot tears to the backs of my eyes.

Our bodies were still damp when we lay down in bed. Jay's lips touched me, and I was once again caught up in the same physical and emotional magic that only he could evoke. The coming together of two souls that recognized and celebrated each other. Jay filled me exquisitely, and we clung to each other and rode the sensations, our mouths and bodies fused. Afterward, he dragged the covers over us and gathered me close. I sank against his heat, feeling safe for the first time since I'd left the church.

"This is way so much better than shopping," I said before sleep carried me away.

Monday morning came too soon for me. The room was still dark when I opened my eyes and found Jay's side of the bed empty. Six thirty a.m. A snoring Mike lay on her back at the foot of the bed, full belly frontal. Jay called it her "Playmate of the Year" look. I stumbled downstairs and was surprised to find him already dressed for work and sipping coffee in front of the television set. He turned the volume down and smiled at me, but I saw the concern in his eyes.

"What's the latest on the fire?" I said, trying to speak around a wide yawn. I sat next to him and reached for his cup.

"It's not good. The wind shifted during the night and sent at least a dozen firefighters to the hospital for smoke inhalation."

I met his gaze.

"No casualties," he said, as though reading my mind.

I sipped his coffee and stared at the screen where a CNN reporter was questioning a fire official. The aerial shots showed the mounting destruction; the flames seemed to lick the heavens. Dozens upon dozens of fire trucks, rescue vehicles, and patrol cars skirted the area, but they resembled toys when compared to the vast ocean of blaze.

Even so, I knew it could get worse.

"How many firefighters are working it?" I asked.

Jay took a sip of his coffee. "Not nearly enough," he said.

I heard the tension in his voice and knew he was imagining what the crews were going through. It was his natural instinct to want to help, but with it being his first day back to work after his injury, he would be on light duty for a while. I was thankful for that, at least.

"How are you feeling?" I asked. "Are you sure you're up to going in?"

He grinned. "If I start feeling bad, I'll dive into the nearest phone booth and slip into my action-hero suit." He gave me a tender kiss. "Did I remember to thank you for nursing me back to health and putting up with my buddies?"

"Last night was a good start."

When I arrived at my office, I went immediately to the small kitchenette in back and put on a pot of coffee. Then I checked my phone messages. A reporter from the *Atlanta Journal-Constitution* had called. He asked me to call him back and left his number. I figured it was related to the shooting the night before and ignored it.

Twenty minutes passed, and I was surprised that Mona hadn't showed. I was about to call her when the phone rang, and she spoke from the other end.

"I've got hives," she said.

"Uh-oh. How bad?"

"Really bad. I used to get them as a kid, so I know how much worse they can get."

"I'm sorry," I said, knowing stress often played a significant role in hives and that I was partially responsible. I should have insisted on going to the anger management group alone. "Is there anything I can do? Would you like for me to take you to the doctor?"

"No. But I can't come into the office looking like I do. You won't have anyone to answer the phone."

"That's why they invented the answering machine," I said.

"It's not just the phones I'm concerned about," she said. "Some of your patients are very jittery when they first come in. I don't like the thought of them walking into an empty reception room. Especially those with abandonment issues," she added.

"That's very thoughtful of you, Mona."

"And what about those with poor self-esteem? Or those with PTSD?" she added. "Kate, these people need to see a smiling face when they arrive."

"I'll try not to let my sessions run over and keep them waiting," I said, although Mona and I both knew there were times it was unavoidable, especially when the patient I was seeing at the time was in crisis.

"Maybe you should hire someone from a temp agency. I know it's costly, but I think it would be money well spent."

I wasn't surprised Mona was so concerned. She had developed a close relationship with a number of my patients, which was why they often told her all their problems before they saw me. Mona then drew on her vast knowledge of psychotherapy from watching *Dr. Phil* and advised them. I had reminded her many times that *I* was the psychologist and it was *my* job to counsel those seeking therapy.

"Please try not to worry," I repeated. "It will only make your hives worse."

And I would end up feeling guiltier than I already felt.

I was still feeling bad for Mona when my first appointment arrived. I'd been seeing Julie Newman for less than a month. She was an attractive woman in her midthirties who worked in advertising. She suffered from borderline personality disorder. I had treated several other borderlines, so I'd recognized the symptoms in Julie right away.

Minor stresses, like discovering the salad dressing in her refrigerator was past the expiration date, could ruin her day, so high anxiety threatened to send her completely over the edge. All she knew of the world was based on her feelings and was not necessarily rational.

I noted the tension in the lines on either side of her mouth and eyes. "How was your week?" I asked.

She shook her head. "I just learned yesterday that the company I work for is downsizing. I'm sure my name is at the top of the list of those who will be laid off." She paused and took a deep, shaky breath. "I paced the floor until all hours last night. I think it would be better to go ahead and resign instead of living in constant dread. Also, it would be less humiliating."

I gave an inward sigh. Borderlines were great at self-sabotage. "Didn't you tell me a couple of weeks ago that you landed a big account, and you received a substantial bonus as a result?"

"Well, yes, but—"

"Why would your company fire one of their top producers?"

She seemed to ponder it.

"You can't afford to let yourself get caught up in a worry cycle," I said, "and risk acting impulsively. You need to channel that energy into winning more accounts."

"So, you think I'm overreacting?"

Duh. "What do you think?"

"I know I often turn everything into a major catastrophe," she said finally, "but what if—"

"What if they *don't* fire you?" I cut in.

"I guess I have a habit of thinking the worst."

"You can change those habits, Julie. You can turn negative, self-defeating thoughts and behaviors into more realistic and positive ones, but it's going to take practice." I realized I sounded like an infomercial. "It can be done," I added.

"I've been like this my whole life. I don't think I'll ever change."

"It depends on how much you want it. Did you make the list I suggested during your last visit?"

"I haven't had time."

"You need to make time. On one side I want you to write down the negative feelings that are making you so anxious and depressed about your job. The worst-case scenario, so to speak," I added. "On the other side, I'd like for you to write down several possible outcomes that are more likely to happen. I want you to do the same thing each time you start dwelling on how terrible something feels."

"I suppose I could do that, even though I don't know what it would accomplish."

"Writing down your fears takes some of the power out of them, and you'll be able to see how, in the end, most of your fears are illogical."

"I guess that makes sense."

"Oh, and don't forget to bring the list to your next appointment so we can go through it."

She took a deep breath. "I always feel so much better when I talk to you, Dr. Holly. You help me put things in perspective. I don't know why I do this to myself."

"In time you'll do it less and less," I promised.

Julie and I finished up, and I saw her out, only to find a TV crew waiting in my reception room. Julie shot me a funny look as she left.

A stately blonde holding a microphone stepped forward. "Dr. Holly?" she said.

"Yes?"

She held out her free hand. "I'm Blair Willow from—"

"I know who you are," I said, taking her hand and shaking it. "I've seen you many times on the six-o'clock news."

She looked pleased. "I tried to call but got your answering machine. I'd like to ask you a couple of questions about the shooting incident last night at St. Francis Catholic Church."

A bright light hit my eyes, and I winced. "I can't discuss it," I said, "for patient confidentiality reasons." I tried to shield my eyes from the light. "Perhaps you could get information from the police."

"Oh, but we wanted to meet you in person," Blair said. "You're being hailed as a hero for what you did. Had you not wrestled the gun away from—" She paused and looked at her notes. "From Beatrice Sully," she said, "her daughter-in-law could have been fatally shot."

"Again, I can't comment one way or the other." I wanted to end the interview. Even if Jay didn't see it on the news, someone at the station would. I looked at the cameraman. "Would you mind turning off that light?"

Blair did not look happy; in fact, she looked as though she could chew the legs off my chairs. Obviously, she was accustomed to getting her way.

"One last question, Dr. Holly," she said, and I could almost swear I saw a sneer cross her lips. "Is it true that you fired the pistol at a picture of Jesus on purpose, and that you're an atheist?"

I was stunned by the question, especially since it had been asked by a professional. "Have a nice day, Miss Willow," I said. I went inside my office and closed the door. I counted the pens in my oversized "Atlanta" coffee mug and was relieved to find an even number.

chapter 3

....

My next patient, Ann Ross, suffered from depression. It began shortly after her youngest child left for college, and the woman discovered that she and her husband of twenty-five years had little in common. It was not unusual for couples to drift apart after spending much of their lives focusing on family and career. In fact, it was fairly normal, and I had stressed as much to Ann countless times, to no avail.

"I have to force myself to get out of the bed in the morning," she confessed, mopping her tears with a tissue. "Now that the children are grown, I don't seem to have a purpose."

She and I had discussed the possibility of her going on an antidepressant until she felt better, but she wanted to try to get through it without medication. "I know you're sad and tired," I said gently, "because depression does that to a person. But if you'll recall, last week we agreed it might be fun for you to take up golf or tennis again." She and her husband had enjoyed playing both early in their marriage.

"It has been so long," she said. "I'm sure I'm quite rusty. I would be self-conscious. I would embarrass myself."

"So take lessons," I said. "You can recapture some of the fun you and your husband shared before the children. And the fresh air, sunlight, and exercise will do you good."

She sighed.

"If you continue to sit in your house and think about how bad you feel, it's only going to get worse. It doesn't have to be that way, because you're not clinically depressed, Ann. It *will* lift," I said, "but you're going to have to do your part." I leaned closer and touched her shoulder, trying to draw her attention so that she could allow my words to seep into the fog that clouded her world.

"You know how it feels when it rains for several days and you think the sun is never going to come out again and everything seems dire and gloomy?"

"Yes."

"The sun will come out again. I promise. You need to do whatever it takes to make that happen."

She nodded, and I saw hope in her eyes.

I finished seeing patients later than usual. On the way home, I swung by a fast-food restaurant for burgers and fries. I always ordered Mike's burger plain. I arrived home and was surprised to find Jay's SUV in the driveway, since he worked twenty-four hours on and forty-eight hours off. I wondered if he'd started feeling bad at work, although it was unlike him to admit it to anyone.

Mike greeted me at the front door. Jay barely acknowledged me from the sofa; his eyes were trained on the television, no doubt checking the status of the wildfire. He
held a newspaper in his hand. Finally, he turned off the
TV and regarded me. He didn't look happy.

"What's wrong?" I asked, thinking the fire must've worsened.

"You were on the six-o'clock news."

I gave a mental gulp. "Really?"

He held up the newspaper. "There's even an article about
you in the paper. Seems you're a real hero," he added.

"You can't believe everything you read, Jay," I said.
"They probably said I was an atheist, too."

"You lied to me."

I shook my head. "I never—"

"You lied by way of omission. You had no intention of
telling me what really happened at that meeting."

"That's not true. I was just waiting for the right moment."

"Last night would have been a perfect time."

"I was too upset to talk about it."

"You were upset, and it didn't occur to you to come to
me?"

"I knew you'd get angry," I said finally. "I just couldn't
deal with that after what I'd already been through."

He tossed the paper aside, stood, and walked into the
kitchen.

I followed. "She wasn't pointing the gun at me, Jay," I
said. "She'd intended to shoot her daughter-in-law."

"Kate, you *stepped* in front of a person holding a loaded
weapon. That is just plain stupid, and you damn well know
it."

"You're saying I should have done nothing?"

"Why is it always up to you to save the day?" he demanded. "Do you have any clue what a thirty-eight can do at point-blank range? Or did you even stop to consider what a person's guts look like once they're splattered to hell and back?" He didn't wait for a response. "The obvious answer is no. And that's where we have a big problem."

I tried to think of a good defense. I considered bringing up the fact that his job had given me a lot of sleepless nights, but the gray duffel bag sitting beside the back door caught my attention before I could do so.

"Are you going somewhere?"

"They need additional men in Florida."

"But you've barely had time to heal," I said. "Why can't you send someone else?"

"I've had experience with wildfires."

As if I needed to be reminded. "But Jay—"

"I've already made up my mind, Kate. I'm only telling you out of courtesy."

My old fears slapped me in the face. "You could have discussed it with me first," I said.

He looked incredulous. "You really think you're in the position to point a finger?"

I didn't try to hide my annoyance. "Give me a break, Jay," I said. "This has nothing to do with me holding back on you last night. You've been itching to get involved with that fire since it started. At least give me some credit for knowing you."

"Then you clearly have the advantage, because there are times when I don't think I know you at all. This happens to be one of them." He wiped both hands down his face. "I'm tired of dealing with your life-and-death dramas."

"Gee, like I don't know how that feels every time you run into a burning building," I said, feeling hurt.

"There's a big difference," he said. "I know what the hell I'm doing. I follow a plan of operation and don't act impulsively. You just jump into dangerous situations with both feet, and to hell with the consequences."

"Oh, right," I said. "You're a real pro. That's why you've been laid up here for six weeks surrounded by all your drinking buddies." I regretted the words the minute they left my mouth.

Jay's face hardened. "I think we've said enough." He picked up the duffel bag and opened the back door.

A wave of panic hit me. "Do you know when you'll be back?"

"When the fire is out," he said. He stepped outside.

The absolute last thing I wanted was for him to leave angry. "Jay, wait."

He turned. "I have to go. I'm meeting a couple of guys so we can ride down together. We've got a four-and-a-half-hour drive ahead of us. I'm already late."

"At least promise to call so I'll know you're okay."

He nodded and closed the door behind him.

I realized I was still holding my purse and the fast-food bag. I slumped in a kitchen chair. Mike's tail thumped wildly as she stared at the bag. She could smell a hamburger before I pulled into the driveway. "How can you eat at a time like this?" I said. "Can't you see I'm in crisis?" I pulled out our food, removed the wrapper on her burger, and handed it to her. She wolfed it down, then stared at my food. I gave her a French fry. I continued to feed them to her as I sipped my soft drink and tried not to feel miserable.

I'd known all along that Jay would be upset when he

learned what had really happened in the anger management group. I'd made it worse by not telling him myself, but even then he would have been mad as hell. There was no way to win, which was probably the reason I hadn't moved back into the loft we had shared before our split.

As if that weren't bad enough, my best friend was battling a case of hives brought on, at least in part, by what Jay had referred to as my drama.

Mike gave a sudden loud belch, and I could almost swear she looked as surprised as I was at the sound. For some reason I found it incredibly funny, and I burst into laughter. I petted her. It felt good to laugh after the harsh words Jay and I had shared, because I knew I was this close to having the mother of all pity parties, and I wasn't sure I had the energy. Besides, it wasn't all bad. My dog loved me, and that had to mean something.

I left my uneaten burger on the table and went upstairs. I changed into my favorite jeans and a sweatshirt, then stuffed my feet into fuzzy bedroom slippers.

I returned to the kitchen, took a bite of my cold burger, and tossed the rest into the trash. If I got really hungry, I could always nuke one of my cardboard-tasting frozen meals. The doorbell rang. I checked the peephole and gave a huge sigh of dread at the sight of my neighbor, Bitsy Stout. She was a religious fanatic who firmly believed I was hell-bound because I refused to attend her church, where the minister brought his congregation to salvation by preaching hellfire and damnation. I decided not to answer the door.

"Kate Holly, you open this door!" Bitsy called out loudly. "I know you're in there, and I'm not leaving, even if I have to camp out in front of your house."

I knew she meant it. I unlocked the door and opened it.

"Bitsy, what a surprise," I said. I noticed the newspaper in her hand.

She didn't look any happier to see me than I was to see her. She shook the newspaper in my face. "So, this is the thanks I get for saving your life," she said. "If I'd known you were an atheist, I wouldn't have bothered."

I stood there and let her rant. In all honesty, she *had* saved my life when I found myself in yet another life-and-death situation one night, but only because she'd been skulking about my yard dropping piles of dog poop across my lawn that she swore Mike had left on hers. She'd heard the commotion going on inside my kitchen and raced home to call 911 and grab her pellet gun.

Bitsy finally stopped long enough to draw breath.

"I'm not an atheist," I finally said, wishing I could smack that mousy Sarah-Margaret for starting the rumor. I would have loved to show *her* how I managed *my* anger.

"It says so right here," Bitsy said, indicating the newspaper. She shoved the page in my face. The photo showed me facedown on the basement floor at St. Francis, my hands folded at the back of my head.

"Oh, gur-reat," I muttered.

"We have *never* had an atheist in our neighborhood. Our property values are going to drop because of you. Even worse, you're doomed for all eternity. What do you have to say to *that*?"

"I would have to say that is the most unflattering photo anyone has ever taken of me. I should call the newspaper and complain."

"You can make all the jokes you want," Bitsy said, "but it's not going to be a bit funny when the devil gets his hands on you." She gave a huff, turned, and marched away.

I closed the door, locked it, and lay on my sofa. Now I was *certain* the day couldn't get worse.

Then I heard it: the rumble of a truck. I moaned out loud. I knew the day was about to get as bad as it could.

I got up and pulled the curtain aside just as my mother's bright red 2007 Navistar CXT monster pickup truck pulled into my driveway. My aunt sat in the passenger seat. The back of the truck was piled high with junk that would ultimately be repaired, painted, or turned into artwork and sold for a ridiculously high price at their studio in Little Five Points.

My mother and aunt climbed from the truck. They had been junk collectors for as long as I could remember, earning the name the Junk Sisters. They knew the location of every Dumpster in Atlanta. They visited the swankiest neighborhoods on trash day in hopes that somebody had thrown out something that could be turned into art. I had been teased unmercifully in school for being part of this family.

They headed toward my front door, two plus-sized identical twins who still dressed alike despite being in their fifties. My grandmother had chosen to name them Dixie and Trixie. They wore their signature overalls—today's color was lemon yellow. Their platinum tresses had been teased and lacquered so that not even hurricane winds could blow their hairdos out of place.

The doorbell rang. I considered not answering it, but I knew my mother would assume I was dead and call the police or break a window and climb through. I opened the door.

"Are you crazy?!" my mother shouted as she and my aunt stepped inside my living room. "Have you lost your d-a-m-n mind?"

My mother spelled out curse words because she thought the man upstairs wouldn't enter them into the Book of Sins if she didn't actually say them outright.

I waited, knowing what was to come.

"We saw the whole thing on the six-o'clock news," Aunt Trixie said, giving me a grim look. She knew I was in for trouble.

"You actually wrestled a thirty-eight from a woman to keep her from shooting someone?" my mother said. "Do you know how dumb that was? What if you'd been shot? I would be talking to a dead person right now. How would that make you feel?"

"Terrible," I said, knowing she wouldn't be happy until she had delivered her daily dose of guilt. I tried to look remorseful.

"That's *all* you have to say for yourself?" she demanded.

"Dixie, you're getting all worked up for no good reason," Aunt Trixie said. "As you can see, Kate is perfectly fine."

My mother looked me over. "And when did you become an atheist? Are you trying to give me a heart attack? Because you almost succeeded," she added. "I'm surprised I'm not in the CCU fighting for my life."

My mother's heart was perfectly fine, so I felt certain she would live another day to chastise me for my behavior. "Mom, I'm not an atheist," I said as calmly as I could.

She walked over to a chair and plopped down. "No mother should have to live like this. I never know if my only child is going to be maimed or murdered by some wacko she's treating. Even worse, I had to hear about it on the news. You couldn't be bothered to pick up the phone?"

"You should be proud of Kate," Aunt Trixie said. "Everybody is calling her a hero."

I smiled at my aunt. She was the peacemaker in our family. I motioned for her to sit.

My mother looked me up and down. "Why are you dressed like a slob? I hope you're not letting yourself go now that you and Jay seem to be working out your problems."

"Dixie, would you shut up?" Trixie said. "You've done nothing but badger Kate since we walked through the door."

My mother gaped at her. It was seldom that Aunt Trixie took her to task. Finally, my mother sucked in a deep breath. "Where *is* Jay, by the way?" she asked.

I joined my aunt on the sofa. "He's headed south to help with the wildfire," I said.

She looked surprised. "Do you think he's up to it?"

"He seems to have healed nicely." I had no intention of telling her about our argument.

"I heard they were calling in additional firemen," Aunt Trixie said. "Everybody is terrified that it's going to be as bad as the one in 2007. They're saying somebody's campfire got out of hand and started it."

"I can't believe you let Jay go," my mother said.

I looked at her. "Since when have I had any control over his decisions?"

My aunt suddenly snapped her fingers. "Oh, goodness gracious, Dixie," she said. "We haven't told Kate our exciting news." She looked at me. "We bought an old trunk at an estate sale last week," she said. "And guess what? While we were cleaning it yesterday we found a secret compartment. Guess what was in it?"

"Money?" I asked.

"Love letters!" she said.

"Written during World War Two," my mother added. "The man, John Smith, was a young naval officer at the time, and the young lady was a schoolteacher. Her name was Lenore Brown. Their last names are so common that it would take forever to locate them in the Atlanta phone book, even if they're still alive. Arnell is trying to find out what he can on his computer."

"If anybody can get information about them, Arnell can," Aunt Trixie said. "You should see him on that computer. Why, there's nothing he can't do."

I nodded. Arnell, real name Arnie Decker, was a patient of mine with a gender identity disorder. He'd spent his entire life feeling trapped in a man's body. When he had decided to pursue sexual reassignment surgery, his family had disowned him. My mother and aunt had taken him under their wings, and he'd moved in with them. They got along surprisingly well in the oversized apartment above the studio.

"Finding those letters was like going back in time," Aunt Trixie said. "It's so romantic."

"You didn't tell Kate why the letters were hidden in the trunk," my mother said. She looked at me. "Miss Brown was engaged to a wealthy young man from a so-called *good* family, and her parents were outraged when she fell in love with an enlisted man and called off the wedding. They forbade her to correspond with Mr. Smith, so Miss Brown opened a post office box, and the two wrote in secret. She promised to wait for him."

"They would be quite elderly by now if they were still alive," I said. "Maybe you should check out a few nursing homes."

My mother and aunt looked at each other. "Why didn't we think of that?" Aunt Trixie said.

My mother sniffed. "I would have thought of it eventually."

"Hey, who wants ice cream?" I said.

Trixie's hand shot up in the air.

"That would be nice," my mother said. "Do you have pistachio?"

It was just like my mother to ask for pistachio. I didn't know a person in the world who liked the stuff, certainly not me. "Sorry, but I only keep chocolate in the house." I stood and led the way to my kitchen. I pulled out three separate pints of Ben & Jerry's chocolate fudge. Some women spent money on shoes; I bought Ben & Jerry's. I put the cartons on the table and went for spoons.

"We're supposed to eat out of the containers?" my mother asked.

"Yep." I grinned.

She opened the lid. "This is a lot of ice cream. I can't possibly eat all of this."

"I plan to eat every last drop of mine," Trixie said, digging in with gusto. "If you can't finish yours, Kate and I will take turns with it."

The doorbell rang. I headed for the living room and found Mike's vet, Jeff Henry, standing on the other side. I threw open the door. "I don't believe it!" I said. "My mother, my aunt, and I are having an ice cream party. You must be psychic." I stepped back so he could come in.

"Actually, I just stopped by to make sure you're okay. I read about your ordeal in the newspaper. That was very brave of you, Kate. Thank God you weren't injured!"

I tried to wave it off as though it was no big deal. I

didn't want my mother to go on another rampage. "Hey, there's a carton of B & J with your name on it."

"Don't mind if I do."

Jeff followed me into the kitchen, where he was greeted by my mother and aunt. Jeff was in his midthirties and handsome. He was also gay, but we never discussed it, so I had no idea if he knew we were all aware of it. I felt it was none of our business.

I served Jeff and reclaimed my chair. He gave us a brief rundown on his day and asked about Jay.

"He's gone to Tallahassee to help with the fire," I said.

"Do you think he's physically up to it?" Jeff asked, echoing my mother's concerns.

I shrugged. "It doesn't matter. Nobody—including me—was going to talk him out of it."

Aunt Trixie finished her ice cream, and my mother, despite her protests that she could never eat a full pint, was scraping the cardboard container clean.

"That was delicious!" Trixie said. "Too bad Arnell couldn't be here."

"You know he's staying away from dessert," my mother told her. She looked at me. "Arnell has been on a diet. He claims he has gained eight pounds living with us, thanks to my fried chicken and biscuits."

Trixie nodded soberly. "He can't fit into his little black dress."

"He doesn't look good in that dress anyway," my mother said. "It's too formfitting, and he doesn't have curves."

"He'll have curves once they start giving him those female hormone injections," Trixie said.

"I hope they sew a butt on him when he has that surgery," my mother said. "Men don't have much of a butt, and Arnell is no exception. I wouldn't mind donating part of mine."

I burst into laughter at the thought of a surgeon sewing my mother's butt on Arnell. Jeff joined me. We were still laughing when the phone rang. I jumped from my chair and ran for it, hoping it was Jay.

Mona spoke from the other end. "I'm in the ER," she said.

"What? Why?"

"My hives got worse. My face is covered with welts!"

"I'm on my way," I said.

chapter 4

....

My mother and aunt insisted on going with me to the
hospital. The three of us piled into the junk-filled monster
pickup truck and took off as Jeff headed back to his office
to check on his surgical patients.

We arrived at the hospital in record time. I glanced about
the ER but didn't see Mona. "I'm going to check at the
reception desk," I said, and headed in that direction.

"Kate!"

I turned at the sound of Mona's voice. Her head and
part of her face were draped in a shawl, so it was no surprise I hadn't recognized her. "Let me see," I said as my
mother and aunt joined me.

Mona led us to a corner of the room where the hard
plastic chairs sat empty and nobody was waiting. She
pulled the shawl aside. "It's hideous!" she said.

I couldn't hide my surprise. The rash, what there was
of it, was barely noticeable. "Mona, it's not bad at all," I
said.

My mother grunted. "You're overreacting."

Mona quickly put the shawl in place. "You're both just saying that to make me feel better."

I shook my head. "Seriously, Mona, I can barely see anything."

"Does it itch, honey?" Aunt Trixie asked.

"Constantly," Mona said, "but I know if I scratch it, I'll have horrible scars. I'll have to spend the rest of my life wearing this . . . this . . . Shroud of Turin." She gave a huge sigh. "Lord only knows when I'll be seen by a doctor."

"Be glad it's not the weekend," my mother said. "That's when people get drunk and knife each other."

The four of us sat. An hour passed, and my mother and aunt went for coffee.

Finally, Mona's name was called. "Would you come with me?" she asked. "I can't bear to go through this alone."

"Of course." I followed her to a pair of metal doors. A buzzer sounded, and the doors opened. A nurse met us on the other side and led us into a treatment room. Mona had to be coaxed into removing her shawl.

"I know it looks awful," Mona said.

The nurse turned to me. "Is she serious?"

"My friend is afraid it will get worse," I said. "Plus, she needs something to stop the itching."

The woman shook her head and left the room.

Mona covered herself once more. "Did you see the expression on her face?" she hissed the moment we were alone. "I repulsed her."

"Mona, I think you're letting fear get the best of you." I was feeling a little fearful myself. If Mona didn't get a grip very soon, the rash would probably get worse, and she would go off the deep end.

She reached for my hand. "Thank you for trying to

make me feel better, Kate. You're such a good friend." She took a deep breath. "Let's talk about something else; otherwise, I'm going to get more depressed. I guess you know you made the newspaper and the six-o'clock news."

"Jay might have mentioned it before he lashed out at me and hit the road."

"Hit the road?"

"He's gone to help with the wildfire."

"I'm sorry." She gave an enormous sigh. "And all this time I've been thinking about myself."

"Plus, everybody thinks I hate Jesus, thanks to that weirdo, Sarah-Margaret. Naturally, Bitsy Stout felt inclined to pay me a visit."

The door to the exam room opened. I recognized the doctor as soon as he stepped inside. It would have been impossible *not* to with his shock of red hair. Dr. Beau Bodine, nickname Bobo, was a friend of Jay's and had performed minor surgery on my wrist when I'd fractured it after falling in the parking lot of my office. I'd been chasing a patient who was suffering a full-blown panic attack at the time.

"Kate, good to see you again," Bobo said. "And this is—"

"Mona Epps."

"Hi, Mona. What brings you here today?"

She parted the shawl so he could see her face.

Bobo stepped closer. "Is that a rash?"

"Hives," she said. "I had them when I was young. Do you think I'll be disfigured?"

Bobo looked at me. I shrugged.

He shook his head. "No, no, you'll be fine. Have you been under stress?"

Bobo obviously hadn't seen the news or read the paper.

"We went through a harrowing event recently," I said. "It's a long story."

"Is the rash confined to your face?" he asked Mona.

"No." She pulled the shawl away so he could see her arms. "I'm broken out all over."

"Show me where."

She pointed to the top of her left hand. Bobo and I both leaned closer. "It itches," she said.

He nodded. "Okay, I'll give you an injection and a prescription to stop the itch and hopefully keep the rash from worsening. I can have the hospital pharmacy fill the prescription; that way you won't have to stop off on your way home."

The color seemed to drain from Mona's face. "I'm terrified of needles," she said.

Bobo nodded. "That makes two of us. I try to stay as far away from them as I can. By the way, the shot is liable to make you drowsy. Did you drive yourself here?"

Mona nodded. "My chauffeur had a hot date."

Bobo grinned as though he thought Mona was making a joke. Of course, he had no way of knowing she really did have a chauffeur.

"I'll drive her home," I said.

"Okay, great." He left the room.

"I'm going to tell my mother and aunt they can go," I said. "I'll be right back." I returned to the waiting room and filled them in.

"I've never seen anything so silly in my whole life," my mother said. "All that fuss over a silly little rash that you can barely see."

"She's just scared," I said, "but there's no reason for the two of you to hang around."

It was another hour before Mona and I left the hospital,

with me behind the wheel of her Jaguar. Mona's house was located in the ritzy Buckhead area. Her late husband had purchased it for her as a wedding gift.

I had lived with Mona for several weeks after I'd left Jay. Of course, I'd honestly thought he would follow me, beg me to come home, and that he'd look for another job. You could have knocked me over with dandelion fluff when he didn't.

I should have known better. Jay came from a long line of firemen, and he had studied fire science in college. He quickly rose to the rank of captain. I don't think I truly realized how important his work was to him until I gave him a choice: the job or me. Jay Rush was not a man who took well to ultimatums.

After four months of being separated, it hit me: My marriage was done for. I filed for divorce. Two weeks before it was to become final, Jay and I met up, and I lost my heart (not to mention my thong) to him all over again. But that was another story.

I tried to push it all from my mind as I helped a sleepy Mona out of the car and toward the house. Although she was presently without a full-time housekeeper, a team of cleaning women came in two or three times a week.

Inside, Mona sank onto one of the two matching white silk sofas in her massive living room. She reached into her handbag for her cell phone. "I'm calling Jimbo," she said. "He needs to come home immediately."

Jimbo was the chauffeur who lived in a spacious apartment over the multicar garage. "I thought he was on a date," I said.

"This is an emergency. I want him to guard this place until my rash goes away. I can't afford to let anyone see me like this."

"You have a state-of-the-art security system," I said.

"That's not good enough under the circumstances," she said.

I sat next to her. "Listen, Mona," I said gently. "It's not as bad as you think. It's just a little rash."

"Stop trying to make me feel better, Kate," she said, growing teary-eyed. I have to deal with the reality of the situation." She punched in a number. "Jimbo, call me," she said. "It's urgent." She hung up.

"Would you like for me to stay with you tonight?" I asked.

"I don't want to be a burden. Besides, you can't leave poor Mike alone."

"I need to run home and grab clothes for tomorrow. I'll bring her back with me. The traffic shouldn't be bad."

"Thank you, Kate. I can't bear going through this alone."

"Have you eaten?" I asked. "I could make you a grilled cheese sandwich before I go. As you know, that's my specialty."

"I'm too upset to eat."

"Why don't you try to rest?" I said. I stood and grabbed a plush throw from the back of a chair. I waited until Mona kicked off her shoes and lay down, then I covered her. "I won't be gone long."

"Please hurry."

I was on my way a few minutes later. I called my mother from my cell and told her I was spending the night at Mona's.

"She is acting irrational," my mother said. "You shouldn't encourage her."

One thing my mom never ran out of was free advice. "I want to be supportive," I said, even though I knew my decision to stay with Mona was partly due to the guilt I felt about having dragged her with me to the anger management group. "I'm just calling to let you know how to reach me if you need to," I added before we disconnected.

I arrived home, petted Mike, and checked my messages. Nothing from Jay, but Jeff had called to check on Mona. I dialed his number as I started upstairs.

"How bad is the rash?" he asked.

"It's not bad at all, but you know how Mona is about her looks. I feel awful. It's all my fault."

"Why is it your fault?"

"The shooting incident was pretty scary."

"Call me if I can help," he said. "If she needs spaying, I'm her guy."

I laughed. "You're nuts, you know that?"

Once we hung up, I quickly packed what I would need in the way of makeup, toiletries, pajamas, and underwear. I grabbed a hanging outfit and matching shoes from the closet and headed downstairs with Mike on my heels. Once I carried everything to the car, I returned for Mike's food, leash, and dog pillow. I helped her into the car, and we took off.

I arrived back at Mona's house to find the outside ablaze with security lights. Nevertheless, Jimbo shined a flashlight on me as I stepped from my car.

"Just wanted to make sure it's you," he said, turning off the light. "I have orders to keep everyone away."

I noticed he was dressed in black. He even wore a black knit cap. "Yes, I know," I said. Mike jumped out, and I reached for my bag and hanging clothes.

"I thought a password would be appropriate," he went

on. "From now on, nobody comes near the house without it. I'm sorry that I'm going to have to include you."

Jimbo was not especially bright, but he was devoted to Mona. I closed my car door. "What's the password?"

Jimbo looked about. He stepped closer. "When I say, 'Who goes there?' you're supposed to say, 'Gee, it looks like we might have rain,'" he whispered.

"I can remember that."

He skulked off into the night.

Despite the high level of security that was supposed to be in place, Mona's front door was unlocked. I stepped inside and found her sleeping on the sofa. I carried Mike's and my things upstairs to the guest room I'd used before, then hurried down to see if there was something I could do for the patient. I found her sitting up.

"How's the itch?"

She yawned. "Not so bad. But the medicine makes me sleepy and thirsty."

"What would you like to drink?"

"Bottled water is fine."

I went into her kitchen. It looked like something Martha Stewart or Julia Child would have designed, with its solid maple cabinetry, granite countertops, and top-of-the-line stainless steel appliances. I opened the refrigerator and pulled out a bottle of water. I turned and found Mona standing just inside, petting Mike. I opened the water and handed it to her.

"Thanks." She took a long drink.

"You should probably eat something," I said.

"I'm too tired. I just want to go to bed. Maybe I'll wake up in the morning and find this was just a nightmare."

She finished her water and dropped the container into a recycling bin. "Do you need to go back outside for anything?"

"I have to take Mike out once more before turning in."

"You know the code to punch in for the security system, right?"

I nodded. I'd learned how to operate it when I'd stayed with Mona after leaving Jay. "I'll see to everything before I come up."

"Well, good night." She started for the door.

"Let me know if you need anything."

"Thanks, Kate." She left the room.

I grabbed a plastic bag and led Mike outside. She spent fifteen minutes sniffing Mona's backyard as I followed. She was in the process of doing her business when a male voice spoke, almost causing my heart to stop.

"Who goes there?" Jimbo stepped out of the shadows.

Mike growled and stopped what she was doing. "Dammit, Jimbo!" I said. "You scared the hell out of me."

"Who goes there?" he repeated.

I tried to remember the stupid password. Something about the weather, I thought. "It looks like it might rain," I said, not bothering to hide my irritation. Mike was going to have to sniff the whole backyard again before she was able to perform.

Jimbo gave a nod and, once again, slipped into the shadows.

Mike finally made her deposit beside a hedge. I gathered it in the plastic bag, tied it securely, and tossed it into a trash can.

Inside, I checked all the doors and punched in the security code. I set up the coffeemaker, turned off the lights, and went upstairs with Mike following.

Despite being so tired, I took a long, hot shower. Mona's bathrooms were spalike, with specialty shampoos and soaps, body lotions, and fluffy towels the size of bedsheets. I would have died for such a bathroom.

I wrapped a towel around myself, sarong-style, and went into the guest bedroom, where Mike was already curled on her pillow, snoring. Mona had only recently completed redecorating the bedrooms, and the white, Canadian goose–down mattress covers and comforters she'd purchased for each room were as opulent as anything one might find in a grand hotel. I slipped into my pajamas, put my cell on its charger, and set the alarm clock. Finally, I turned off the lamp and climbed into bed.

I sighed with pleasure as I sank into what felt like a cloud. I was certain I would conk out right away, but it didn't happen. I thought of Jay and hoped he was okay. I'd forgotten to watch the news to see if there had been any progress with the fire. I sent up a prayer and finally drifted off to sleep.

I was awakened some time later by a shriek. I bolted from the bed, my heart thumping wildly in my chest. Mike growled, and I hushed her. Fear seized me. Was there an intruder in the house? Had I punched in the wrong security code? Had I forgotten to make certain the system was armed before I walked away?

Another shriek. I groped for the phone and quickly dialed 911. The dispatcher promised to send a patrol car immediately. I dropped the phone on the bed and tried to think of what I could use as a weapon. I remembered the tall, decorative vase on the dresser.

I wasted no time crossing the room, trying to be as quiet as I could. I grabbed the vase, surprised by how heavy it was, and turned for the door. I took great care opening it as soundlessly as possible, then headed down the dark hall with Mike beside me.

I tried to get my bearings, but I couldn't see my hand in front of my face. I didn't dare turn on the light and alert the possible intruder that there was someone else in the house. I gripped the vase, ready to swing it as hard as I could the minute I got close enough.

I didn't see the figure headed my way until I slammed right into it.

I don't know who screamed the loudest, Mona or me. I dropped the vase, and it hit my big toe. Surprisingly, the vase didn't break, but I was pretty sure my toe was broken. I bit my bottom lip to keep from howling. Instead, I whimpered.

The light came on. "What are you doing?" Mona demanded. "And why is my vase on the floor?"

I looked down to see if my toe was still attached to my foot. I leaned down and touched it gently. "I heard you scream," I said, blinking back tears of pain. "I thought somebody was in the house. I was going to hit him with the vase."

"I had a nightmare," she said. "I must've cried out, because I woke up. Then I couldn't go back to sleep because I was itching. I went into the bathroom to take my medicine, and on my way out, I accidentally saw my face in a magnifying mirror. You'd scream, too, if you'd seen what I saw."

I looked up at her. I didn't notice any changes.

"You need to calm down, Mona. Stress is only going to make your hives worse."

"Calm down?! Did you say calm down? I dreamed I

had leprosy, for Pete's sake! What if that's a sign of things to come?"

"You don't have leprosy," I said, trying to be patient with her. I checked my wristwatch. Five thirty a.m. I was still tired, but nothing short of a morphine drip would have eased my pain enough to fall asleep, plus, I was too shaken to think of going back to bed. I picked up the vase, turned, and headed toward the guest room.

"What's wrong with your foot?" she asked.

"I dropped the vase on my toe."

"Does it hurt?"

"What do *you* think?"

I returned the vase to the dresser and headed downstairs to grab a couple of Tylenol. Mona followed. In the kitchen, I took a closer look at my toe. It was red, but fortunately, I was able to move it.

"You should put ice on it," Mona said.

I opened my mouth to answer when I heard a vehicle outside. I glanced out the window and saw a patrol car pull into her circular drive. "Uh-oh," I said.

"What are the police doing here?" Mona asked.

"Um."

"You called them?"

"I thought you were being murdered in your bed!"

"I've already explained what happened," she said.

"How was I to know?"

"Oh, hell!" Mona said. "My shawl is upstairs. I need something to cover my face." She looked about frantically before hurrying to the breakfast table, where she whipped off the tablecloth and covered herself.

We heard a shout from outside, and we both jumped at the same time.

"What was that?" Mona said.

"I have no idea."

We peered out the window over the sink, but couldn't see anything. After what seemed like forever, the doorbell rang.

Limping, I followed Mona to the front door, where she checked the peephole before punching numbers into the alarm panel. She opened the door. Two policemen stood on the other side. Beside them, Jimbo was cuffed.

"We found your intruder," the older of the two officers said. "He was hiding in the hedges."

"He's not an intruder!" Mona cried. "He works for me."

Jimbo gave the officers a smug look. "See? I told you."

The policemen looked confused. "Why were you hiding?" the younger officer asked.

"I was performing security checks," he said. "Now, if you would kindly remove these handcuffs, I can go back to doing my job."

"I'm the one who called," I said as the officer freed Jimbo. "I thought I heard someone in the house. I'm so sorry I bothered you." They were staring at Mona, as though unsure what to make of her shroud.

"Who owns this place?" the other policeman asked.

Mona raised her hand. "I do. My name is Mona Epps. This is Dr. Kate Holly. She's taking care of me while I'm ill." Her words were muffled by the linen tablecloth. "Thank you for coming, but as you can see, everything is fine."

They insisted on taking a report; fortunately, it was quick. They said good-bye, and Jimbo returned to his patrol duties. Mona closed the door. She yawned widely.

"I'm going back to bed. I'm sorry I can't work today. Even if I didn't look like I'd just slithered out of some swamp, I can barely keep my eyes open because of the medication."

I noticed Mike standing at the back door. Obviously, she had to do her business. I gave a sigh, grabbed her leash, and led her out, still favoring my toe. I was relieved not to run into Jimbo, because my mood had definitely soured. After sniffing every tree, hedge, and flower, Mike squatted. When we reentered the kitchen, I saw that the automatic coffeemaker had come on, and the pot was almost full. I took two Tylenol, poured a cup of coffee, and sat at the kitchen table. I drank three cups before heading upstairs to get ready for the day.

I checked on Mona, who was sleeping soundly, thanks to good drugs. She looked quite regal tucked beneath her stark white comforter, which contrasted nicely with walls that were a soft powdery blue. The decorator had outdone herself and chosen only the highest quality of everything.

I slipped from the room, praying that Mona's rash would be gone when she awoke but knowing it wasn't likely.

I arrived at my office shortly before my first appointment was due in. I put on a pot of coffee—I really love the stuff—and checked my messages. Nothing from Jay. I began to fret. I counted the pens in my coffee mug. An even number. Good. I returned a call from a patient who sounded anxious.

Then I went into my kitchenette and poured my coffee. I heard the door to the reception room open and hurried down the hall to greet my first patient of the day. I stopped short at the sight of my mother standing beside Mona's desk.

"Surprise!" she sang out. "Guess who's going to be your receptionist while Mona is out?"

chapter 5

....

I opened my mouth to speak, but nothing came out. I didn't know what to say.

"I knew you would be surprised," she said. "Mona called me. She was concerned that you had no one to answer your phone or greet your patients. I told her I would be more than happy to help out."

She was dressed in her nicest outfit, and her platinum hair was teased and lacquered with hair spray, as usual.

"What about the studio?" I asked.

"Trixie and I worked it out," she said.

"Thank you for coming to my rescue, Mom," I said, trying to appear grateful, even though I feared her presence would only create more stress for me. I wondered if Mona had called her as a way to get even with me for causing her hives.

"What did you expect me to do?" she said. "We're family, and families stick together. But I have to tell you, Kate, I was hurt that you didn't personally call me. If you can't count on your own mother, who *can* you count on?"

Let the guilt-trip begin, I thought.

She set her purse on the desk and glanced about. She thumbed through the magazines on my coffee table and peeked inside the supply room.

"I can see that I have my work cut out for me," she said.

I gripped the handle on my coffee cup. "What do you mean?"

"Well, that supply room definitely needs organizing," she said. "And do you realize that some of the magazines on that coffee table are almost a year old? They really need to be tossed. And that poor plant is dying," she added, pointing to my bamboo plant near the window.

The thought of her changing and rearranging everything in my office struck fear in my heart. "You don't need to do all that, Mom. If you could just answer the phone and try to make my patients feel at ease when they arrive, that'd be great. Some of them are pretty anxious when they come in."

"Of course!" she said. "I'll make them feel right at home. Oh, this is going to be so much fun," she added. "I'll finally be able to see what you do all day. I just wish I could sit in on a couple of your sessions so I could watch you in action, but I'm sure that's a big no-no."

"You're right," I said. I noticed a stack of envelopes sticking out of her purse. "What's all that?"

"RSVPs for Bump and Lou's twenty-fifth wedding anniversary party on Sunday night at the VFW. I hope you didn't forget."

How *could* I forget, I wanted to tell her. I'd been dreading it for weeks. I had met Aunt Lou's family, all hog farmers, at a reunion five years ago and had learned more than I'd wanted to know about the process of mating, castration, and dressing of hogs. I hadn't been able to look at a pork chop for months.

"How many people are you expecting to attend?" I asked.

"About forty," she said.

"That's a lot of people," I said. "Where are they staying?"

"At the Comfort Inn. We were able to get everybody a big discount. Oh, and there's no need to dress up for the party. It's casual."

Which meant there was going to be a lot of polyester at the VFW on Sunday night.

Just then, the door opened, and a man in his fifties walked in. He wore jeans and a sweatshirt. "I'm Robert Nells," he said. "I have a nine o'clock appointment."

It was his first visit. "I'm Kate Holly." We shook hands. "Please call me Kate."

"I'm Robert."

"Would you like a cup of coffee?" I asked.

"That would be great. I take it black."

It didn't take long for him to complete the necessary paperwork I required all my new patients to fill out. I invited him into my office and closed the door. I scanned the form quickly and discovered that he had lost his job with a major corporation six months prior. His body language—slumped shoulders, hangdog look—said it all.

"I had no idea it was coming," he said, not wasting any time getting to the heart of the matter. "I was the executive vice president for twelve years."

"Were you given an explanation as to why they were letting you go?" I asked.

"Profits were down. The company was cutting back. At least that's what I was told. I later learned they hired a guy to replace me. He's probably twenty years younger than me and costs them a lot less. I received a nice severance, but I feel they screwed me. It's not easy starting over at fifty-five. Not only am I older, I'm overqualified for most jobs, and when potential employers take one look at the salary I was being paid, they back off."

"So how do you fill your time these days?" I asked.

"Frankly, I'm bored out of my mind," he said. "It wasn't so bad in the beginning, because I was able to do a lot of things that needed doing around the house. I cleaned out the attic and the garage, got rid of a bunch of stuff. I painted several rooms and redid the landscaping in our yard. My wife loved it. But I've run out of projects. Nowadays, I mostly sit around the house and wait for the phone to ring."

"Do you ever get together with friends or colleagues?" I asked.

"No. I guess I'm embarrassed."

"You must feel very isolated these days."

He shrugged. "Yeah."

I jotted down a few notes before speaking. "Robert, I'd like to play a little game," I said. "It may sound or feel silly, but I think you could benefit from it."

He shrugged. "I suppose. It's not like I have someplace I need to be."

I set my clipboard aside. "I want you to close your eyes and imagine what it would feel like if you were offered a good job. The *perfect* job," I added.

He gave me an odd look but closed his eyes. "I'm not feeling very imaginative today," he confessed.

"I'll help you out. I want you to pretend that you're sitting in the CEO's office of a reputable company," I added. "I want you to imagine what the office looks like and form a picture of the man who just hired you. Take your time."

Robert frowned. It was obvious he was struggling. Finally, after several minutes, he nodded.

"Tell me what you see."

"Top-of-the-line office furnishings, and a guy in a nice suit. Custom tailored," he added.

"And you're wearing your best suit, right?"

"Yes."

"How are you sitting?"

"What do you mean?"

"You're feeling good about getting the job. You're at the top of your game, so to speak. How does someone in that position sit?"

He looked thoughtful. Finally, he sat up straight in the chair. "Like this?" he asked.

"Excellent," I said. "Now I want you to keep your eyes closed and really concentrate on how that feels. Throw back your shoulders and see just how tall you can sit. Hitch your chin high." He worked at it. "Come on, Robert, you can do better than that. Puff out your chest." He finally achieved the pose I'd been looking for. "Tell me how it feels," I said.

"Different," he said, "but nice."

"You're feeling pretty proud and confident, aren't you?"

"Yes."

"Do you remember a time when you felt like that in the past?"

"Yes."

"Great. I want you to concentrate solely on what that was like. If other thoughts come to mind, just nudge them aside."

I sat very still and watched the changes come over him. The lines on either side of his mouth and eyes relaxed. His breathing became deep and even. After almost ten minutes, I spoke.

"I'm going to ask you to open your eyes, but I want you to remain sitting just as you are."

He looked dazed.

"What are you thinking?" I asked.

"I'm thinking maybe I came across poorly in some of my interviews. Maybe I appeared depressed or desperate."

"You're right," I said. "So from now on, I want you to get up early during the workweek, take a shower, and put on your best suit."

"Even if I have no place to go?" he asked.

"Right. I also want you to make a list of friends or colleagues you can invite to lunch. You don't have to go to expensive restaurants, but I'd like for you to go to lunch with someone at least three days a week. It's called networking.

"In the meantime, I want you to work at what you enjoy doing outside of being an executive. Can you think of anything?"

"I'm pretty good at landscaping. That's how I put myself through college. Even my neighbors are impressed. A couple of them wanted to hire me. And to be honest, it feels good being outside after spending years cooped up in an office. Plus, I'm getting exercise."

"That's an excellent idea!" I said.

"You know, I could even start my own business."

I nodded. He appeared enthusiastic at the thought.

He gazed at me for a moment. "You know, for someone so young, you really know your stuff."

I smiled. "Thank you for calling me young. You just became my favorite patient."

He chuckled. I suspected it had been a while since he'd laughed. I felt we'd made progress.

"You had a couple of phone calls," my mother said once I'd scheduled Robert for the following week and saw him out. I noticed a bounce in his step that he hadn't shown before. My mother handed me two pink message slips. "This lady, Mrs. Bryant, sounded like she was going off the deep end."

I arched one brow.

"You know, like maybe she shouldn't be allowed near a bridge because she might bail. I was able to calm her down, though."

Mrs. Bryant was an elderly woman who had been grieving her husband's death since he was laid to rest almost a year ago. She hadn't been able to get on with her life. "What do you mean, you calmed her down?" I asked.

"I talked some sense into her," she said.

"That was really very thoughtful of you, Mom, but you should not try to advise my patients." I could tell she wasn't listening.

"As you can see, the other call was from your pervert ex-boyfriend," she went on. "I don't know why you even talk to him."

"Thad Glazer and I share several patients."

"How can you share patients?" she asked.

"He provides medication therapy for mine, and I see some of his for talk therapy."

"Why doesn't he talk to his own patients?"

"Thad doesn't like to listen to other people's problems."

"That's because he's shallow and self-centered. I'm surprised Jay allows the two of you to work together."

"It's strictly business, Mom." She gave a grunt. I checked my wristwatch. "I have someone due in shortly. I'd better return these calls."

I entered my office and closed the door behind me. I dialed Mrs. Bryant's number, and she answered on the first ring.

"I understand you're having a bad day," I said, trying to sound as sympathetic as I could. "Would you like to move your appointment up?"

"Oh, I'm much better now that I've talked to your receptionist, Dixie," she said. "I can't believe how self-involved I've been. Like Dixie said, most women aren't lucky enough to celebrate forty years of marriage. I can't believe what a whiner I've been. You should have told me."

I sighed. Leave it to my mother to create problems between my patients and me. "Everyone grieves differently and in their own time, Mrs. Bryant. You and your husband had an exceptional marriage. You were best friends. I'm not surprised his passing was so difficult for you."

"Well, it's like Dixie said, he wouldn't have wanted me to sit around feeling sorry for myself. I need to get off my behind and do something for somebody else. When you do for others, it takes your mind off your own problems."

I listened politely. I couldn't begin to count the times

I had suggested Mrs. Bryant look into volunteer work. "I'm glad you've decided to take that step," I said. "Did you want to reschedule or come in on your regular day?"

"Actually, after giving it some thought, I'm not going to require your services anymore."

The next thing I heard was a dial tone. "Thanks, Mom," I muttered to myself. I suddenly noticed Thad's message was marked "urgent." I dialed his number. His receptionist, Bunny, informed me in her Betty Boop voice that Thad was meeting with his attorney, and she didn't know when he would be back.

"I don't know what the meeting is about," Bunny said, "but Thad was upset when he left here."

"Would you please tell him I tried to call him back?"

"Oh, for sure," Bunny said.

I barely had time to hang up before my phone rang. Mona was on the other end. "How is your mom working out?"

"She just cured one of my patients."

"No kidding?"

"There goes a paying customer." I tried to make light of it, even though I was annoyed as hell. I had gone through about a gazillion boxes of tissues trying to pull Mrs. Bryant from her grief, but she had dug in her heels and refused to budge. Then, with one word from my mother, she had been fully restored.

"I probably should have checked with you before calling her, but I felt terrible leaving you in the lurch."

"Don't worry about it," I said, knowing Mona's heart was in the right place. "How is the rash?"

"Jimbo agrees that it has gotten much worse," she said. "I have an appointment with my dermatologist right after lunch. How's your toe?"

"Still sore, but it doesn't hurt as bad as it did."

"I have a confession to make," she said with a laugh. "I've been cracking up all morning thinking about it."

"Gee, I'm glad I could provide a little comic relief. If it'll help, I can come by and drop the vase on my other toe."

"Only a true friend would offer to do something like that," Mona said.

I was glad her mood was better. "Let me know what the dermatologist says," I said before we hung up.

I got up from my desk, opened my door, and found Ellen and Gerald Holmes, a couple I had been counseling for several weeks, talking to my mom as she thumbed through the telephone book. Ellen and Gerald smiled at me, which was rare, because they had trouble being in the same room without fighting. Some three or four months ago, Ellen had walked into Gerald's office and found him in a compromising position with a coworker. She automatically assumed they were having an affair, although Gerald swore it was all very innocent, that he was merely trying to comfort the woman, who'd recently lost a loved one. I did not know where the truth lay, but I was not sure their three-year marriage would survive Ellen's doubts and suspicions.

"Ready to come in?" I asked them.

They headed my way. Ellen paused and glanced at my mom. "You'll let us know what you find out?" she said.

She nodded. "I should have all of the information before you leave."

They came in and I closed the door. I waited until we were seated before questioning them. "What kind of information are you looking for?"

"Well—" Ellen slid forward on the sofa. "We got to talking to Dixie, and the next thing I know, I'm telling her the reason Gerald and I have been seeing you. I mean, she's so easy to talk to, you know? She came up with a great idea."

"Oh?"

"She suggested that we take a second honeymoon."

"I see."

"Maybe she's right. She says we need a clean slate."

Gerald nodded. "Plus, Dixie has a friend who is a travel agent. She's going to see if she can get a good deal for us. We want to go to the hotel in Hawaii where we spent our first honeymoon."

I looked from one to the other as I tried to keep up.

"Are you sure you're ready for that?" I asked. "I mean, we've only had a few sessions."

They both nodded eagerly, but I didn't share their enthusiasm. I knew Ellen was no more convinced of Gerald's innocence than she was the day they first walked into my office. She had huge trust issues, and Gerald resented her accusations.

"Not that I don't think a second honeymoon is an excellent idea," I said quickly, "but it would probably be better if the two of you had more sessions under your belt." I knew Ellen would never heal until she stopped accusing Gerald of every vile thing under the sun and considered that he might just be innocent of any wrongdoing.

Ellen looked hurt. "I thought you'd be happy for us."

"I am *very* happy," I said, "but I want the experience to be wonderful for you."

"It *will* be wonderful," Gerald said. "Not to mention

romantic," he added. He smiled at his wife. "Moonlit walks on the beach, dancing under the stars, the smell of suntan lotion on warm skin."

It was obvious they had already made up their minds, and I was not going to be able to convince them otherwise. "Okay, if you're both determined to go, I think we should set up a few boundaries."

"For example?" Ellen asked.

"I think the two of you should make a pact not to discuss your problems while you're away."

Ellen arched one brow. "Are you saying I should pretend the affair never happened?"

"There was no affair," Gerald said tightly.

"That's what I mean," I said. "Just go and have a good time, and we'll work on the problems when you get back." I looked at Ellen. "Do you think you can do that?"

Ellen was prevented from answering when there was a knock at my door. My mother peeked inside. "Guess what? My travel agent can get you a forty percent discount if you can leave within seventy-two hours."

Ellen and Gerald looked at each other. "That's a huge savings," Gerald said. "We'd be crazy not to jump on it."

Ellen suddenly looked anxious. "It doesn't give me much time to get ready," she said. She looked at me. "Could we cut this session short? I won't be able to concentrate, knowing I have so much to do."

"Of course," I said. I followed them out. I noticed my mother had moved some of the furniture in my reception room and was presently making travel arrangements for Ellen and Gerald. I went into my supply room for a new legal pad and found a mess. Obviously, my mother was in the process of getting things in order, only it looked as though it would get much worse before it got better.

Back in my office, I grabbed the Atlanta phone book and thumbed through the listings until I found what I was looking for: Midtown Temps. I dialed the number, and a professional voice on the other end introduced herself as Bernice.

"Hello, Bernice," I said and told her who I was. "I'm in urgent need of a receptionist."

I waited until my mother and I were alone before I broke the news to her. "Guess what?" I said. "I called a temporary employment agency and found a receptionist. She's coming in this afternoon."

My mother looked shocked. "Why on earth would you do that?" she asked. "Do you have any idea how much those places charge?"

"I can afford it, Mom, now that I have a few new patients. Besides, Aunt Trixie needs you at the studio. Don't you have some sort of spring thing you're working on?"

"It's called the Spring Fling," she said, giving a proud smile. "It's a whole new line of furniture and junk art in pastel colors."

"Plus you have to get ready for the anniversary party on Sunday night."

She looked thoughtful. "Well, yes, but—"

"Besides, Mona is only going to be out for a few more days."

"I don't want you to feel as though I'm abandoning you," she said.

"That's the farthest thing from my mind! I know if things don't work out with this girl, I can call you."

"Absolutely!"

It took twenty minutes to finally usher her from my

reception room and into the elevator. I stood and waved as the double doors closed. I hurried back inside my reception room and moved the furniture back in place but decided to straighten the supply room later. To celebrate my mother's departure, I grabbed my wallet and keys, locked up, and went downstairs to the sandwich shop, where I ordered a roast beef and cheese with the works. I returned upstairs to find a slender blond woman standing outside my door.

"May I help you?" I asked.

"Are you Dr. Kate Holly?"

"Yes."

"I'm Abigail Davis," she said. "The temp agency sent me."

"Wow, that was quick!"

"I was actually interviewing with them when you called, so they sent me straight over."

She looked to be in her midthirties. She was neatly dressed and attractive but wore little makeup. I unlocked the door to my reception room and motioned her inside. I followed. "Have you eaten lunch?" I asked.

She shook her head. "I had a late breakfast, so I'm okay." She looked around. "This is a nice office," she said.

"Thank you," I said, setting my wallet, keys, and bag on Mona's desk. "This is where you will sit," I told her, wasting no time on preliminaries since I would barely have time to finish my sandwich before my next patient arrived. "Your main duties will be to answer the phone and greet patients when they come in. I usually have coffee in back in case they want a cup. A couple of them prefer hot tea."

"That sounds easy enough."

I picked up the appointment book. "Each morning,

we'll want to compare our appointment books for the day," I said. "If someone cancels or wishes to reschedule, make sure I get the message so I can take care of it and coordinate with you. That way I won't end up double booked."

"I hope you weren't looking for someone with great computer skills," she said, motioning to the desktop computer. "I'm not real good at that sort of thing. In fact, I'd probably break it."

I thought it odd that she had little computer knowledge. It seemed everyone had a home office or carried a laptop with them these days. "My receptionist sends out monthly bills," I told her, "but you won't be doing that. Like I said, I just need someone to answer the phone and greet my patients when they come in. I should warn you, some of them might try to discuss their problems with you while waiting to see me. I would appreciate it if you would discourage such behavior."

She gave a rueful smile. "I seriously doubt that anyone would ask *me* for advice. I have enough trouble managing my own life."

I didn't know how to respond. I didn't know if she was joking or if her self-effacing manner was part of her personality. "Some of my patients, especially the new ones, are a little anxious when they come in. A smile and a cheerful word go a long way toward calming them down."

"I promise to make them feel welcome."

"You can put your purse in the bottom drawer of the desk or beneath the sink in the kitchenette," I said. "Whichever makes you feel more comfortable," I added.

"I don't have enough money on me to worry about it," she joked. She opened the desk drawer and shoved her purse inside.

I showed her the kitchenette, which held a small refrigerator and microwave. "If you don't feel like bringing your lunch, there's a sandwich shop downstairs. They also serve coffee and pastries in the morning so they're usually open by seven a.m. If you don't want to go to the trouble, you can grab something from the vending machines on the first floor. It's not healthy, but it's fast."

"How long is your receptionist going to be out?" she asked.

"I'm not sure. Oh, and feel free to bring a book. You might get bored sitting around waiting for the phone to ring. Mona, my receptionist, likes to shop online." I opened the small refrigerator. "I keep soft drinks in here," I said, "in case you get thirsty. The vending machines charge too much." I offered her one, but she shook her head. I chose my usual diet drink and closed the door. I looked up to find her standing close and staring at me intently. I instinctively took a step back. "Is something wrong?"

She blushed. "I don't mean to gawk," she said, "but I wasn't expecting you to be so young. Not to mention pretty," she added. "I figured you would be middle-aged and wearing spectacles and sensible shoes."

I decided it was a good day since I'd been called young twice. "I've never been the sensible type," I said. "I'm sort of a fly-by-the-seat-of-your-pants kinda gal."

"You have more going for you than that, or you wouldn't have your own practice," she said. "I really admire that."

I still felt she was standing too close, crowding my personal space. "Thank you, Abigail," I said, wishing she would move so I didn't have to push past her. I wondered if I was making too much of it.

"I'm sorry if I seem a little nervous," she said. "I just moved to Atlanta, and this is my very first job with the temp agency."

"Where are you from?"

"California."

"Wow, that's quite a distance. Do you have family here?"

"No. I recently divorced, and I wanted to move as far away as I could. You know, make a fresh start."

The therapist in me wondered if there was more to it, if maybe her husband had created problems for her or if she had felt threatened by him. It never failed to amaze me how angry and bitter some couples became after a divorce. "It must've been scary coming all this way and not having any friends here."

"I prefer to think of it as an adventure."

"So you've already found a place and you're all settled?" I asked.

She shook her head. "It's only temporary. I want to take my time looking. I'd like to find a place where the traffic is not so bad."

"Good luck," I said. Then I added, "I hope you don't think I'm rude, but I'd better hurry up and eat my sandwich before my next appointment arrives." She stepped aside, and I started for the door. "Feel free to ask me any questions," I mentioned as I moved away.

She followed me down the hall. I paused at the reception desk and grabbed my stuff.

"May I see your office?" she asked.

"Sure."

I opened the door and went in. Abigail stood in the doorway. "It's very nice."

I pulled my sandwich from the bag and unwrapped it. "A couple of friends did it. I have trouble decorating a Christmas tree." I took a bite of my sandwich.

"Yes, but look at what you *are* capable of. You help those who are hurting." She pointed to a picture of Jay on my credenza. "Is that your significant other?" she asked.

"Yes." I decided not to go into the complicated details of our accidental divorce.

"He's quite a hunk."

"I think so." I touched the picture frame as though it would somehow bring him closer to me. "He's a firefighter." I heard the pride in my voice. Even though Jay's job made me anxious, I had always been proud of him. I suddenly missed him so much that my heart ached. It didn't help that we'd argued. More than anything I wanted to clear the air between us.

"My ex was an insurance adjuster," Abigail said, interrupting my thoughts. "How boring is that?"

It was on the tip of my tongue to tell her I would gladly welcome boring, that I'd prefer it to having Jay running into burning buildings, but I could not imagine him sitting at a desk punching numbers into a calculator all day.

"I caught my ex having an affair with my best friend," Abigail said.

"That must've been painful."

"It was more painful losing my best friend." She smiled. "Best friends are hard to come by. Crummy husbands are a dime a dozen."

I chuckled and took another bite of my sandwich.

"I'll bet you've heard your share of sad stories," she said. "Does it ever get to you?"

"Sometimes. There are certain cases I refuse to treat because I know I can't be objective."

I took another bite of my sandwich and wished she would stop asking questions so I could finish my lunch.

"Have any of your patients ever committed suicide?" she asked, only to cover her mouth the minute the words came out.

I stopped chewing.

chapter 6

....

Abigail's cheeks turned a bright red. "I'm so sorry," she said. "I can't believe I asked that. It was so out of line. Please, I don't expect you to answer."

The question had caught me off guard. It was like asking a soldier how many people he'd killed on the battlefield.

I finally swallowed. "I haven't lost anybody yet," I said, trying to make light of it. Even so, I was reluctant to share with her that I had been trained long ago in what signs to look for and how best to handle a suicidal person. She had asked enough questions for one day.

I noticed my answering machine was blinking, and I wondered if Jay had tried to call while I'd been in the sandwich shop. It would give me an excuse to cut off my conversation with Abigail. "Oops, I probably should check my messages," I said. "Would you please let me know when my next patient arrives?"

Abigail nodded and put her hand on the doorknob. "Dr. Holly—"

"Call me Kate."

"Again, I'm sorry if I asked too many questions."

"Don't worry about it." She nodded and closed the door. For some reason, I was relieved to see her leave my office. I pushed the button on my answering machine. I was annoyed that my next patient had canceled. Most therapists charged for a missed session if they didn't receive a twenty-four-hour notice, and I was tempted to put that policy in place. The machine beeped, and I listened to my next call. It was from my patient Bill Rogers, who suffered from obsessive-compulsive disorder. He claimed he was in crisis and desperately needed to see me. The last call was from Thad, asking me to call him back on his cell phone. Nothing from Jay.

I returned Bill's call first. He was clearly agitated.

"I just had a cancellation," I said. "How soon can you be here?"

"Ten minutes."

"I'll see you when you get here, then."

I called Thad. "I've had it with Liz Jones," he said.

Uh-oh, I thought. Thad and I shared a patient with multiple personality disorder. The host personality, Alice Smithers, was a senior accountant and something of a prude. Liz Jones, one of her alternate personalities, was the bad girl in the bunch and had the hots for Thad.

"What happened?" I asked finally.

"She showed up this morning minus her panties. Again," he added. "I told her she would have to find another psychiatrist."

"And?"

"She threatened to file a complaint against me for inappropriate sexual behavior."

"Oh, gur-reat." I knew Thad was innocent of any wrongdoing. He might be the worst kind of womanizer, but he would never cross the line with a patient.

I would have loved to smack Liz Jones. The only problem was that I'd have to hurt the likable personalities as well. "Maybe she's just blowing hot air," I said. "Why don't you give me a chance to talk to her?" Even as I said it, I wondered if Liz would even "come out" for me. She didn't like women, but she especially didn't like me.

"I just left my attorney's office," he said. "I have to be prepared for the worst. I can't let her destroy my reputation."

I knew it was a serious matter. The mere whisper of any wrongdoing on Thad's part could devastate his career. "Just let me try to reason with her, okay?" I repeated. "I promise I'll do everything I can."

He begrudgingly agreed. He rang off without his usual flirting, which proved how anxious he was. Liz Jones had been a thorn in our sides from the beginning. I hated to lose Thad as the case psychiatrist, because Alice Smithers, the host personality, did not handle change well, and she and I had been making progress. I called Alice's home number and left a message for her to call me back as soon as possible.

I finally finished my lunch.

I heard a tap at my door. Abigail peeked inside. "May I come in?"

"Yes."

She stepped inside my office and closed the door. "There's a guy out front who is acting very weird."

"That would be Bill Rogers," I said, getting up and going to the door. I put my hand on the doorknob, but Abigail quickly covered it with hers. I looked up.

"Is he dangerous?" she whispered.

"No, he's just upset."

She looked relieved. "Well, while we're on the topic, what if one of your patients became dangerous and attacked you?"

Her hand felt heavy on mine. "Are you afraid?" I asked.

"No, but I'd like to have a plan in place in case something like that ever happened. I mean, what if a patient went off the deep end and locked your door so that I couldn't help you? Is there a key?"

I noted the concern in her eyes. Surprisingly enough, there were still people, including my mother, who thought all people in therapy were crazy and/or dangerous. I figured we owed our thanks to Hollywood, which often portrayed psychiatric patients as evil or homicidal.

"*If* it were to happen," I said, "I would yell for you to call security. The number is listed under "S" in the Rolodex on the desk." I avoided her question about the key. There was a spare key to my office, but only Mona and I knew where it was. "You really needn't worry, though. My patients aren't dangerous. They simply have problems." I decided not to tell her about George Moss, the nutcase who had brought nitroglycerin into my office, nor would I mention the explosion that followed, since I was responsible for it.

"That makes me feel better," she said and moved her hand. "Oh, I should probably tell you the guy out front is wearing about a gallon of cologne."

I opened the door and stepped into the reception area, where I found an impeccably dressed Bill Rogers pacing the floor. He was in his late thirties with a receding hairline. His cologne slapped me in the face.

He stopped pacing. "Oh, Dr. Holly, thank you for agreeing to see me on such short notice," he said.

I smiled. "No problem." I motioned him toward my office. "Please come in."

He hurried in and sat on my sofa. I didn't bother to grab his file; instead, I quickly took the chair beside him.

"What has you so upset?" I asked, wishing I could throw open a window and let some air in.

Bill began wringing his hands, and I noted they were chapped as usual, from so much washing. "It was a nightmare," he said, his voice trembling. "I had to inspect a sewage treatment plant early this morning."

Bill worked for OSHA and investigated complaints of possible safety hazards. "And?" I said.

"I slipped and fell in a vat of excrement."

I blinked back at him. "But how—"

"It wasn't properly covered, which is why I was called in to investigate. Any of the employees could have fallen in. I almost drowned, Dr. Holly! I *would* have drowned if a couple of guys hadn't fished me out." He covered his face with his hands. "I freaked out. I mean, I totally lost it. I'm sure everybody at that company thinks I'm completely insane. They showed me to a locker room so I could shower. I spent an hour trying to scrub off the germs. They gave me a pair of coveralls to wear home because my clothes were ruined, and—"

"Bill—" I touched his arm. I could see he was in panic mode. Sometimes a simple touch could calm people. "I'm sorry you had to go through that," I said. "I know it must've been awful."

"Awful doesn't come close to describing it," he said. "It was one of the most traumatic experiences I've ever been through. I can't seem to get the smell of sewage off me. I even put on cologne."

Duh, I thought.

"I'm afraid I carried some of the germs inside my house, so I sprayed the place with a disinfectant. I used an entire can," he added, "but I don't think it was enough. I used another whole can on the inside of my car."

"Bill?"

"Yeah?"

"Let's pause and take a couple of deep breaths." I waited for him to do so. "Okay," I said gently, "while I know the experience was really hard on you, it's over. You're going to be okay."

He shook his head. "You don't understand. I'll never get rid of the germs."

"You said you showered carefully at the plant."

"I even cleaned my ears and under my fingernails and toenails. I blew my nose several times."

"I'm sure you were very thorough. So the odds of you transferring germs to your car and house are very slim, don't you agree?"

He looked doubtful.

"Plus, you took the added precaution of disinfecting everything."

"But what if it wasn't enough?"

"What more do you think you could have done?"

"Maybe I should hire a cleaning crew to come through. I could get my carpets cleaned and take my drapes to the dry cleaners."

"And after that?" I asked.

"What do you mean?"

"You could move to a different house, and you would still worry that you'd carried the germs from your old place. You could buy a new car, and it wouldn't be enough."

He was quiet for a moment. Finally, he nodded. "I know it's irrational, Dr. Holly, but I'm afraid. Do you think I've gone crazy?"

"No. Have you been listening to your relaxation and visualization tapes?"

"Probably not as often as I should."

It annoyed me that some of my patients frequently had to be forced to take part in their own recovery. It was as if they expected me to wave a magic wand and pronounce them healed. If I had a magic wand, I would have used it on myself long ago.

"Don't you think you should make time?" I asked coolly. He didn't respond. "I can't do it for you, Bill."

"I'm afraid," he confessed, "because I know where you're going with this. Eventually, you're going to put me in fearful situations. You're going to make me touch dirt or garbage, or something equally germy."

"I would never push you to do something like that," I said, "but if you don't follow my instructions, I can't help you."

"I promise to do better," he said.

He had calmed down by the time I walked him out half an hour later. From the corner of my eye, I saw Abigail snatch a couple of tissues from a box and press them to her nose. Bill didn't miss it; in fact, he looked stricken.

"Oh, no!" he said. "I thought I had managed to scrub off the foul odor. I have to go home and take another shower." He threw open the reception room door and shot out like a bottle rocket.

"Bill, wait!" I called, wanting to tell him it was his cologne and not the sewage smell he imagined, but he crossed the hall and walked straight into an open elevator filled with passengers who stepped as far away from him as they could. Obviously, he noticed. He seemed to shrink inside himself as the doors closed.

I reentered my reception room and found Abigail standing there wearing a guilty look. "I'm so sorry," she said. "It's just that I'm very sensitive to smells, and I was getting nauseous. Was he trying to come on to you or something?"

"No. Why do you ask?"

"I thought maybe that's why he put on so much cologne. I'll bet half your patients have a crush on you. I'll bet they make passes at you all the time."

I shook my head. "I'm careful to keep boundaries in place," I said.

Mona called as I was getting ready to leave for the day. "What did your dermatologist say?" I asked.

"He agreed it looks like I have hives, but he didn't understand why the medicines weren't helping. I told him it was getting worse. He sent me straight to an allergist, who performed all these scratch tests on me. I'm allergic to cat dander, chicken feathers, latex, and other stuff that I haven't even been around. Long story short, he chalked it up to stress and gave me a couple of prescriptions, but if you ask me, I don't think he knew any more than the dermatologist."

"I know this must be frustrating for you."

She gave a huge sigh. "Well, the real reason I'm calling is to see if you planned to stay here again tonight."

I heard the hopefulness in her voice. "I'll be happy to stay if you want me to," I said.

"You're just saying that because you feel sorry for me," she said. "Because you suspect I will be disfigured before it's over."

"You are *not* going to be scarred or disfigured," I said a

little more forcefully than I'd intended. Abigail peeked into my office. "I have to go," I told Mona. "It'll be at least an hour before I can get there. I need to run by the house and grab Mike and a change of clothes. How about I stop by our favorite Chinese place on the way?"

"That would be great."

"Do you have chocolate in the house?"

"Have you ever known me not to?"

"Sorry, I forgot who I was talking to for a minute."

I hung up. Abigail smiled. "I'll bet that was Mona. Sounds like you guys are planning a big evening. I miss not having a best friend."

"I'm sure you'll meet a lot of new friends," I said, grabbing my purse from my bottom desk drawer.

Her smile faded. "I don't think I could ever trust anyone to get that close to me again."

I didn't respond, mainly because I did not want to encourage Abigail into thinking it was okay to tell me all her personal problems, which some people tended to do when they learned I was a psychologist. Also, instinct told me that Abigail probably had more problems than most. Instead, I went about locking my files and drawers.

"Do you want me to come back in the morning?" she asked.

I glanced up. She seemed to be holding her breath. "That was the plan I worked out with the temp agency," I said, surprised that she would ask. "I told them I'd need someone until my receptionist returned."

Abigail looked relieved.

My telephone was ringing as I walked through my front door. My mother was on the other end of the line.

"How did the temp girl work out?" she asked.

"Not bad, considering it was her first day," I said, deciding it was best to leave out the part about Abigail being a little weird.

"Well, that makes me feel better," she said. "Have you heard from Mona?"

"She claims her rash has worsened."

My mother gave a grunt. "That woman spends too much time worrying about her looks. She won't always be young and beautiful."

"Please promise me you'll never tell her that."

"I have more important things on my mind," she said. "Now, you know I'm not one to interfere with your life, but I've been doing a lot of thinking."

Just hearing those words sent a shudder of fear through me. "Yeah?"

"I know you're concerned about Jay, and I have always found that prayer helps me through difficult times. I'm not trying to preach to you, but I don't like that you've strayed from your faith."

I pressed the ball of my hand against my head. Just what I needed, another Bitsy Stout in my life. "Mom, I'm not an atheist, okay?"

Silence at first. "If you say so."

I managed to cut the call short. I changed into my favorite jeans and decided on an outfit for the following day, then I grabbed Mike's food, and we took off. At the Chinese restaurant, I filled two take-out containers from the buffet. I figured I would give Mona as many choices as I could.

I arrived at her house twenty minutes later and found her wearing loose pajamas. I was shocked to see that her rash had indeed worsened, but I pretended not to notice.

"I know it's a little early for pj's," she said in a dejected tone, "but I can't stand for anything to rub against my skin. So I figured satin wouldn't be as bad."

"You should wear whatever is comfortable," I said. I smiled and held up the to-go bag from the restaurant. "I hope you're hungry, because I chose a little of everything."

"Thank you," she said.

We prepared our plates, and I grabbed bottled water from the fridge.

"So how was the girl from the agency?" Mona asked, once we sat down at the kitchen table.

"She did okay," I said, again keeping my feelings to myself. I smiled. "Of course, nobody can fill your shoes."

Mona gave me a weak smile, but her thoughts seemed elsewhere. "Who knows, maybe I'll be able to come back to work sooner than I thought."

"Oh?"

"I called my mama," she said, "and told her about this god-awful rash. I don't know if I even mentioned it to you, but she's a healer and a midwife."

Mona had told me very little about her past. I knew she'd been born and raised in the Tennessee mountains and that her father had hit the road when he'd learned Mona's mother was pregnant with her.

"I've never met a healer or a midwife," I said. "That sounds so exciting."

Mona didn't look enthusiastic. "She had to tie up a few loose ends, but she promised to hit the road as soon as she could. I just hope that old VW van makes it," she added. "Lord knows I've offered to buy her something new, but she won't hear of it."

Once we finished dinner, I wrapped the leftovers, rinsed our dishes, and loaded them into the dishwasher.

"Hey, I know what will cheer you up," I said.

"Get totally drunk and puke in my hair?"

"How come *I* never come up with these cool ideas?" I said, giving my forehead a bop with my palm. "I was just thinking we could watch Popeye cartoons."

Mona gave a wistful smile. "Mr. Moneybags loved those cartoons. We used to watch them for hours. I miss him."

"I know."

Mona and I headed for the media room, where an enormous flat screen was attached to the wall. The other walls were devoted to shelves where hundreds of DVDs had been categorized and alphabetized. Comfy overstuffed chairs and sofas dominated the room.

I went straight to the animated section and pulled out one of the Popeye collections. I popped the DVD into the player, and Mona and I settled on the sofa with Mike at my feet. We spent the next couple of hours watching Popeye and Brutus fight over Olive Oyl. Mona and I had long agreed that Olive Oyl was one of the most unattractive women we'd ever seen and wondered why Popeye wasted all those cans of spinach so he could pound Brutus into the ground and win Olive's affection.

Sometime later, I awoke and realized Mona and I had both fallen asleep. It was after midnight, but Mona was sleeping so soundly that I hated to wake her. Instead, I covered her with a plush throw and took Mike out to do her business. I was not surprised to find Jimbo shining his flashlight at the hedges.

"Who goes there?" he called out.

I gave a massive eye roll. "It's me, Jimbo!" I said.

He stepped out of the shadows. He was dressed like a ninja. "Did you forget the password?" he asked.

"I'm not going to use a password," I said, wondering

why I didn't make things easier on myself and play along. But I'd had my fill of weird people for one day. "You know damn well who I am, and I don't have time to deal with stupid passwords."

He looked put out.

"Furthermore, Mona's mother will be arriving soon. She shouldn't have to use a password either."

"Are you saying I'm going overboard on this security thing?"

"You think?" I said.

I left him standing there and reentered the house through the back door, pausing at the counter to grab a dog biscuit from a box where I kept Mike's treats. I offered it to her, and she gobbled it. I looked about the room, wondering if there was anything I should do to get ready for the arrival of Mona's mother. The pantry and refrigerator were filled with food, since Jimbo had purchased massive amounts on his last grocery run, and I knew the twice-weekly cleaning crew saw that the upstairs guest rooms and baths were maintained.

I was considering taking a quick shower and putting on my pajamas when I heard a vehicle pull into the driveway. I looked out the window as a vintage VW van parked beside my car.

I hurried out the front door. A woman in a flowered skirt, peasant blouse, and shawl climbed from the driver's side. I noted a long gray pigtail hanging down the center of her back. She was no bigger than a minute; it was obvious where Mona had inherited her size-three frame.

"You must be Mona's mother," I said, giving her what I hoped was a welcoming smile.

She returned it. "That's right. And you're Kate. Mona has told me all about you. I'm Willie-Mae Dalton."

I held out my hand. "It's very nice to meet you, Mrs. Dalton."

"Call me Willie-Mae," she said, squeezing my hand affectionately. Just then, the passenger door opened, and a very pregnant young woman climbed out. "Meet Tiara Tuttle," Willie-Mae said. "I had to bring her with me on account of I'm her midwife."

Tiara looked to be in her midtwenties. She and I shook hands, even as she gawked at Mona's house. "Holy cow, this is a big place," she said. "How many people live here?"

"Just Mona," I said. "I'm here for emotional support."

"My whole family could fit in this house," Tiara said, "and I'm related to half the people in Tennessee." She looked at Willie-Mae. "How come you didn't tell me your daughter lived in a mansion? She must be really rich."

"It didn't cross my mind," Willie-Mae said as she opened the back door of the van. "But then, money has never meant much to me."

"I'm glad I brought my camera," Tiara said. "I've got to get pictures of this place. My friends won't believe it."

Jimbo joined us and introduced himself to Willie-Mae. "I'm Mona's chauffeur," he said, "although I help out in other areas." He glanced at me. "I have been instructed to keep everyone away from the house until Mona's rash heals, so I'm trying to keep the place secure."

"I hope it's okay that my patient and I are here," Willie-Mae said, glancing my way. "Mona asked me to come."

"You're more than welcome," I said. "We've been expecting you."

Jimbo nodded. "Please allow me to take your luggage." He reached for a large black satchel.

"Don't touch that!" Willie-Mae said so loudly that Jimbo

snatched his hand away as though he'd just grabbed a hot coal. "That's my medical bag," she said.

"Nobody is allowed to touch her medical bag," Tiara whispered to me. "It's *sacred*."

We headed toward the front door of the house with Jimbo on our heels, bearing suitcases, and Willie-Mae clutching her black bag.

"When is your baby due?" I asked Tiara.

"Not for a couple of weeks." Without warning, her face scrunched up and she burst into tears.

"Hush up, Tiara," Willie-Mae said. "We don't have time for nonsense. Besides, it's not good for the baby."

"Did I say something wrong?" I asked Willie-Mae.

Willie-Mae shook her head. "It's her hormones."

"That's not the only reason," Tiara said.

"Her husband is in the armed forces," Willie-Mae said. "He was deployed six months ago."

Tiara sniffed and swiped at her tears. "He won't be here when the baby comes," she said. "It's our first."

"I'm sorry to hear it, Tiara," I said, feeling genuinely sad for her.

Willie-Mae's look softened, and she rubbed Tiara's back. "That's why I brought my digital camera. We'll take plenty of pictures and e-mail them to Wayne."

A sleepy Mona met us at the front door, and we went inside. Willie-Mae set her bag down and hugged her daughter, but Mona's gaze was fixed on Tiara. "Let me look at you," Willie-Mae said, taking a step back. She frowned. "I thought you said you had a terrible rash."

"What do you call this?" Mona said, pointing to several small red patches on her face.

Willie-Mae looked from Mona to me. "She has always

put too much stock in her looks," she said. "I don't know how many times I've told her, real beauty comes from the inside."

"I don't think inner beauty would have won me all those beauty pageants," Mona quipped, "or the money that came with them. If not for the outer kind of beauty, I would still be living in the mountains."

Willie-Mae gave a snort. "Like that's a bad thing," she muttered.

They bickered back and forth for several minutes, and I couldn't help but wonder if it was normal for mothers and daughters to argue all the time. Their relationship wasn't so different from the one I had with my own mom.

"Where do you want these suitcases?" Jimbo asked Mona.

Mona didn't seem to hear him; her focus was on Tiara. She turned to her mother. "I don't mean to be rude, but why did you bring a very pregnant woman with you?"

"I'm her midwife, honey, and it's my job to see that she takes care of herself."

Mona didn't look pleased. "When is the baby due?"

"Not for two weeks," Willie-Mae said, "but you know how first babies are. They're always late."

Mona didn't change her stance. "Mama, you'd better be right about that, because I am *not* going to assist you in birthing a baby. I told you when I moved out that I'd had enough of that sort of thing to last me a lifetime."

Tiara burst into tears. "I shouldn't have come."

"Now look what you've done," Willie-Mae accused Mona. "You've gone and upset my patient." She turned to Tiara. "Stop that bawling right this minute, young lady!" Willie-Mae looked at me. "See what I mean? She cries at the drop of a hat. Darn those hormones. They're flip-flopping about like a fish out of water."

"Would somebody please tell me where to put this luggage," Jimbo said.

Mona looked at him. "There are four empty guest rooms upstairs," she said. "*You* decide."

He nodded and started up the tall staircase.

"Mona, I've been a midwife for thirty years," Willie-Mae said, "and I have never been wrong about a woman's due date. Not once!" she added.

"There's always a first time," Mona said. "Oh, great! Just thinking about it makes me itch. I should have known something like this would happen." She started for the kitchen.

"Where are you going?" Willie-Mae asked.

"To take my anti-itch medicine," Mona said.

I decided Mona was in no state to see to her guests, so I took it upon myself to play hostess. "May I get you something to eat or drink?" I asked Willie-Mae and Tiara.

"I'm always hungry," Tiara said. "I would kill for a pizza with all the works, including anchovies."

Willie-Mae rolled her eyes. "I have to watch her like a hawk; otherwise, she'd be eating junk food with tons of salt, which is not good in her condition. She's already ten pounds over the normal pregnancy weight because she sneaks French fries and milk shakes behind my back."

"I can make you a grilled cheese sandwich," I offered Tiara.

"Don't trouble yourself," Willie-Mae said. "I'll prepare a light snack to tide her over. Something healthy," she added.

The three of us went into the kitchen and found Mona tossing back a pill, followed by water. Willie-Mae pulled a chair from the kitchen table and motioned for Tiara to sit, then turned to her daughter. "What is that you're taking?" she asked. "You know how antidrug I am."

"It's just crack cocaine, Mama," Mona said. "I bought it off the street corner."

Willie-Mae didn't look amused. She held out her hand, and Mona handed her the prescription bottles she'd received from the hospital.

Willie-Mae pulled a pair of glasses from her purse and put them on. "I wouldn't give this stuff to a lab rat!" she said, tossing the bottles in the trash.

"What do you think you're doing?" Mona demanded.

"I'm going to have to insist you get off all medication if you expect me to heal you," Willie-Mae told her.

Mona pressed her lips together in irritation but said nothing. I had a feeling I should have stayed home.

Willie-Mae went to the refrigerator, opened it, and peered inside. "You may have cottage cheese and fruit," she told Tiara.

The young woman gave a huge sigh. "I thought being pregnant would be fun. Frankly, it stinks."

Mona and I joined Tiara at the table as Willie-Mae prepared the snack and set it before her. Willie-Mae took a closer look at Mona's rash, examining her arms and legs as well. "Are you sure you haven't been bitten or stung by an insect?" she asked.

"I'm positive," Mona said. "I know I have hives," she added. "I broke out after a particularly stressful event. I remember breaking out every time I had to help you deliver a baby."

"You broke out because you had allergies," Willie-Mae said. "You were allergic to just about everything, including my chickens and that kitten you wanted so badly." Willie-

Mae looked at me. "She was even allergic to baby powder, and the only soap her skin could tolerate was Ivory." She turned to Mona. "I'm going to give you a topical cream to get you through the night, but before we can attack the problem, we need to cleanse your system of toxins. I'll have to start you on a regimen of colonics first thing in the morning, starting with a liver cleansing."

Mona instantly paled.

"What's a colonic?" Tiara asked.

"Don't ask," Mona said.

chapter 7

....

I overslept the next morning and was forced to rush. I barely had time to shower and throw on my clothes, walk Mike, and toss back a cup of coffee before I loaded my belongings and my dog into the car and hit the road for home. I figured Mona would not need me now that her mother was there.

I dropped Mike off and drove straight to my office. I was surprised to find the door to the reception room unlocked and Abigail sitting at the front desk.

"How did you get in?" I blurted.

"I forgot to mention it yesterday, but I took the key from the center desk drawer. I hope you don't mind."

I did mind. True, Mona had her own key and came and went as she pleased, but I'd known Abigail less than twenty-four hours.

"Uh-oh," she said. "I can see by the look on your face that you're not pleased."

"You should have told me," I said. "I prefer knowing where all the keys are."

She looked surprised. "It's not like I took the key to your private office," she said. She suddenly opened the bottom desk drawer and pulled out her purse. She reached inside and brought out a key and dropped it on the desk. "There," she said. "Only it's going to be a bitch for me tomorrow, because I don't know what time I'll get here or how long I'll have to wait until you let me in."

"What do you mean?"

"I take the city bus," she said, "so I'm a slave to its schedule."

"Don't you have a car?"

"Yeah. Only it was old before I drove thousands of miles to get to Atlanta. I never know when it's going to break down, and right now I can't afford to have it fixed."

"Why didn't you tell me?"

"Companies don't hire people unless they have adequate transportation."

"How were you able to get here so quickly yesterday?"

"I took a cab."

No telling what that had cost, I thought. I was beginning to feel bad for her. "So how long have you been here this morning?" I asked.

She shrugged. "A little over an hour. I used the time to straighten the supply room and clean out the refrigerator. There was a jar of mayonnaise that expired two years ago. I'm surprised it didn't kill somebody."

I smiled. "So you saved my life."

She shrugged. "Could be."

"Here," I said, shoving the key across the desk toward her. "I'm sorry I overreacted. How about I make it up to you over a cup of coffee?" I suggested. "It won't take me long to make it."

"I've already made it," Abigail said, "and I bought donuts from downstairs. They're on the kitchen table." She picked up a sheet of paper and handed it to me. "I made a list of items you are running low on, both in the kitchen and the supply room. You're almost out of coffee, and if you don't buy toilet paper soon, we're all going to be sorry."

I nodded and skimmed the rest of the list. "Thank you, Abigail," I said, genuinely appreciative. "Mona usually makes the list and gives it to me. I wouldn't have thought to look."

Abigail smiled. "You're just being nice because I bought donuts."

"You're right," I said.

"So what are we waiting for?"

Five minutes later we were both sitting at the kitchen table with coffee and a donut in front of us. "I should probably tell you," Abigail said, "that the temp agency called only minutes before you got here. This lady named Bernice wants to know if I'm working out okay," she added. "I told her I thought you were pleased with me, but I suspect she's going to call back." She paused. "Are you?"

"Am I what?"

"Pleased with my work?" she asked.

"Oh. Well, yes," I said. Which was true. I had no complaints as far as how she performed her duties. I just thought she was strange. "I hate that you had to sit around for an hour this morning," I said.

She shrugged. "I didn't have anything better to do, but I plan to look more closely at the bus schedules for this area. Hopefully, I'll find something more convenient." She paused. "You know, if Mona decides not to come back, you'll be able to hire me full time. I know the agency will charge a fee for that, but I'll gladly pay it."

Her comment surprised me. "Please don't get your hopes up, Abigail. There is no reason to believe Mona isn't coming back."

She looked disappointed. "I just want you to know I'm available."

My first patient of the day was claustrophobic and had a fear of heights. I had treated numerous patients for the same problem. Unfortunately, this patient worked on the top floor of a tall building, and her office was surrounded by glass. Not only did she avoid looking out the windows for fear of having a full-blown panic attack, she was forced to use the stairs because of her fear of elevators.

As with many of my patients, I'd made a relaxation tape for her. Unlike others I treated, she actually practiced the techniques. She could take short trips on the elevator. If she sat in her chair and placed her hands flat on her desk, which gave her a feeling of being grounded, she could peek at the windows. I felt confident there would come a time when she would be able to look out the windows and admire Atlanta's skyline instead of hiding from it.

My next appointment, Arnie (aka Arnell) Decker, suffered from gender identity disorder. He'd spent his life feeling trapped in a man's body before he'd decided on sexual reassignment surgery. In order to qualify, he had to see a therapist for eighteen months, during which time he would live as a woman.

Most people don't understand the confusion, distress, depression, and self-loathing that often accompanies GID, especially for someone like Arnie, an ex-Marine. He had been devastated when his family, specifically his father, had disowned him. My mother and aunt, on the other hand, had opened their hearts and their home to him, accepting him just as he was.

As proud as I was of them, and although I genuinely liked Arnie/Arnell, I felt I had to avoid a close friendship with him, lest it get in the way of our patient-therapist relationship.

Today he was dressed in an attractive rust-colored skirt and jacket, accessorized by a flattering scarf. Arnell had exquisite taste, proof that my mom and aunt did not accompany him to the mall.

"How are things going?" I asked him once we were seated in my office. Arnell was the head chef at a five-star restaurant, and he was always coming up with new recipes. Since our sessions were strictly confidential, I was often privy to the secret ingredients he used.

"I know people make fun of me behind my back," he said. "Especially at work," he added. "I try to ignore it, but sometimes it's hurtful."

"Most people don't understand GID," I said, "and those who do may not be so accepting."

"I don't think it's any of their business," he said.

I nodded. "You're right. A person's sexual preference is a personal decision, but we both know that some people are going to be uncomfortable with it. You can't control what other people think, Arnell. You can only control how you choose to deal with it."

He gave a grunt. "That's what I keep telling myself, but

sometimes it's hard. The owner of the restaurant finally called me into his office day before yesterday. I was shaking in my high heels that he was going to tell me to take a hike."

"And?"

Arnell grinned. "He said he didn't care if I came to work in a hoop skirt as long as I kept the customers coming in."

"Excellent!" I said. "By the way, have you looked into a support group?"

"I'm still checking. I'd really like to meet people like me. Not that I don't get a lot of support from your mom and aunt," he added. "They're great. I just wish my own family could accept me as I am."

"Give it time, Arnell."

"We both know my father isn't likely to come around."

Arnell's father was a colonel, a die-hard military man who'd pressed his son to join the armed forces in hopes of turning him into a man's man. Arnell had served proudly; he'd even kept his gender issues top secret, but it had been a miserable existence for him. As had the heterosexual relationships he'd tried to form. It wasn't until Arnell was on the verge of suicide that he came to me for help.

"You and I both know we can't live our lives according to other people's wishes," I said. "If that were the case, you'd be attending monster truck rallies with your father, and I'd be Dumpster-diving for junk."

We both laughed. Arnell knew my mother had wanted me to be part of the family business for years. She had never understood why I'd chosen to become a psychologist instead of a junk dealer.

The session ended, and Arnell and I set up a time for the following week. After he left, I remained in my chair, staring out the window. I wondered if Jay was okay and if he was getting enough rest. I wondered if he was still annoyed with me and if he was ready to toss in the towel as far as our relationship went. My patients were able to distract me from dwelling on my worries, but once they were gone, it all came back to me. The least he could do was call.

I went into the bathroom and washed my hands three times.

Abigail knocked on my door at noon. "I was thinking of grabbing a sandwich downstairs," she said. "Would you like something?"

I had to admit a sandwich sounded better than cheese crackers from the vending machine. "Sure," I said, reaching for my purse.

"No, no," she said, holding up both hands. "It's my treat."

"Don't be silly," I told her, suspecting she had financial problems after hearing about her car.

"I'd really like to buy your lunch today, Kate. It would mean a lot to me."

"Okay," I said. "Next time, it will be my treat." I gave her my order, and she hurried out.

I was trying to organize my files when Abigail returned. At least half the files, paperwork from patients I no longer saw, needed to be put through the shredder. I finally closed the file drawer and joined Abigail in the kitchenette.

"Boy, that Arnell guy sure knows how to dress," she said. "He looks so put together, if you know what I mean," she said. "It all has to do with accessorizing, I think."

I nodded but waited for her comment, to see whether she would have a problem dealing with some of my more outlandish patients, for lack of a better word.

"I never know what's in style," she confessed. "I'll bet he subscribes to one of those high-fashion magazines."

"I don't keep up with the latest styles," I admitted.

She looked surprised. "But you look so professional, so tailored. Does someone make your clothes for you?"

I laughed. "Yeah. Jaclyn Smith from Kmart."

"No way!"

"Uh-huh. Also, thirty percent off," I added proudly, pointing to the navy blue suit I wore.

"That color looks good on you, and the style has a certain, shall I say, understated elegance? I'll bet the guys find it sexy."

"Wow, I'm going to have to write to Jaclyn Smith and thank her." I picked up my sandwich. "You should see how my receptionist dresses," I said. "She shops at all the best stores."

"She must have money."

"Yup. Plus, she's a size three and can eat anything without gaining weight."

Abigail shook her head. "Don't you want to slap people like that?"

I laughed. It felt good. Perhaps I'd been too hard on Abigail.

On the way home, I stopped by the grocery store to pick up the supplies Abigail had said we needed. I checked my messages. Again, no word from Jay. I felt my heart sink to the soles of my feet, but I was annoyed as well. The man couldn't pick up the damn phone for five minutes? I had a real problem with that.

I gave Mike her daily dose of attention and opened my freezer so I could decide what I was having for dinner. I had a choice between Salisbury steak with mashed potatoes or turkey and stuffing with mixed vegetables. I liked having a variety from which to choose. I popped the turkey and stuffing into the microwave and tried to reach Alice Smithers again, the patient whose alter ego, Liz Jones, was giving Thad trouble, but there was no answer. I went upstairs to change clothes.

Mona called shortly after I'd finished my dinner. "How did it go today with the temp?" she asked.

"She's not so bad," I said, "but I hope your mom is able to cure you quickly so you can come back to work."

"Mama is determined to rid my body of toxins." Mona sighed. "We're working on cleansing my liver."

"I didn't know livers got dirty," I said.

"She claims she can't treat an illness until the body is cleansed. She also threw away half the stuff in my pantry. She'll probably put me on a diet of bean sprouts and seaweed before it's over."

"How is Tiara?"

"Miserable. She complains constantly. She says she feels bigger than the Mall of America. Plus, her feet are swollen. When she's not complaining about how crummy she feels, she's complaining about being hungry. I should have known Mama would bring one of her patients. Like I don't have enough to deal with," she added.

"You sound resentful."

"Maybe I am," she said. "I never call Mama for help, but the one time I do, she has to bring the most pregnant woman in the world with her. It's not like she's the only midwife in Tennessee. She could have asked someone else to take over Tiara's care. You should see how she fusses over her."

"I'm sorry," I said, knowing Mona was hurt because she was playing second fiddle to a woman she barely knew.

My doorbell rang. I said good-bye to Mona and peered through the peephole. Two neatly dressed women, one middle-aged, the other one a bit younger, stood on the other side. Obviously, they were selling something. I unlocked my door but kept the chain in place. "I don't know what you're selling," I said politely, "but I'm not interested."

"We're selling eternity," the older woman said.

The younger one spoke up. "Actually, eternity is free for the asking."

"Let me guess," I said. "Bitsy Stout sent you."

"She's worried about you," the older woman said. "She asked us to pay you a visit and pray with you. We would also like to invite you to Sunday services. Even someone like you is welcome in the Lord's house."

"Someone like me?" I asked.

"A nonbeliever," she said.

I gave a sigh. "I'm really busy right now."

"Too busy to accept Jesus into your life or end up in hell?" she asked.

"I already know what hell is like," I said a bit louder than I'd meant. "It's living across the street from Bitsy Stout." They looked shocked as I closed the door in their faces.

Thad called and asked if I had reached Alice Smithers.

"I've left several messages on her answering machine," I said, "but she hasn't returned my calls. I'll keep trying."

"She's probably out trying to screw up somebody else's life," he said. I heard the irritation in his voice.

"Thad, you and I both know that this has nothing to do with Alice," I told him.

"It doesn't matter," he replied. "I could still lose my license." He ended the call on a sour note, and I wasn't in such a great mood either. Seemed all I did was wait for the stupid phone to ring.

The first thing I did the next morning, even before I poured my first cup of coffee, was try to reach Alice Smithers. Hopefully, I could catch her before she left for work. When she didn't answer, I left a curt message for her to call me back right away.

My annoyance quickly turned to surprise when I arrived at my office and found Abigail scrubbing the bathroom. "Why on earth are you cleaning?" I asked. "That is not part of your job description. Besides, there's a cleaning crew that comes in every night."

"They don't do a very good job," Abigail said, "and I have this thing about bathrooms and kitchens. I think they should sparkle. By the way, your coffee is ready."

The kitchenette had been cleaned as well and smelled fresh. I poured a cup of coffee, added cream and sugar, and took a sip. Perfect.

A smiling Abigail joined me a few minutes later.

"We need to talk," I said, and watched her smile droop.

"You're not pleased with me."

"You're trying too hard. I wish you'd relax."

"I have to make a good impression with the temp agency," she said. "I really need a job."

"You're doing fine," I said.

She looked relieved. "Thank you. That means a lot to me."

I got up and poured another cup of coffee, hoping it would clear the cobwebs in my brain. I had wakened several times during the night wondering why Jay hadn't bothered to pick up the phone and let me know he was okay. I rejoined Abigail at the kitchen table and saw that she was staring at me. "Is something wrong?" I asked.

"You have dark circles under your eyes. Are you not sleeping well?"

I had tried to conceal the circles with makeup. Obviously, it hadn't worked. "I have a lot on my mind," I said.

"I'm a good listener."

I decided it would not do any harm to tell her. "Jay is among the firefighters working the wildfire in the Apalachicola National Forest," I said without going into details of how I fretted constantly over his job.

I noted the sympathy in her eyes. "I'm sorry," she said. "I've been watching the fires on the news. People are afraid it's going to be as bad as the one here in 2007."

"That was a monster," I said, shuddering mentally at the thought that the present fire might prove just as deadly.

"That's why it's important to have a lot of support right now," she said, "so you don't feel you're going it alone." She put her hand on mine. "Please remember that I'm here for you. When I make friends, I make them for life."

The phone rang in the reception room, and Abigail bolted from the chair and hurried from the room. As odd as it sounded, I still felt the imprint of her hand on mine. I knew she meant well, but something about her made me uncomfortable, and I couldn't put my finger on it. Maybe it was me.

Abigail returned a moment later. "There's an Alice Smithers on the phone."

I wasted no time going into my office and reaching for the telephone. "Why haven't you returned my calls?" I demanded.

"I was in the shower and didn't hear the phone ring," she said. "I was on my way out the door when I saw I had a message. I had to wait until I arrived at work to call you back. Is something wrong?"

"I've called you a half dozen times," I said.

Silence at first. "I didn't know."

It didn't take a rocket scientist to realize that Liz Jones had erased my messages. "I need to see you immediately."

"I have to attend meetings this morning. I could come during my lunch hour."

"Fine. Just make sure you show up."

I saw several patients back-to-back before Alice arrived. She apologized profusely. "My answering machine is old," she said. "I guess I'm going to have to replace it."

"Don't rush out and buy one," I said. "I have a feeling Liz has been erasing the messages."

The color drained from Alice's face. Although the alter personalities were able to keep up with Alice's comings and goings, she was only aware of their actions through me. "Has Liz done something?"

I told her about Liz's threats against Thad. "I need to speak with her, please," I said, although there was no guarantee that Liz would give me the time of day.

Alice sat there quietly, but within a few minutes I noted the subtle changes in her face and demeanor. Liz had a hard look about her that was often seen on much older women who'd lived a not-so-pleasant life. One side of her lip curled upward into a half sneer.

"Hello, Liz," I said. "It has been a while."

"I know why you want to talk to me," she said. "It's about Thad."

I wasn't surprised Liz referred to Thad by his first name. "I understand Dr. Glazer wants to set you up with another psychiatrist."

"Just let him try."

"And that you've threatened to file charges against him for inappropriate sexual conduct," I added.

She didn't reply.

I didn't let her silence dissuade me. "You're aware that Dr. Glazer is one of the most prominent and reputable psychiatrists in Atlanta," I said.

She met my gaze. "I don't care if the man walks on water. It's his word against mine. I can be very convincing."

"What are you going to do if one or more of the personalities comes forth and denies your charges?"

Again, she didn't reply, but I could see the anger and uncertainty gathering in her eyes like darkening clouds.

"Dr. Glazer's colleagues will back him up, as will his impeccable reputation," I said. "You'll look foolish."

"You're a real bitch," she said.

"You've worn out your welcome, Liz," I told her. "The others don't need you anymore. You're of no value. You're like a guest who has overstayed her visit."

Hatred burned in her eyes. I realized I was taking a great risk by goading her. She was clearly a narcissist. When you call narcissists on the carpet, expose them for what they are, they either get depressed or fly into a rage. I had no idea what to expect from Liz.

I went on. "Surely you realize that if there's a hearing,

your past will come to light. How you had an affair with your old boss, how you and your ex-boyfriend tried to extort money from him, how that same boyfriend attacked me in my office," I added. "It won't bode well for you, Liz."

"I had nothing to do with that attack. You can't pin it on me."

I leaned closer. "Don't screw with me, Liz. You want to make trouble, go ahead. I'll draw up commitment papers so fast you won't know what hit you. You're going to hate being locked up."

She smirked. "You'd never do that to the others."

"Try me."

I caught a flash of uncertainty, then she was gone.

Abigail had messages waiting for me. I was not surprised that one of them was from Thad. I called him back on his cell phone.

"I can't say for certain," I told him, "but my gut tells me that Liz Jones isn't going to bring charges against you after all."

He gave a sigh of relief. "How did you manage that?"

"I can be a real badass when I put my mind to it."

Thad chuckled. "I've seen that side of you."

"Only once," I reminded him, "when I caught you in your hot tub with another woman and realized you had commitment issues."

"That was a long time ago, Kate. I keep telling you I've changed. I've matured. The fact that I'm not asking you what kind of panties you're wearing should be proof, even though I can't help but be curious."

I laughed. Same old Thad.

"So what's the possibility of us getting together later?" he asked, his tone changing and becoming almost somber. "I need to talk to someone, and I'd prefer that person be you." He paused. "It's not about Liz Jones; it's something else."

"Sounds serious," I said, noting his tone.

"I'd like your advice on a matter. Maybe we could grab dinner tonight."

"I don't know, Thad. You'll probably try to ply me with wine and get me to go home with you."

"That's what the old Thad would have done," he said. "You're talking to the new and much-improved Thad. Anyway, I owe you for taking on Liz Jones."

"That's true. Where would you like to have dinner?"

"How about that French restaurant you like so well," he suggested.

"That's a bit intimate, don't you think?"

"I'm trusting that you'll be on your best behavior. I'll make reservations for eight o'clock."

I was gathering files and stuffing them in my file cabinet so I could leave for the day when Abigail knocked on my door.

"I was wondering if you'd like to get a bite to eat," she said. "I have a coupon for Waffle House. Buy one meal, get the other one free."

"Thanks for the invitation, but I've already made plans," I said, annoyed that I couldn't find a file and hoping I hadn't misfiled it. Crap.

"I guess you and Mona are getting together," Abigail said.

"Huh? No, I'm meeting Dr. Glazer for dinner." I gave a

sigh, half relief, half frustration, when I found the damn file lying on top of the cabinet.

"The guy who keeps calling here?" she said. "Where are you going?"

I paused and looked at her. "I'm sorry, I wasn't listening."

She shrugged. "I asked where you're having dinner?"

I shoved the file in place, closed the cabinet, and locked the drawer. "No place special," I said, feeling the less Abigail knew about my personal life the better.

"Well, don't worry, my lips are sealed."

I looked up. "Excuse me?"

"Jay won't hear it from me," she said.

I was both surprised and annoyed by her response. "Don't give it a second thought, Abigail," I said. "The last thing you need to concern yourself with is my personal life."

"In other words, mind my own business, right?"

I gave her a tight smile. "Something like that, yes."

I swung by Mona's on the way home. Willie-Mae met me at the door. She wore baggy denim overalls, a flannel shirt, and her long hair had been pinned up and covered with a bandanna. She looked happy to see me.

"How is Mona today?" I asked once Willie-Mae stepped aside so I could enter.

"She's down in the dumps. Maybe you can cheer her up."

I found Mona in the sunroom at the back of her house, feet propped on an ottoman, white pads on the soles of her feet. She didn't look happy. I was surprised to find a dark red splotch on her neck, but I would have bitten my tongue clean off before mentioning it.

"What are those things for?" I asked, pointing to the pads.

"They're supposed to draw toxins from my body." She shook her head sadly. "I sort of regret calling my mama," she added. "You'd feel the same way if you had to drink her tonics."

I sat near her. "What is in them?"

"I have no idea, but they're nasty. I'd give anything for a burger and fries."

"I would try to smuggle them in if I thought I could get away with it."

"There are no secrets in this house," Mona said. "My mama is all-knowing." She gave another sigh. "So how is what's-her-name doing?"

"Her name is Abigail. I guess you could say she's a little strange."

"Well, then, she should fit in well at the loony bin."

Mona could be irreverent as hell when the mood hit her. "She asks a lot of questions. Some are way too personal, in my opinion."

"She obviously has boundary issues."

"Ah, I take it you've been watching *Dr. Phil*."

Willie-Mae joined us in the sunroom. "Kate, would you like to stay for dinner?" she asked.

"Thanks for asking, but I already have plans."

"Well, just so you know, you have a standing invitation," Willie-Mae said before hurrying out.

"Who are you having dinner with?" Mona asked.

"Thad."

"Uh-oh."

"He's been through a couple of tense moments lately. One of his patients threatened to bring charges against him for inappropriate sexual behavior."

"That's ridiculous," Mona said. "Thad could have just about any woman he wanted. He's not dumb enough to get involved with a patient. Besides, he's still got the hots for you."

"That's in the past."

"Anything from Jay?"

"No. And guess what? I'm going to stop worrying about it."

"Good for you."

"Right now I'm more concerned about you. I don't like that you're isolating yourself."

"I can't let people see me like this," Mona said. The expression on her face told me she wasn't about to budge on her decision. We chatted for close to an hour before I checked my wristwatch. "I should get going," I said. "I'll try to stop by after work tomorrow."

"That'll be great," Mona said. "I'm expecting my mood will be even worse."

As *always, Mike* was happy to see me. Of course, there was no way to know if she was just showing devotion to her master or if she was hoping for a burger.

I saw that I only had little more than an hour before I was to meet Thad, and I needed to upgrade my outfit. I hurried upstairs, chose the little black dress that women everywhere knew was indispensable because it worked for high-end restaurants, cocktail parties, and funerals. I added a single strand of pearls that my grandmother had given me, stepped into black pumps, and started downstairs.

The doorbell rang.

I peered through the peephole and found a man on the

other side whom I did not recognize. Since I didn't make a habit of opening my door to strangers, I tiptoed away.

I was standing at the kitchen sink freshening Mike's water when someone knocked on the back door, almost causing me to jump out of my skin. I pulled the curtain aside and found the same stranger staring back at me. I unlocked the dead bolt but kept my chain in place.

"May I help you?" I asked.

"My name is Brother Love," he said, drawing the words out with a flourish and reminding me of a preacher I'd once heard shouting scripture from a street corner. "Your neighbor, Bitsy Stout, is concerned about you."

I didn't believe for one minute that his last name was Love. "Look, I'm in a bit of a rush," I said.

"Sister Stout can't sleep at night because she worries about your wicked ways."

"My wicked ways?" I said, then frowned. "Are you sure you've got the right house? There's just not that much excitement going on around here."

"You have been blinded by the devil to your own sins, Sister Kate. But there is no reason to lose hope. I can show you the way."

I was quickly getting irritated. I was more interested in showing *him* the way off my property. "Listen up, Brother whatever your last name really is. First of all, I'm not your sister. Secondly, you don't know anything about me. So you need to remove yourself from my property and leave me alone."

I closed the door and locked the dead bolt. I had to wonder if there was a sane person in Bitsy's church.

* * *

Thad and I arrived at the restaurant only minutes apart. He was his usual gorgeous self, blond and tanned and wearing a suit that probably cost more than all my monthly bills combined. We were led to a table for two, and Thad pulled my chair out for me. I smelled soap and aftershave. He'd showered beforehand.

"You look lovely as always, Kate," he said.

"Thank you."

Thad took the chair across the table from me and smiled. "This reminds me of that quaint little place we used to go to when we were at Emory. What was the name of it?"

"Antoine's," I said. "That was a long time ago," I added.

"Not so long."

Our waiter appeared. Thad reached for the wine list. "I wonder if they have that white wine you like so well," he said.

"You don't need to order a bottle on my behalf," I told him and looked at the waiter. "I'll just have a glass of your house chardonnay."

Thad looked disappointed. "Scotch and water for me," he said. "Preferably Dewar's."

"Of course, sir." The waiter nodded and moved away.

I glanced at Thad and noted the amusement lurking in his eyes. "What?"

"I forgot to mention that I saw your picture in the newspaper."

I gave a heartfelt sigh. "So did everyone else."

"You did a brave thing."

"Thank you," I said. "You're the first person who hasn't called me an idiot."

"Including Jay?"

I did not like talking to Thad about Jay. "He wasn't

thrilled that I stepped in the line of fire. He can be weird like that."

"Doesn't he know you're not the type to just stand by and watch something bad happen to another person?"

"It didn't seem to matter."

"Well, I'm not him. I applaud your bravery, Kate."

I saw that he was sincere, but I tried to prevent my dangling nerve endings from wrapping themselves around the tenderness in his voice. Thad could play me, and every other woman, like a fiddle. I opened my menu and studied it closely. The waiter appeared with our drinks.

"Would you care for an appetizer?" the man asked once he'd served our cocktails.

Thad nodded. "Indeed we would. The lovely lady and I would like to start with the goose liver pâté," he said. "Extra capers on the side, and please dice the onions smaller than usual." He looked at me. "Is that okay with you?"

"Sounds great," I said, suddenly remembering how fussy Thad was when it came to dining out.

"Would you like to hear the specials?" the waiter asked.

"Of course," Thad said.

I smiled as the man began a litany of food dishes that were preceded by adjectives like *succulent* or *tender* or *luscious.*

"I already know what I want," I said, only to have the waiter give me a hurt look, as though he thought I found his recitation dull. "I'll take the filet mignon with béarnaise sauce. Medium rare," I added. "Bleu cheese on the salad."

He wrote it down and turned to Thad.

"I'll have the succulent bay scallops with the tender new potatoes," Thad said.

The waiter gave him a broad smile. "Excellent choice."

Finally, Thad and I were alone. I took a sip of my wine and tried to relax. "So?" I said lightly. "What did you want to talk to me about?"

"Us," he said, reaching across the table and taking my hands in his. "You and me."

chapter 8

....

I yanked my hands away. "Dammit, Thad! You misled me *again*, and I was dumb enough to fall for it, *again*."

"I didn't mislead you," he said quickly. "I *do* have something important to discuss with you, but it's equally important that I know where you and I stand. You're the only woman I've ever told I loved and meant it."

"Gee, wouldn't that make you the world's biggest jerk?"

"We could have made it, Kate," he went on, "if you had given me a second chance. If you hadn't run off and married Jay on the rebound."

I closed my eyes for a few seconds and took a deep breath. "Thad, how many times do I have to tell you that I did not marry Jay to get back at you? I married him because I loved him."

"And yet the two of you have lived separately for how many months now? And dare I bring up the fact that you're still legally divorced?"

"You know darn well I had planned to stop the divorce from going through," I said.

"Nevertheless, I'd have thought two people madly in love would have remarried by now."

"We're still seeing a marriage counselor," I said, wondering why I was trying to defend my relationship with Jay. Actually, our marriage counseling had been put on hold temporarily, so the therapist and I could work together on some of my issues. "I've already explained all of this to you, Thad. Why do you insist on rehashing it?"

He sat back in his chair. "I'm seriously thinking of closing my practice and moving to West Palm Beach."

I blinked several times. "Why would you do that? You have a very lucrative practice here."

"An old friend of mine is looking for a partner. You wouldn't believe how much psychiatrists make in West Palm. I could work half the hours for twice the money."

"You already work half the hours for twice the money."

"West Palm Beach is a beautiful place, Kate. I could get in more golf and tennis and sailing." He stirred his glass of scotch with a swizzle stick. His smile faded as he lifted the glass to his lips.

"Does this have anything to do with Liz Jones?" I asked. "Because I've already told you, the woman appears to be giving it second thoughts. She doesn't want to look like a fool." I gave him a brief rundown of the conversation I'd had with her.

He leaned back in his chair. "As much as I appreciate you taking care of that matter, it has nothing to do with West Palm." He sighed. "The thing is, I'm thirty-six years old. I need a change."

Our pâté arrived. Thad spread some of it on a wafer, added capers and chopped onions, and offered it to me. I thanked him. I waited until he'd prepared a cracker for himself before tasting mine. It was delicious. Still, I was trying to digest the news he'd just given me.

"You don't look very happy," he said. "Does that mean you would miss me if I went away?"

"Are you nuts? Of course I would miss you." It was true that Thad's first love was himself, and he was as shallow as they come, but he had come through for me many times when I'd found myself in a jam. I suppose I'd never considered how much he actually meant to me, once I'd gotten past how angry I'd felt when I caught him cheating on me in his hot tub.

"You could always come with me," he said.

Our gazes met. The candle on our table tossed a soft glow on Thad's face, and he looked almost vulnerable; his brown eyes appeared lighter in color, as though shot with gold. Our waiter picked that moment to arrive with our salads. I was glad to have a moment to myself.

I cleared my throat. "That's not going to happen, Thad," I said once we were alone.

He took a sip of his drink. There was no teasing light in his eyes anymore, just a flat stare. I suddenly felt very sad. Like when I'd graduated from high school and my friends and I went our separate ways, on to various colleges. Same with grad school. Saying good-bye had always been hard for me, because my worst fear was loss. It didn't take a genius to figure out why.

"What are you thinking?" Thad asked.

I shrugged. "I guess I assumed you'd always be around."

"I have been around, Kate. You just haven't noticed."

"That's not fair."

"I made one mistake, and I'm going to pay for it for the rest of my life."

"There was more to our breakup than your propensity to get women naked in your hot tub," I said, "but I don't want to discuss it. It's too late for us, Thad."

We both sipped our drinks in a tense silence.

The waiter retrieved our uneaten salads. He seemed to sense the unease at our table, because he made no sound.

"I shouldn't have come," I said. "This was a mistake."

"Why? Because I'm asking the hard questions that you can't or won't ask yourself?"

"What do you mean?"

"I want to know if you have any feelings left for me."

I grappled for an answer. "How could I not?" I said finally. "You were my first real love." Much to my embarrassment, I felt a tear slide down one cheek. I swiped at it.

"Oh, crap, you're not going to cry, are you?" he said. "Please don't do that."

"I'm not crying," I said, trying to blot my tears with my napkin. This time when Thad reached for my hand, I let him hold it. Something inside of me hurt so much, it felt like one of my organs had been cut out and the wound was still exposed and raw. "You're right about Jay and me. We should have worked things out by now. It's just *stuff* keeps getting in the way. Why is that?"

His smile was rueful. "I don't know, Kate. I can't even figure out my own life."

"I've got to get out of here," I said as fresh tears overtook me. "I'm sorry, but I don't feel like eating anything right now."

Thad motioned for the waiter, and the man seemed to appear out of nowhere. If he noticed my tears, at least he pretended not to.

"Would you box our food and bring the check?" Thad said. "The lady and I would like to take a walk."

Thad and I walked for ten minutes before I could pull myself together. He held two take-out boxes in one arm, and the other was draped over my shoulders, as though he feared I might run screaming off into the night.

"I am so glad you could attend my meltdown," I said, my voice hoarse from crying and my head pounding.

"It's probably a delayed response to the shooting," Thad offered.

I shook my head sadly. "I'm *so* not in a position to treat people with emotional problems," I said. "Nothing is going right, and my anxiety level is at an all-time high. Mona's got hives, and I know I'm partly to blame because of all the stress I bring into her life. I've got religious fanatics knocking on my door, trying to save me from going to hell because they think I'm an atheist and a jezebel. And wouldn't you know it, the girl I hired to fill in for Mona is a weirdo."

"What do you mean?" Thad asked.

"I don't know. I can't put my finger on it. Maybe she's just nosy, but she asks more questions than my mother, and she stands too close." He gave me an odd look. "You know, she's in my personal space," I added. "It's enough to give someone a bad case of heebie-jeebies.

"Why don't you ask the agency for a replacement?" he said.

"I don't know," I said, between a sigh and a whine. "She needs the money, and she's so down on herself that I hate to give her another reason to feel bad."

"Yes, but if she's not working out—"

"She's trying so hard, Thad," I said, remembering how she had cleaned the kitchenette and bathrooms. "And she has no family or friends in town. It's complicated." I tried to ignore my pounding head. "And that's not even the worst of it," I added. "I've got to attend a family reunion this weekend with a bunch of hog farmers. Hog farmers! And God forbid Jay should pick up the phone and let me know he's okay. Is that too much to ask?"

"Aw, Kate, no wonder you're stressed." Thad pulled me closer and dropped a kiss on the top of my head.

"And now you're talking of leaving," I said and began sobbing in earnest. "Perfect damn timing, Thad," I said, giving him a punch in the arm.

He stopped walking and looked at me. I could see him clearly under the streetlamp. "I will never be so far away that you can't pick up a phone and reach me immediately."

"Oh, sure, that's what everyone says. People swear they'll stay in close touch, but they eventually drift apart."

"That's not always the case," he said.

"I need to go home and take something for my headache," I said. "I'm sorry I burdened you with my problems."

"You've never been a burden to me, but I should take you home. I don't want you driving right now."

"I'm okay now." He looked doubtful. "Really," I said. "Once I get a good night's sleep, I'll feel better."

He and I turned around and headed toward our cars. Thad opened my door and handed me the box containing my uneaten meal. "Call me when you get home so I'll know you made it okay. Even better, I should follow you."

"No, no, I'm fine." He waited until I had closed the door and locked it before walking toward his own car.

I had only driven a few miles when a flash of light hit my rearview mirror, and I realized I was being followed. "Oh, Thad," I said, hating that I'd made him worry, at the same time wishing he would turn off his high beams. On second glance, though, I realized it wasn't Thad's Mercedes behind me. It was difficult to get the exact make and model of the car with the blinding light. I slowed, hoping it would pass me. Instead, the car lagged back and remained at a distance. Then, all at once it sped up and passed me, an older model white sedan. The only thing I could really make out was that the driver wore a baseball cap.

I arrived home and checked my answering machine. There were several hang-ups, which I found odd, and Jeff had called to check on Mona. The machine beeped, and my heart did a little happy dance when Jay's voice came on. It was difficult to make out the entire message because of the static.

"Wanted to touch base . . . bad reception . . . I'll call . . . back."

I gave a huge sigh of relief, knowing he was okay. I quickly dialed his cell phone, but there was no answer.

At least he'd called. That meant a lot.

I returned Jeff's call and gave him the latest on Mona. "Um, I sort of need a date for Sunday night," I said, "but I'll understand if you say no."

"Where are we going?"

I told him about my aunt and uncle's anniversary party.

"Isn't that the aunt who carries an ice pick in her purse?" he asked.

"Yeah, but I don't think she's ever stabbed anyone."

He hesitated. "Okay, where and what time?"

"Seven o'clock at the VFW. I'll meet you there. Oh, and dress casually."

"That's a relief. It will save me the trouble of having my tux dry-cleaned."

"Thanks, Jeff. I owe you."

I reached the office the next morning and stopped short when I saw Abigail's outfit. It was the exact one I'd worn the day before.

"Guess what?" she said, giving a small twirl as if to model the suit. "Fifty percent off!"

"No kidding?" I didn't know what else to say.

"I went to Kmart to buy panty hose, and there was a whole rack of Jaclyn Smith on sale. I bought three outfits!"

"Good for you." I tried to sound enthusiastic, but frankly, I felt a little creeped out.

Abigail must've sensed my displeasure. "I hope you don't mind," she said. "I needed clothes, and it was such a good deal. If you have the same outfits, we can wear them on different days. You could call me the night before and—"

"Don't worry about it," I interrupted.

"I just don't want you to be upset with me," she said. She paused. "Um, your coffee is ready."

"Thanks." I headed toward the kitchen. I poured a cup and glanced through my appointment book, trying to prepare myself mentally for the day. I heard a noise and looked up. Abigail stood in the doorway with a vase of red roses.

"These just came for you," she said.

I immediately thought of Jay, and my heart lifted. I reached for the card and opened it. It was from Thad.

I enjoyed dinner last night. Hope you're feeling better.
Call me if you need to talk.

"From your husband?" Abigail asked with a smile.

"No." I stood, refilled my cup, and dropped the card into the trash. To my astonishment, Abigail retrieved it. Right in front of me.

"Oh, they're from Thad Glazer," she said, "thanking you for dinner last night. Wow, that must have been some dinner, considering how much roses cost these days."

She looked up. The expression on my face must've reflected my annoyance, because she immediately tossed the card back into the trash can.

"I'm sorry," she said. "I wasn't thinking."

I stood. "Put them in the reception room so my patients can enjoy them," I said shortly and left the room.

I went into my office and closed the door. I wasn't sure why I was so ticked off with Abigail, only that I was. If Mona had done the same thing, it wouldn't have mattered. Was it me? I wondered. Was I being difficult to get along with? I dialed Mona's number. She sounded funny.

"It's hard to talk," she said. "Mama mixed up this gunk and put it on my face and neck. It's hard as plaster."

"What's in it?"

"I'm afraid to ask."

"I'm sure she knows what she's doing," I said, trying to lift her spirits. I decided not to mention the incident with Abigail.

"She said to invite you to dinner tonight. Please say yes."

Mona sounded desperate. "Okay." There was a knock at my door. "I have to go."

Abigail peeked inside. "There's an Ellen Holmes on the

line," she said. "She's calling from Hawaii. I should tell you, she sounds upset."

I picked up the phone. "Hi, Ellen," I said. "Are you and Gerald having fun in Hawaii?"

She burst into tears. "It's awful, Dr. Holly. I caught Gerald flirting with a hotel employee."

"I told you I wasn't flirting," Gerald yelled in the background. "I was trying to get information on parasailing."

"Yeah, right," Ellen said caustically. "Which is why you almost jumped out of your skin when I stepped off the elevator and saw the two of you together," she added.

"That's because I knew you would suspect the worst!" he said loudly. "I can't help it that you're so suspicious. Maybe one of these days you'll learn to trust me."

"Well, that's not going to happen any time soon, buster."

Here we go again, I thought. I had been afraid from the beginning that Hawaii was not a good idea for them just now. "Ellen, you need to calm down," I said. "We agreed to leave the problems behind so that you and Gerald could concentrate on having a good time," I reminded her.

"Obviously, Gerald is having more fun than I am."

"Let me speak to him, please," I said.

He got on the phone. "This whole thing was a mistake," he said. "We've got this gorgeous suite right on the ocean, but every time I try to get romantic with Ellen, she shuns me."

"Maybe I'm afraid you'll give me herpes," Ellen shouted.

"See what I mean?" Gerald said. "Last night I slept on the couch. I would check out today and fly home if I could get a refund, but it's a package deal."

"Is there a second phone in the suite?" I asked.

"Yeah," Gerald said.

"Please ask Ellen to pick up." I waited until I had both

of them on the line. "Okay, as I see it, the two of you have a choice," I said. "You either try to put your problems on the back burner until our next session, or you cut your losses and fly home."

Silence.

"Maybe Ellen and I should do our own thing while we're here," Gerald said after a moment. "I could go deep-sea fishing or play golf, and she could shop or whatever."

"What a perfect idea," she said to him. "That way you'd be free to run amok."

They began arguing again. I wished I could put my mother on the phone, since she was the one who had suggested they go away together in the first place. "I've already given you my opinion," I said. "Do you think you could call a truce?"

Again, silence.

"I'm willing," Gerald finally said.

Ellen sniffed. "I guess so."

As the three of us disconnected, I couldn't help but wonder how long their little peace treaty would last.

chapter 9

....

I arrived at Mona's and was shocked to see that her rash had worsened. Her eyes were red and swollen. Obviously, she'd spent the day crying.

Willie-Mae came into the room. "I've tried everything," she said.

"Do you think it will ever clear up?" I asked, then realized I had ulterior motives. I wanted Mona to come back to work so I didn't have to deal with Abigail.

"Eventually," Willie-Mae said.

Mona sniffed. "I'll probably be scarred for life."

Willie-Mae looked frustrated. "You're making it worse," she told her daughter, "by overreacting. All it does is cause you more stress, and you know that's not good for you."

I tried to think of a way to change the subject. "How is Tiara?" I asked.

"She's taking a nap," Willie-Mae said. "The baby kicks all night. Poor girl is exhausted. I'm glad you're having dinner with us. I cooked a big pot of vegetable soup and my famous corn bread."

"Sounds delicious," I said.

I heard a noise on the stairs and saw Tiara slowly and carefully picking her way down. "I'm starving," she said.

Willie-Mae gave a grunt. "What else is new? Were you able to rest?"

"Yes. I guess the baby is tired from staying up half the night."

The four of us went into the kitchen, Tiara waddling like a duck. I set the table while Willie-Mae filled four bowls and put them in each place setting, along with a plate of hot corn bread.

"Dig in before it gets cold," she said.

I spooned some of the soup into my mouth. I smiled at Willie-May. "This is awesome!"

She looked proud. "I made a gallon of it," she said. "I'm going to send some home with you."

"You're spoiling me," I said.

"You girls could use some spoiling. I'd love to spoil my daughter, but I don't get many invitations to visit. And heaven *knows* she can't be bothered to visit her mama."

Mona remained silent.

"I don't know why you don't come back to Tennessee, now that Henry is gone," Willie-Mae said. "Lord knows you don't need a house this large. And you wouldn't believe how our little town has grown. We have a Walmart Supercenter. *And* we've got our share of eligible bachelors. I don't like seeing you all alone."

Mona shot me a frantic look.

"We'd hate to lose Mona," I told Willie-Mae. "I don't know if she's told you, but she's involved in a project to curtail gang violence in Atlanta and build youth centers in hopes of keeping kids off the streets."

Willie-Mae looked surprised. "I didn't know that!" She looked at her daughter. "Why didn't you tell me you were involved in community work? I'm so proud of you!"

"It's the least I can do, Mama," she said. "Henry left me more money than I'll ever spend. It's only right that I give back. You're the only one who refuses to let me do anything for you."

Willie-Mae waved off the remark. "I don't need nary a thing, sugar. My house and van are paid for, and I'm in excellent health. What more could a person ask for?"

"That cabin you live in is as old as the mountain it sits on," Mona said.

Willie-Mae looked hurt. "I love my cabin!"

Mona ignored her. "You wouldn't have to work so hard if you'd let me help you."

"I don't consider what I do work. Besides, staying busy keeps the aches and pains away."

Mona looked at me. "See how stubborn she is?"

After dinner, Willie-Mae ordered Mona and Tiara from the kitchen so they could rest, and I helped her clean up. I asked her about life in Tennessee, and she regaled me with funny stories about some of her neighbors and patients. It felt good to laugh.

"Mona told me your husband is part of the crew working the wildfire," she said. "We've been keeping up with it on the news. Those poor firefighters can't seem to catch a break, what with all that wind and no rain in the forecast. Yet they keep pressing on. Do you talk to him often?"

"He tried to call me last night, but I was out."

"I'll keep him in my prayers." She filled a quart jar with soup and wrapped several pieces of corn bread in foil. "Soup always tastes better the day after it's made," she said.

"Thank you, Willie-Mae," I replied. "For everything," I added.

I awoke Saturday morning to the sound of gospel music. I buried my head under a pillow but could not drown it out. I looked at the alarm clock. Six a.m. Finally, I staggered from the bed, pulled my curtain aside, and found Brother Love sitting in a lawn chair in my front yard, a boom box beside him blaring "What a Friend We Have in Jesus."

I marched outside in my white pajamas with pink flamingos and gave him my fiercest look. "What do you think you're doing?" I yelled, trying to make myself heard over the music. "Do you know what time it is? You're going to wake the whole neighborhood!"

He gave a wide smile. His teeth were too perfect to be his own. "And what better way to wake people than to greet them with the Lord's music."

"You're crazy!" I said. "You're also trespassing. You've got five minutes to pack your chair and music and hit the road, or I'm calling the cops."

He shrugged. "I'm willing to go to jail if it means bringing a lost soul to our Lord. You need to repent and give up your life of sin."

"Okay, it's your decision," I said loudly. I went inside, but I could still hear the music. Even Mike looked irritated. Finally, I picked up the phone and called the police. They took their time; I suppose they didn't feel my situation was dire. As they parked in front of my house, Brother Love didn't so much as budge from his spot nor did he turn down his music. I went outside again, still in my pajamas. Across the street, Bitsy Stout was standing on her sidewalk, hands planted on her hips. If looks could kill, I would have dropped dead on the spot.

I explained the situation to the policemen.

"You're trespassing," one of the officers said to Brother Love. "The lady has asked you to leave. I suggest you pack up your things and clear out."

"I can't do that," Brother Love said. "The Lord has sent me here on a mission. This jezebel woman must be saved."

"How dare you call me a jezebel!" I shouted. I turned to the officers. "Do these look like the kind of pajamas a jezebel woman would wear?"

Both gave me a long, hard look.

"Just calm down, ma'am," the other officer told me before turning his attention to Brother Love. "I'm only going to ask you once more to get off this lady's property. If you refuse, I'll have no choice but to arrest you."

"I can't leave a lost sheep," the preacher said. "I'm a disciple of the Lord, and I must spread his word."

"See, he's nuts!" I said. "He and his whole church group are crazy religious fanatics."

The officer handcuffed the minister while his partner spouted off his Miranda rights. Brother Love did not resist arrest as he was led to the police car.

Bitsy Stout had obviously gone inside for her camera; she was snapping pictures as fast as she could.

"You're going to be sorry," she yelled at me.

I was already sorry for having moved across the street from her.

Sunday arrived, and I dreaded the anniversary party I was supposed to attend. I tried to think of a sudden illness I could come up with in order to get out of going. I even went so far as to search through my *Mayo Clinic Family Health Book*, but nothing short of a heart or lung transplant would have been acceptable in my mother's eyes.

After cleaning the house and catching up on my laundry, not to mention running various errands—which included buying more frozen dinners—I dressed in jeans and a plaid shirt.

I drove to the VFW and waited for Jeff to arrive. He'd called to say he might be a few minutes late, and I did not want to enter the VFW alone.

I would not have noticed the white sedan parked on the far side of the parking lot if I had not been watching for Jeff's car. Nor would I have thought anything of it had the driver not made a point to park along the very edge of the asphalt, facing the road, as though trying to maintain a safe distance. I told myself I was being paranoid; after all, the car was not unique. I probably passed a hundred white sedans each day on my way to the office, so that didn't mean it was the one that had followed me the other night, with its bright lights glaring into my rearview mirror.

Still, the funny feeling in my stomach wouldn't go away. A small voice told me I should check it out. I started my car, pulled from the parking slot, and turned in the direction of the white sedan. I didn't get far before it screeched from the parking lot, turned onto the road, and sped off. It confirmed my suspicions that somebody was following me.

Jeff picked that moment to pull in.

He stopped beside my car and rolled down his window. "You're not thinking of bailing, are you?" he asked, wearing a grin.

"I'm just looking for a good parking place in case I do

decide to bail," I said. "I think we should park our cars facing the road."

He laughed. When he climbed from his car, I saw that he had chosen his outfit wisely—worn jeans and a checkered shirt.

I could hear my cousin, Lucien, and his band blasting their music even before Jeff and I reached the building. They called themselves the Dead Artists. They should have called themselves Pierced and Tattooed. They had more holes in their bodies than a pincushion. "Are you sure you're ready for this?" I asked Jeff.

"It can't be that bad."

"Wanna bet?"

We opened the door and were almost knocked over by the loud music. Inside was an enormous, dimly lit, no-frills room with a bar lining one end of the room and battered tables and chairs scattered about.

Jeff put his mouth at my ear. "I almost never get invited to these high-class social events," he said loudly.

"See what happens when you know the right people?" I said.

I found my aunt and uncle right away; they weren't hard to miss, because they were the only ones dressed up. My uncle wore a tux, and my aunt Lou, who'd decided to become a redhead since I last saw her, wore her wedding dress.

Jeff followed me over. "Congratulations!" I said to them, trying to make myself heard over the music. I hugged them both. My aunt's lipstick had bled into the lines surrounding her lips. "You look beautiful," I said, noting there was more orange in her hair than red.

"Can you believe I was able to get into my wedding dress?" she said.

"That's wonderful!"

"Yeah. Two weeks of laxatives and water pills," she said. "I don't have any liquids left in my body, and my intestines are completely empty."

"Wow," I said. "I would never have thought of doing that."

Jeff just stared.

"Thank you for coming, Kate," Uncle Bump said, leaning close so I could hear him. "It means a lot to have our friends and family celebrate with us."

"I wouldn't have missed it for the world!" I introduced Jeff, who shook their hands and wished them well, although I was almost sure they couldn't make out what he was saying. "Jeff is a veterinarian," I said loudly.

"Have you ever worked with hogs?" Aunt Lou asked.

Jeff shook his head.

"I can tell you everything you need to know about hogs," she said.

I leaned close to Jeff. "My aunt learned to castrate hogs at a very young age."

Jeff nodded at her. "I'll bet you were really good at it."

"I held my own," she said.

"I've seen her do it," Uncle Bump shouted. "Once a man has seen something like that, he never forgets."

"I need a stiff drink," Jeff said.

I used sign language to let my aunt and uncle know we were going to the bar, sidestepping an assortment of people who looked like they'd once played on *Hee Haw*. Jeff and I ordered beer.

A man leaning against the bar beside us filled two shot glasses from a quart-sized Mason jar. "Have a shiner," he said, shoving the drinks toward us.

"What's in it?" Jeff asked.

"A little of this and a little of that."

I shook my head. "Um, no, thank you."

"Scaredy cat," the man said, his eyes bright with merriment. He turned to Jeff. "How 'bout you, pawdner? Show the little lady what you're made of."

Jeff looked uncertain. "Well, I—"

"Just toss them back, real quick like."

"You don't have to drink that, Jeff," I said. I barely got the words out of my mouth before Jeff put the first shot glass to his lips and chugged it back. The man handed him the second one, and Jeff did it again. I just stared. Two seconds later, his eyes rolled about, he wheezed, and fell to his knees. I gave a squeal and knelt beside him. "Are you okay?" I cried.

His face was as red as a stop sign. He choked and coughed. "Water," he managed.

The grinning bartender had a glass waiting. I took it from him and handed it to Jeff, who drank it straight down. I glared at the man standing on the other side of Jeff. "What did you give him?" I demanded.

"Moonshine," he said. "I made it myself."

I picked up the empty shot glass and sniffed. "It smells like turpentine!"

"It haint gonna kill him. Just give him a good buzz."

I helped Jeff to his feet. "I think it singed my esophagus," he said, hanging on to the bar as though he weren't sure he was going to be able to stand.

"Why did you drink it, you idiot?"

"I didn't want to look like a sissy," he whispered.

The music stopped, and my cousin hurried toward us. "Hey, Kate," he said. "You look hot! If we weren't related, I'd—"

"Never mind," I interrupted, knowing Lucien wouldn't

let something like being blood relatives stand in the way of jumping my bones. The guy with the quart jar offered him a drink.

"I wouldn't drink that," Jeff managed with another wheeze.

Lucian ignored him and gulped it back. He gave a huge shudder. "Man, that's good stuff!" he said as Jeff and I stared in disbelief. I didn't know if Jeff was impressed that Lucien was able to drink the moonshine and still remain standing or if he was taken by surprise by the huge ring through Lucien's nose.

"There's more where that came from," the man with the quart jar told Lucian.

"Cool band," Jeff managed to say.

Lucien puffed with pride. "We write our own stuff. Hey, I gotta take a whiz before we start the next set." He hurried away.

"Are you really related to him?" Jeff whispered. His eyes were glazed.

"Scary, huh?" I said.

"Kate!"

I turned at the sound of my mother's voice and gave her my brightest smile. As usual, my aunt Trixie was close behind. They wore matching leopard-print overalls.

"It's good to see you again," my mother said to Jeff. "Thank you for joining us on this auspicious occasion."

"I'm honored," he said.

"Great party, Mom," I told her. I knew she and my aunt had worked hard to put it together.

"Have you seen the hors d'oeuvres?" Aunt Trixie said. "Arnell made all your uncle's favorites."

"Really?" That meant the menu would include pickled eggs and Vienna sausage. "We'll have to check it out."

"Too bad Jay couldn't be here," my mother said.

I nodded. "I know he'll be disappointed that he couldn't make it."

Aunt Trixie looked excited. "Guess what? We're going to have square dancing later. One of Lou's brothers is going to teach us."

"Sounds like you two thought of everything."

"Well, we'd best mingle with our guests," my mother said. She pointed to the man with the moonshine. "If he offers you a drink, tell him thanks, but no thanks. That stuff will rot your gut."

"Uh-oh," Jeff said as they hurried away.

"Why don't we find a place to sit?" I suggested. "Do you think you can walk?"

He looked uncertain. I linked my arm through his and led him to a table. He sat down. "I can't feel my face," he said, touching his cheeks.

I figured I'd better get some food in him. "You need to eat something. Will you be okay here by yourself for a few minutes?"

"Huh?"

"Stay here, okay? I'll be right back."

I made my way to a long table piled high with fried food. The waiter stood on the other side slicing something. "What is that?" I asked.

"Spam. Would you like some?"

"No, thanks." I filled a small paper plate with cheese cubes and crackers and returned to the table to find Jeff slumped in his chair. "Here," I said, setting the food before him. "You'll feel better once you get something in your stomach."

He reached for a piece of cheese but missed his mouth. He dropped it, and it hit the floor. "Oops," he said.

I retrieved the cheese and dropped it in an ashtray on the table. "I'll help you," I said. "Open your mouth."

He did so, and I put a cheese cube on his tongue. "Do you think you can chew?" I pushed his jaw up so his mouth would close. He chewed.

"I shouldn't have asked you to come with me," I said. "We can leave as soon as you're able to walk."

"I don't want to be a party pooper."

I looked up and found Arnell headed our way carrying three bottles of beer. He was dressed in a red-sequined pantsuit and matching heels. His makeup was perfect, but he looked anxious.

"May I join you?" he asked, placing a beer each in front of Jeff and me. "I'm trying to shake off that guy in the white cowboy hat."

"Have a seat," I said, looking past him. I saw the cowboy staring.

"Is he looking this way?" Arnell whispered.

"Yup."

"I hope he doesn't try to join us."

"Right now he seems to be worshipping you from afar."

Arnell looked at Jeff. "You don't look so good."

"He accidentally drank some moonshine," I said. I popped another piece of cheese in Jeff's mouth. "Chew," I said.

"I shouldn't have worn this outfit," Arnell said. "I'm sending out the wrong message. Do I look like a cheap slut?"

"No, you just, um, stand out a little." The cowboy headed toward us. "Uh-oh, here he comes."

The man reached our table. He swept off his hat and smiled at Arnell. "May I get you something to drink, little lady?"

Arnell shook his head. "No, thank you."

"Mind if I sit down?" He motioned to the empty chair next to Arnell but didn't wait to be invited. He turned the chair around, straddled it, and leaned his elbows on the back, his gaze fixed on Arnell all the while. "I'm Hoss," he said. "What's your name?"

"Arnell. And I'm waiting for my date to arrive."

"That's a purty name. I like your outfit. Do you come here often?"

Arnell just looked at him. "If my boyfriend sees you sitting here when he comes through that door, he's going to rip out your gizzard."

"Might be worth it," Hoss said, then turned to Jeff and me.

I made the introductions, and Hoss offered Jeff a meaty handshake.

"Are you related to Lou?" I asked.

Hoss nodded. "We're cousins."

"Are you a hog farmer?"

"Nope. I have my own trucking business. I don't mind telling you, I make a good living." He smiled at Arnell. "Folks'll tell you I can be very generous." The band started playing a slow number. "You wanna dance, honey?" he asked.

Arnell shook his head. "No, thank you."

Hoss stood. "Aw, c'mon, just give me one little dance." He took Arnell's hand.

"I don't know how to dance."

"All you have to do is follow my lead." He pulled a frantic-looking Arnell to his feet and led him to the dance floor.

"I've never met anyone named Hoss," Jeff said, putting another piece of cheese in his mouth. His words were slurred.

"I should probably take you home," I said.

"I'm having a good time," he said, picking up his beer and taking a swig. "I haven't been to a fun party since I don't know when."

"Um, Jeff, I don't think you're supposed to mix beer and moonshine." I took his bottle.

"You're no fun."

The music stopped, and Hoss and Arnell returned but remained standing.

"We should blow this joint," Hoss said to Arnell. "I have a room at the Comfort Inn."

Arnell looked shocked. "Excuse me, but I don't even know you."

"You come to my room, and we'll get to know each other real good."

Arnell crossed his arms. "I'd like for you to leave."

"Now, honey, you don't mean that."

"Get lost, pal."

Hoss smiled. "You're just playing hard to get."

Arnell gave Hoss his best smile. "I have a surprise for you."

Hoss grinned. "I like surprises."

"Give me your hand."

Hoss did as he was told.

Arnell placed the man's hand against his crotch.

Hoss's faced drained of color. "What the hell is *that*?" he demanded.

"It's called a penis."

Hoss looked as though he might be sick. "Let me tell you something, you freak," he said between gritted teeth.

"You tell anybody I came on to you, and I'll put a bullet in both of your kneecaps."

"It was very nice meeting you, Hoss," Arnell said sweetly. "We'll have to do this again soon."

Hoss spat on the floor and stormed off.

"I'd better get out of here," Arnell said, "in case that redneck decides to pull a gun on me after all."

"We'll walk out with you," I told him, standing.

"You don't have to leave because of me."

"Trust me, we're ready to go. You're going to have to help me with Jeff. He's not able to walk by himself." We managed to get Jeff to his feet and out the door. "Deep breaths," I said.

Jeff gulped in air.

"If you could just help me get him to my car, I would appreciate it," I told Arnell.

"Where are we going?" Jeff asked.

"I'm taking you home."

"What about my car?"

"We'll have to come back for it tomorrow morning. You're in no condition to drive."

Jeff swayed, but Arnell caught him and, between the two of us, we managed to get Jeff inside my car. "Don't forget to put on your seat belt," I said.

"Oh, shur," he said. He struggled to pull it around, then couldn't manage to lock it in place. Arnell and I watched for a moment, both of us shaking our heads.

"All right already," I said and reached inside to snap it in place.

"Wow," Jeff said. "You make it look so easy."

Arnell and I looked at each other. "Should I follow you and help you get him inside his house?"

"No, I'll manage."

Arnell waved as I drove away.

"Did you have a good time at the party?" Jeff asked.

"It was okay," I said without enthusiasm.

"You sound depressed. You're missing Jay, aren't you? You know what I think? I think you should visit him."

"He sort of has his hands full with the fire."

"I'll bet he gets time off."

I didn't reply. The next thing I knew, Jeff was asleep. Fortunately, I knew where he lived. The traffic was light, and I made the drive in record time. "You're home," I called out once I'd parked in his driveway. He sat up and looked around as though trying to get his bearings. I helped him to his door, unlocked it, and followed him to his bedroom. Inside, I ordered him to sit on the bed so I could remove his shoes. I went into his bathroom and checked the medicine cabinet for a bottle of aspirin. I filled a plastic cup with water and returned to his bedroom.

"Here, take this," I said. "You should feel better in about a week." He popped the two tablets in his mouth and drank the water.

"Okay, lie down," I said. I found a blanket in the closet and covered him. He was snoring when I left the room.

I watched my rearview mirror as I headed home, but I didn't notice anyone following me. My stomach growled as I drove, and I realized I hadn't eaten. I remembered the quart of soup in my refrigerator and was thankful Willie-Mae had sent it home with me.

As usual, Mike met me at the front door. After I'd heated and eaten my soup and a large chunk of corn bread, I called Mona and told her about the party. Despite her low mood, she howled with laughter when I told her about Hoss and Arnell.

"Did you undress Jeff before you put him to bed?" she asked.

"No, but I removed his shoes. Does that count?"

"Damn, Kate, it would have been the perfect opportunity to see him naked. I don't care if he *is* gay, he's still a hunk with a great body."

"What is your mom putting in those tonics?" I asked.

"Humor me, Kate. I'm bored out of my mind."

"And yet, your life is still more exciting than mine." As if to prove my point, I yawned. "Oh, I forgot to mention it to you. Thad is thinking of moving to West Palm Beach."

"For real?"

"An old friend has offered him a partnership. The money is supposed to be great."

"I'm not surprised. West Palm is a ritzy place to live."

"Yeah, I suppose."

"You don't sound very happy about it."

"I would miss him. We go way back, you know?"

"Hold it," she said. "Is this the same shallow, insensitive man you were engaged to, whom you caught in his hot tub with his twenty-something-year-old receptionist?"

"We were never officially engaged, and he isn't as shallow and insensitive as he used to be."

"Kate, are you listening to yourself?" Mona said. "You sound like you still have feelings for Thad."

"I was in love with him once." I sighed. "How can I explain it to you when I can't even explain it to myself?"

"You know what your problem is? You're missing the hell out of Jay."

"Duh."

"You should call him."

"It's difficult to reach someone who is trying to put out a massive wildfire," I said, feeling as irritable as I sounded.

"So leave him a message to call you back when he's got a few minutes to talk. It's not like they're working twenty-four-seven."

"I'll think about it."

Once Mona and I hung up, that's exactly what I did. I thought about it. Finally, I picked up the phone. I took a deep breath and dialed Jay's cell. His voice mail came on. I hung up.

I was preparing for bed when the phone rang. The caller ID belonged to Jay. I snatched up the phone before it could ring a second time.

"I saw that you called," he said. "I was in the shower. Why didn't you leave a message?"

"I figured you were busy with the fire," I said, glad that he didn't sound angry. Perhaps he'd gotten over our fuss. "I've been keeping up with it on the news."

"Yeah, it's a real bitch."

"Where are you?"

"I'm calling from the motel where we're all staying. I've got twenty-four hours of R & R before I get back. I was going to phone you after I grabbed something to eat." He paused. "Is everything okay?"

I didn't miss the tinge of uncertainty in his voice. "Everything is fine," I said. "Couldn't be better," I added, and thought I heard a sigh of relief from his end. "I saw on CNN that the National Guard has been called in."

"They've ordered mandatory evacuations. A lot of people are going to lose their homes."

"That is so sad," I said.

"Yeah, but there haven't been any casualties, and that's what counts. You see something like this, and suddenly your priorities fall into place. At least for most people," he added. "There are always those who run back into a burning house for the family silver."

I heard the fatigue in his voice and knew I should get off, but I wanted to hang on to his voice a little longer. "How bad do you think it's going to get, Jay?" I asked. "Do you think it will be as bad as the one in 2007?"

"I don't know. Everything is dry and brittle. We've got high winds kicking up sparks all over the place. The one thing in our favor is that we learned a lot from the last big fire."

I waited for him to say more, but he didn't. "I'm going to get off now, Jay," I said. "Go grab something to eat so you can crash for a while."

"Thanks for calling, Kate."

"Okay, I—"

The next thing I heard was a dial tone. I stared at the phone. He'd hung up before I could tell him I loved him. I should have been quicker. I was suddenly angry with myself. Why the hell hadn't I said the words? Why hadn't he? Instead we'd been as polite as two strangers meeting on the street. I wanted to call him back and make everything right, but I knew this wasn't the time to discuss our relationship.

Maybe I was making more of it than I should. The man was flat-out exhausted and needed to see to his basic needs instead of dealing with a neurotic woman. I turned off the light. Mike was already snoring at the foot of my bed. I listened to her long into the night.

The next morning I drank my coffee in front of the TV, where a news anchor was stationed not far from the fire.

"We don't have the names of the injured as yet," he was saying.

My ears perked up.

He went on. "All we know is that the wind took another sudden turn about five a.m. this morning and sparked new fires. Two firefighters were trapped for twenty minutes. Hospital officials have listed their conditions as stable but guarded."

I closed my eyes and said a little prayer. I was fairly certain that Jay would have been at the motel. I felt bad for the families of those who had been injured.

I poured another cup of coffee and went upstairs to shower. The phone rang as I was getting ready to walk out the door. I snatched it up quickly. Jeff spoke from the other end. He didn't sound well.

"How are you feeling?" I asked.

"Terrible. I can't believe I actually drank moonshine, but I'm paying for it today, believe me. The reason I'm calling is to let you know my neighbor gave me a ride to the VFW so I could pick up my car."

I gave my forehead a mental slap. I'd totally forgotten about his car.

"I'll call you once my head stops hurting," he said before hanging up.

I was about to walk out the door again when my mother called. "You made the newspaper again."

"Oh, great," I muttered. "What did I do this time?"

"The article said you had a preacher arrested. There is a picture of him in handcuffs."

No doubt Bitsy had supplied the photo to the newspaper. "Just what I need," I mumbled.

"It gets worse," she said. "They interviewed that nosy neighbor across the street."

"Bitsy Stout?"

"Yes. She claimed the preacher was trying to lead you to the Lord, since you're a confirmed atheist." She gave a long-suffering sigh.

"Mom, I know it looks bad, but we're talking about a couple of kooks, okay?"

"Whatever you say, Kate."

I was not in the best of moods when I arrived at my office. I went inside, took one look at Abigail, and felt my jaw drop. She had obviously spent a good amount of time in a hair salon over the weekend, because she'd had her hair colored and cut so it matched mine. She was wearing one of the Jaclyn Smith outfits as well. Looking at her was almost like looking at myself in the mirror.

"Surprise!" she said, giving me a broad smile.

I just stood there, not knowing what to say.

"I woke up Saturday morning feeling down in the dumps, and I decided to re-create myself," she said. "I told the stylist I wanted a whole new color, something really different. It wasn't until I chose the color and cut that I realized it resembled yours."

"It's more than just a resemblance, Abigail," I said carefully.

Her smile faded. "Are you upset?"

"Well. . . ." I hesitated. "I find it a bit odd." It was more than odd, in fact. It had finally hit me that my receptionist was not only strange, she was a wacko.

I went into my office, closed the door, and called Mona. Once I told her what Abigail had done, she agreed that it was way more than just weird.

"That would creep me out," Mona said.

"I don't know how she managed to get the exact color and cut."

"I do," Mona said. "She took one of the flyers I had made up to promote you. It has a large color photo of you."

I hadn't thought of that. Part of Mona's PR plan to launch me to stardom included an open house the first Monday of the month. Not only did Mona pay for the caterer, she handed out goodie bags that contained glossy flyers singing my praises as a psychologist. "Do you think I'm overreacting?" I asked.

"No. I think you should call the temp agency and ask them to replace her."

"I'm afraid it would send her off the deep end," I said. "I think she's pretty unstable."

"Duh!" Mona said. "Listen, Kate, the last thing you need is another crazy person in your life." As I listened to her, Abigail knocked on the door and peeked in. "Mr. Eddie Franks has arrived for his nine o'clock appointment."

"I have to go," I told Mona.

I invited Eddie inside my office. He was a distinguished, smooth-talking man in his fifties who'd spent time in prison for milking a number of older women out of their retirement. He was also sweet on my aunt Trixie, so much so that they had almost eloped. In the end, Eddie had experienced a moment of guilt and told her the truth about his past. Aunt Trixie had promised to wait until he took care of his old business. Still, my mother referred to him as Slick Eddie.

"So, how is it going?" I asked. It was impossible not to like him, even though he and Aunt Trixie had scared the spit out of my mother and me with their elopement scheme. I'd come down on him pretty hard afterward.

"I'm staying on the straight and narrow, Dr. Holly," he

said. "I'm working as many hours as I can so I can save up for my own store one day."

Eddie worked in an exclusive menswear store and had quickly been promoted from salesman to manager. "I have no doubt in my mind that you'll accomplish your goals," I said.

"I appreciate that you believe in me. You know, in the beginning I only came here because it was a condition of my parole, but you probably already figured that out."

"I can be clever when I put my mind to it," I said.

"But I don't ever want to go back to being the person I used to be."

I was glad that Eddie felt remorse for what he'd done because, in the beginning, he had seemed more concerned about how much *he* had suffered instead of what he'd put his victims through.

"You've made restitution, and you've served time for your crime," I said. "You seem to have learned your lesson."

He nodded.

"So how are things with you and my aunt?"

"I'm going really slow," he said. "I'm not out to hurt her, Dr. Holly."

"That's good, because I know somebody who would shoot you in the kneecaps for fifty bucks."

He grinned. "I don't doubt it for a moment."

Once we'd finished our session, he leaned closer to me. "What's the deal with your receptionist?" he asked. "I almost mistook her for you."

"She is going through a difficult time," I said. I led Eddie out and said good-bye. Abigail must've been in the bathroom, because she wasn't at her desk. The phone rang, and I picked it up. Thad was on the other end.

"Why the hell haven't you called me back?" he demanded.

"I didn't know you phoned me."

"I've left about ten messages. I told that bitch receptionist of yours that it was a matter of life and death, but she refused to put me through to you."

"What's wrong?"

"Alice Smithers took an overdose this morning. I'm at the hospital now."

I felt as if I'd been punched in the chest. "Is she—?" I couldn't say the word.

"She's still alive. They pumped her stomach."

"I'm on my way."

chapter 10

....

I raced into my office, grabbed my purse and keys, and locked my office door. Abigail came out of the bathroom. "Why the hell didn't you tell me Thad Glazer called?" I shouted.

She blinked several times. "The guy who sent the flowers?" she asked.

"Also the psychiatrist with whom I share patients," I said, gritting my teeth.

"You were with Mr. Franks," she said. "This is the first chance I've had."

"Dr. Glazer told you his call was urgent. You should have alerted me immediately!"

"I thought he was just using that as an excuse. I didn't think you'd want to be disturbed with personal calls."

"It was not a personal call and, besides, that's not for you to decide. I almost lost a patient this morning, dammit! I still don't know if she's going to make it."

Abigail covered her mouth with one hand. "I'm so sorry," she said as I crossed the reception room to the door.

"Sorry doesn't cut it, Abigail. Cancel my morning appointments. I have to go to the hospital. You and I will talk later."

"Please don't be angry with me," she said.

I ignored her as I threw open the door and hurried out.

I made it to the hospital in record time. I arrived at the ER and was buzzed through the metal doors leading to the treatment rooms. Thad was standing in the hall talking with one of the physicians. He introduced me to Dr. Meyers.

"We evacuated the contents of Miss Smithers's stomach," the doctor said. "I expect that she'll pull through."

"May we see her?" I asked.

"She's a little groggy, but you're welcome to go in." He paused and looked from me to Thad. "You're probably going to want to make some kind of arrangement once she's stable. There's no guarantee she won't try it again."

Thad and I nodded. We both knew that Alice would have to go to the psych ward for treatment and observation. Dr. Meyers was paged. He excused himself.

"This is my fault," I said. "I came down on Liz Jones too hard. I'm willing to bet my license that she is responsible for the overdose."

Thad checked his wristwatch. "I'll start the commitment process, but I have to be at the airport at two p.m."

I felt a sinking sensation. The look on my face must've shown it.

"What's wrong?" he asked.

"You're going to West Palm Beach, aren't you?" It sounded like an accusation.

"That's the plan. I'm sorry to leave you at a time like this, but I've already rearranged my schedule. I'll only be gone a few days. A week at the most," he added. "In the meantime, I suggest you find another psychiatrist to take my place."

"How can you just walk out on me?"

He gave me a funny look. "She's not my patient anymore," he said. "The only reason I'm here is because nobody could reach you, and Alice's alter personality, Sue, managed to tell someone I was the attending psychiatrist. By the way, she was the one who called the ambulance."

"Have a great trip, Thad," I snapped and walked away. I slipped quietly into the exam room and found Alice sleeping. An IV pumped fluid into her veins as a nurse checked her vital signs. I sat in the chair beside the bed. It hadn't been so long ago that I'd sat in another exam room in this very hospital when Jay was injured. It felt like I'd spent a lot of time in the ER. I was beginning to think I deserved my own parking space.

I'm not sure how long I sat there before Alice finally stirred. I stood and leaned over her. "Alice, can you speak to me?" I asked.

She opened her eyes and blinked several times, as though trying to focus. "Where am I?"

"You're in the emergency room," I said. "You took an overdose."

She frowned. "I wouldn't do something that stupid," she said.

"Do you remember anything?"

She lay there quietly for a moment, and I could see her thoughts churning. "I was getting ready for work. I don't know what happened after that." Her voice was hoarse from having suction tubes shoved down her throat.

"I need to speak with Sue," I said.

"But—"

"It's important." Sue was the take-charge person who often stepped in when life became too difficult for Alice.

Alice nodded, and I witnessed the subtle changes take place in her demeanor.

"Hello, Dr. Holly," Sue said. "That was a close one."

"Can you tell me what happened this morning?" I asked.

"Liz swallowed a bottle of sleeping pills," she said. "I called for help."

"Where did Liz get the sleeping pills?"

"From the back of the medicine cabinet. Alice's family doctor prescribed them a long time ago because she was having trouble with insomnia."

"I need to talk to Liz."

I waited, but Liz refused to appear.

"I guess she doesn't want to talk to you," Sue said. "Maybe she's embarrassed."

"I'm sorry to have to tell you, but Dr. Glazer is in the process of getting commitment papers drawn up."

"Alice is going to be upset," she said.

"I have no choice when a patient tries to commit suicide. We can't risk another attempt, because the next one might be successful." I gave a heartfelt sigh. "I suppose I should talk to Alice."

I arrived back at the office after lunch and found Abigail sitting at the desk thumbing through a magazine.

"It's not working out, Abigail," I said.

"I am so very sorry about what happened this morning. I'm sorry for everything." She looked on the verge of tears. "I really thought Dr. Glazer was calling for personal reasons, especially since he took you to a romantic restaurant for dinner, then sent you roses."

Something didn't feel right. I frowned. "How do you know he took me to a romantic restaurant?" I said. "I never told you where we had dinner."

"Oh." She glanced away quickly. "I guess I just assumed—"

"My personal life is none of your business, Abigail. Grab your purse and get out. And while you're at it, hand over the key."

"You don't understand," she said, tears filling her eyes. "I was trying to protect you. I know how much you must miss your husband, and I know how some guys might try to take advantage of that."

I held out my hand. "The key, Abigail."

She opened the bottom drawer and pulled out her purse. "I thought you were my friend. Friends stick together."

I waited.

She reached inside her purse. Finally, she handed the key to me. "You should give me another chance to prove myself. If you knew how much I cared about you and respected you, you wouldn't do this."

I could see that she was on the verge of losing it. "Don't make me call security, Abigail."

She stood and walked to the door. She gave me one last look before she opened it and walked out. I was relieved to be done with her.

I saw two patients back-to-back before I called to check on Alice. She had been moved to a private room. "How are you feeling?" I asked.

"I'm worried about my job." Her voice was shaky.

"You're going to have to call your boss and tell him you're ill."

She gasped. "You mean, tell him about the suicide attempt?"

"No," I said. "You'll have to come up with something that will prevent you from going to work for a week to ten days."

"I'm supposed to *lie*?"

I gave an inaudible sigh. I knew Alice would never lie, and even if she tried, she'd never pull it off. "Sue can call for you."

She burst into tears. "Maybe I *would* be better off dead," she said and slammed the phone in my ear. The next thing I heard was a dial tone.

I hung up and sat at my desk quietly. There were times I wondered if I could help Alice. Each time I felt we were making progress, Liz stepped in and screwed up everything.

I was glad to see the workday come to an end. I planned to grab something sinfully fattening on the way home, change into my comfortable jeans, and crash on the sofa with the remote control. Maybe I'd find a decent movie on TV, something lighthearted to take my mind off the crap that was my life.

My mood brightened when Mike greeted me with her happy dance. I changed clothes and shared my junk food with her—fried chicken strips with thick honey mustard and French fries. It was then that I noticed the wall clock was a couple of hours slow. How had that happened? I had recently put in a new battery, and it had been working fine.

I went into the laundry room and grabbed a new battery from the shelf over the washer and dryer, then reached for the clock. I opened the plastic cover to exchange batteries and froze at what I saw. Or what I didn't see. There was no battery. The hair prickled on the back of my neck. As hard as I tried, I could not come up with an explanation. I checked the rest of my house but saw nothing out of place.

I sat on a kitchen chair feeling confused and disoriented. The only people who had keys to my house were Jay and Mona. Of course, there was my spare key, outside beneath a brick in my flowerbed, but nobody would know where to look unless I told them. Then I remembered the spare house key in Mona's desk drawer. It was unmarked, and because it had been made by a locksmith, it would have been difficult to reproduce. Difficult, but not impossible.

I grabbed my purse and headed out the front door once again. I drove straight to my office, took the elevator to the fourth floor, unlocked the door to my reception room, and felt for the light switch. I hurried toward Mona's desk and opened the middle drawer. The keys were where they were supposed to be, including my house key. I took them out and put them in my purse. It was then that I noticed my Rolodex was gone, as were the roses Thad had sent. I felt a chill race up my spine.

Back at home, I was in the process of putting a new battery in my wall clock when my cell phone rang. Mona spoke from the other end. "Are you okay?" she asked, her voice trembling.

"Why wouldn't I be?"

"I just got a call from some woman who said you were in a bad car accident."

I sank onto a kitchen chair. "Did she identify herself?" I asked.

"She hung up on me before I could ask. I thought it was strange, so I decided to call your house before I started checking hospitals. What the hell is going on, Kate?"

"I fired Abigail today," I said. "She didn't take it well. It wouldn't surprise me if she made the call." I paused. "I think she has been in my house, Mona." I told her about the clock. My phone beeped. "Jay is calling," I said. "Let me get back to you."

I answered the call. I could barely hear Jay over the static.

"Katie, how badly are you hurt?"

"I'm perfectly fine, Jay," I said. "Did you get a call from a woman saying that I was in an accident?"

More static. "I just got off the phone with her. What the hell is going on?" he asked, echoing Mona's words.

Even though I hated to worry him, I knew I had no choice but to come clean. I told him about Abigail. "She took my Rolodex," I added. "She has been making prank calls."

"I only heard about half of what you just said," he told me.

"Somebody stole my Rolodex and is making prank calls," I said loudly. "If she calls back, hang up."

"Are you in danger?" he asked. "Do you think it's that lunatic from the anger management group?"

I hadn't thought of that, but my gut said no.

"You need to call the police," he said. "I don't want you to try to handle this alone. Promise me you'll file a police report," he said.

"I promise," I shouted into the phone, trying to make myself heard above the static.

"I'm serious, babe." Then the phone went dead.

I arrived at my office the next morning only minutes before my first appointment was due in, leaving me barely enough time to make coffee, toss back a cup, and check my messages. Gerald and Ellen had called again from Hawaii. Ellen was crying. It wasn't working out. They were catching the next plane home.

Mr. and Mrs. Freemont had lost an adult son in a traffic accident the year before, and their twenty-five-year marriage was suffering. Tragically, a high percentage of marriages failed after the loss of a child, even if the child was an adult. One reason the relationships deteriorated was because each parent was so caught up in his or her own grief that they couldn't help the other. That was the case with the Freemonts. Bonnie Freemont had insisted on seeking therapy, and husband Len had begrudgingly agreed. It was the only time he talked about Jason, their deceased son.

Bonnie spoke first. "As you know, Saturday is the anniversary of Jason's death," she said, her bottom lip quivering.

I did not need a reminder; the three of us had been preparing for it, just as we'd worked hard to get through their first Thanksgiving and Christmas without their son.

"Have the two of you made a decision as to what you plan to do to make it a little easier?" I asked, not for the first time. They couldn't seem to agree how to handle it.

"I still want to take a long weekend and get away," Len said, "but Bonnie continues to insist on staying home and attending church so she can be with family and friends."

She looked at him. "You don't understand," she said. "You don't even try to understand. It comforts me knowing there are people in our lives who cared about Jason," she said. "I don't want to take a vacation and pretend it never happened."

I looked at Len.

"I'm tired of people patting me on the back and saying stupid things that are meant to make me feel better," he said. "Like how lucky Bonnie and I are that we have two other children, or how Jason is in a better place because, had he lived, he would have been severely handicapped for the rest of his life." Len sighed. "It's bullshit, because I don't feel a damn bit lucky. I've been screwed out of a son."

"Why can't you stop being so angry?" Bonnie said, tears gathering in her eyes. "It's not going to bring Jason back. And we do have two other children who need us. You are so caught up in your feelings that you haven't stopped to consider theirs. They need a father," she added, "but every time we mention Jason, you shut down."

Len looked away. I could tell he was struggling with his emotions. Although Bonnie had shed an ocean of tears, which I think had been healthy for her, Len had grown bitter.

"Bonnie, you've just given me a great idea," I said.

She looked hopeful. "I'm open to anything that will help."

"I think you should spend the anniversary of Jason's death celebrating his life." They looked at me as though my hair had just caught on fire. "Seriously," I added.

"You mean throw a party?" Len said.

"Yes, a party for those who knew and loved Jason. A party where each person could maybe stand up and tell the others what was so special about your son."

They continued to stare at me in disbelief.

Bonnie finally looked at her husband. "It's not a *bad* idea," she said. "We could invite Jason's friends. We could take our favorite photos of him and make posters. I could cook his favorite foods." She swiped at a tear.

Len propped his elbows on his thighs and clasped his hands together. His face was masked with pain. "I don't know, Bonnie."

She touched his arm. "Len, we've done nothing but grieve since we lost Jason. I think I would much rather spend the anniversary date celebrating his life than mourning his death."

Len didn't answer right away, but his eyes glistened. Finally, he covered her hand with his and nodded.

I saw two more patients. By noon, I was famished and trying to decide what to select from the vending machine. I heard a noise at my door and looked up. Abigail Davis stood there holding two sacks from the sandwich shop downstairs.

"Surprise!" she said.

I was more than surprised; I was stunned. "What are you doing here?" I said in a none-too-friendly tone.

"I brought lunch," she said. "I thought about it, and I decided that even though our working relationship didn't turn out well, we could still be friends. Plus, I was in the building. I filled out a job application for a receptionist position in the bank this morning, and guess what? I'm pretty sure I got the job! Which means we can get together for lunch anytime we like," she added.

Words escaped me. If I'd suspected that she was off her rocker before, I was now convinced.

"You can't imagine how surprised I was when I came across the job in the classifieds," she went on. "I mean, what's the likelihood of that happening? Frankly, I saw it as a sign, so I called immediately. After I told the personnel manager, Mr. Cox, that I'd been working for you, he gave me the impression I was a shoo-in, so I'm counting on you to give me a good reference."

I continued to stare, speechless, even as my brain ran through a list of possible diagnoses.

"The main thing I want you to tell him is that I got on well with people," she said, "because I'm going to be dealing with a lot of bank customers."

My confusion suddenly turned to annoyance, then outright anger. I took a deep breath. "Abigail, why the hell would you give my name as a reference when I fired you?" I asked. "Don't you find that a bit odd?" I held up a finger. "Wait, odd simply isn't strong enough. How about deranged? That's more like it."

She looked hurt. "Just because *you* didn't appreciate my services doesn't mean they won't appreciate me at the bank. Besides, I need this job, Kate."

"You threw out the roses Dr. Glazer sent," I said. "You stole my Rolodex."

"Why would I do something like that?" she asked innocently.

"So you could scare the hell out of my friends and family," I said, "by calling them to say I was in a car accident. Why would you do that, Abigail? Did you get some kind of sick pleasure out of it?"

"How do you know it wasn't one of your patients?"

"None of my patients dislikes me that much. *You* took the Rolodex, Abigail. You have a choice. Either return it immediately, or I'm going to file a police report against you for theft. And while I'm at it, I'm going to add breaking and entering. I know you were in my house."

"And how would I have accomplished that?" she asked.

"You made a copy of the keys in Mona's desk."

She suddenly looked angry. "Go ahead and call the police," she said, "but you can't prove I had anything to do with it."

She stood there for a moment. I could tell she was trying hard to get her emotions under control. "I came here hoping we could clear the air between us. When you're ready to apologize, let me know." She placed the lunch sack on my desk and walked out.

chapter 11

••••••••••••••••••••••••••••

I arrived home, pulled into my driveway, and cringed when I spotted Bitsy Stout headed my way. She did not look happy; in fact, she looked mad enough to spit the fire and brimstone she preached. But I'd had enough bullshit for one day. She waited until I climbed out of my car and closed the door before speaking.

"I have kept quiet as long as I can," she said, "because I knew I had to calm down before I came over or I would say things unbefitting a Christian. But you have gone too far this time, Kate Holly, by having Brother Love arrested."

"Maybe you'll think twice before you send your army of religious crazies to my door," I replied.

"Is that what you call people who care about your soul? Brother Love can't sleep for worrying about you."

"Tell Brother Love that my soul is just fine, and he needn't fret."

"You're going to regret this come Judgment Day. There is a special place in hell for people like you."

"Listen to me carefully, Bitsy, because I'm only going

to say this once. I want no part of your religion, including the wrathful God you worship. Now, I've had a long day, and I don't feel like talking to you, so I'm going to ask you as nicely as I can to get the hell out of my yard and stay out." I turned for my house, unlocked my front door, and went inside. Mike was waiting, her tail wagging eagerly. I petted her and gave her a treat, then checked my phone messages. My mother's voice came on.

"Kate, you'll never believe what happened. Call me the minute you get home!" She sounded excited.

I dialed her number. "So, give me your news," I said when she picked up.

"We found him!" she said. "We found John Smith."

"Who?" I asked.

"Remember, Trixie and I told you about the love letters we came across in that old trunk?" she said. "Letters that Mr. Smith wrote to his sweetheart during World War Two?"

"That's great, Mom," I said. "How did you manage to locate him?"

"Trixie and I have been calling nursing homes. We'd almost given up. Then, yesterday, we phoned this facility called Magnolia Place, and the receptionist put us right through to him. Sadly, his fiancée died of influenza while he was away, but he never forgot her; in fact, it was the reason he never married. Isn't that romantic?"

"It certainly sounds like true love," I said.

"Trixie and I are taking him to dinner tonight. We wanted to invite you. I know it's short notice and all."

I immediately began combing my brain for an excuse, then decided I needed a night out. "Where should I meet you?"

"Pizza Hut," she said. "The one not far from our studio," she added. "Mr. Smith said they almost never serve pizza at Magnolia Place because the residents complain of heartburn."

We settled on a time. I had less than an hour to dress and drive over, so I hurried upstairs to change. Twenty minutes later, I was on my way.

My mother, my aunt, and an elderly gentleman were already seated at a table when I entered Pizza Hut. My mother immediately introduced me to Mr. Smith.

He stood. "I've heard all about you, Kate," he said. "I'm happy to meet you."

"Likewise," I said. We shook hands. Although he was frail, his eyes were alert, and he wore a kindly expression.

He waited until I sat before taking his own chair beside me. "I understand you're a psychologist," he said.

"All her patients are crazy," my mother said.

"They're not crazy," Aunt Trixie told him. "They're troubled."

I smiled at my aunt, who was trying to be kind. Although most of my patients *were* simply troubled or confused, I'd had some real lulus as well.

The waitress arrived and took our order. We decided on a large pizza with the works. The woman walked away, and my mother leaned forward. "John was at Pearl Harbor when it was bombed," she said.

I turned to him. "I can't even imagine what that must have been like."

"I would not want to go through the experience again," he said solemnly.

"I was sorry to hear your fiancée died while you were away serving our country," I said.

"Lenore was the love of my life. Would you like to see a picture of her?" he asked, reaching for his wallet. "It's old, of course."

"I'd love to."

His liver-spotted hands trembled as he pulled the photo from a plastic sleeve in his wallet and handed it to me. "It was love at first sight," he said.

Although the photo was worn and faded, I could still make out the face of the woman who had posed for it. "She was very attractive," I said.

"My biggest regret, next to losing Lenore, was not having children," he said. "I'm the end of the line."

I passed the photo to my mother. She and Aunt Trixie studied it. "Such a lovely woman," Trixie said.

"How long have you been living at Magnolia Place?" I asked.

"Going on ten years now," he said. "It's a very nice facility. Of course, many of the people who were there when I arrived have passed on." His smile faded. "Don't ever take your family and friends for granted. They are more precious than jewels."

"That's what I keep telling Kate," my mother said, eyeing me as she passed the photo back to John, "but young people today are too busy with their careers and have little time for anything else."

He gave me a kindly look. "I suspect Kate's work can be demanding at times. She is working with people who are hurting. That is more than just a job. It's a calling."

"Thank you, Mr. Smith," I said, touched by his insight.

"Call me John," he said. "And now I want to hear about this brave husband of yours who is fighting that awful wildfire."

I told him about Jay, leaving out that we were separated. "I worry about him," I added, "but he's doing what he loves."

"I'll bet he has saved a few lives in the course of his

job," John said. "What a wonderful feeling that must be."

"Did I mention my own husband was a firefighter?" my mother asked.

John shook his head. "I don't recall that you did, but my memory isn't so good these days."

"He was very brave," she said, "but he lost his life in the line of duty when Kate was about ten years old."

"I'm sorry," John said. "I'm sure it was very painful for both of you."

"It was," she said, "but he and I loved each other deeply. I feel blessed to have known him, even though he was taken from us."

Trixie smiled. "Kate was a daddy's girl. They were inseparable."

John gave me a sympathetic look. "That explains why you worry so much about your husband."

Our pizza arrived, and John closed his eyes the minute he took a bite. "This is so much better than the food we're served at Magnolia Place," he said, looking from my mother to my aunt. "I really appreciate the two of you taking the time to make an old man happy."

"You'll be seeing us on a regular basis," my mother said. "In fact, Trixie and I always go to the movies on Thursday night because it's senior's night and we get a discount. We can swing by and pick you up on the way. Oh, and you'll have to come for dinner sometime so you can meet our roommate, Arnell. You will like him, even though I should warn you that he's a little, um, different. I'm only telling you so you won't be caught off guard."

"He hasn't had it easy," Aunt Trixie said. "Inside, he feels like a woman, but on the outside he's a man. He claims he has spent his entire life trapped in a man's body."

John looked confused.

"It's called gender identity disorder," I told him, although I did not mention Arnell was a patient of mine.

"He will eventually have some kind of surgery that will turn him into a woman," my mother said, then looked at me. "What do they call it?"

"Sexual reassignment," I replied, and hoped we could change the subject. I did not feel right discussing Arnell's personal issues.

"I would love to go with the two of you on Thursday night," John said, "and I look forward to meeting this Arnell person. I learned long ago not to judge people."

We finished our pizza, and my mother and aunt told John all about their junk business. "We decided to try and turn it into art."

"Of course, we had to learn how to weld," Aunt Trixie said, "but it was well worth it, because our little studio does a booming business."

"You wouldn't believe how much people are willing to pay for junk," my mother told him.

"I'd love to see it sometime," John said.

I said good-bye to John in the parking lot. He insisted on giving me a hug. "One thing I've learned," he said, "is that you can never give or receive too many hugs."

I found myself smiling as I drove home, and I was glad I'd accepted my mother's dinner invitation. I was also happy that she and my aunt had sort of adopted John Smith, just as they had Arnell.

I was so caught up in my thoughts that I did not see the car barreling toward me until its bright lights shone in my rearview mirror, blinding me and making it impossible to see the make and model. It passed me at a high speed, and I recognized the white sedan.

I pulled into my driveway, and as I climbed from the

car, I looked up and down the street, just in case I was being followed. Inside my house, I left the lights off and sat near the window overlooking my street. It was well past midnight when I saw the car cruise by, but I could not get a look at the driver. I didn't have to; I knew in my gut it was Abigail. Had she lied about her car being in the shop, forcing her to take the bus? Had she made up the whole thing so I wouldn't be angry when I discovered she had taken the key to my office without my permission?

I had an eerie feeling. I had seen what she was capable of. Just how far would she go?

It was still dark when I woke up the next morning. I tried to go back to sleep, but my mind was spinning. I showered and dressed. At seven thirty I drove to the hospital to check on Alice. She was depressed and worried about her job. I asked to speak to Liz, but as I expected, she didn't show.

I was suffering a bad case of jitters when I arrived at the office. I looked in each room, wanting to make certain all was as it should be. I barely had time to make coffee and drink my first cup before Mona called.

"Somebody slashed my damn tires," she said.

I didn't know what to say. I finally found my voice. "When do you think it happened?"

"Obviously, sometime during the night. Jimbo just informed me."

"I thought he was watching the house."

"He can't be expected to keep an eye on things twenty-four-seven," she said. "He has to sleep at some point. Do you think it was that bitch, Abigail?"

"She's the first person who comes to mind," I said.

"How the hell does she know where I live? And how did she get my number to call me the other day? It's unlisted."

"I didn't want to drag you into this, Mona, but she took the Rolodex from your desk. I'm really sorry." Actually, I was more angry than anything. It was one thing for Abigail to harass me, but to go after someone I was close to really pissed me off.

"What does that lunatic have against *me*?" Mona asked. "I've never laid eyes on her."

"I know this is going to sound strange, but I think she's jealous of our friendship. I think she has been following me."

"That's scary, Kate. We need to call the police."

"I have no proof, and I don't know her address. The temp agency might have it, but they're not likely to give it to us."

"They'll have to give it to the police," Mona said. "What's the name of the agency?"

"Midtown Temps."

"I'll call you back later," Mona said, "after I've talked to the police."

I barely had time to hang up before Frank Cox from the bank phoned me.

"Kate, I'm glad I caught you," he said. "Do you have a minute?"

I knew why he was calling. "Of course," I said.

"It's about the young lady who has been working for you. Abigail Davis," he added. "I have several good applicants I'm considering for the position we have available, but Miss Davis listed you as a reference, which I consider a big plus. What do you think of her?"

I debated what to say. I wasn't going to lie and sing Abigail's praises when I knew she was a kook. I had too many friends who worked at the bank. "Miss Davis worked for me only briefly, Frank," I said, "but I had to let her go."

"Really?" He sounded surprised.

"Which is why I'm totally baffled to learn that she listed me as a reference. I think hiring her would be a huge mistake. I hope this is off the record," I added.

"Absolutely, and I appreciate your candor. I'll simply tell her we decided to go with someone who had more experience."

We said good-bye. I was certain I'd done the right thing by warning Frank.

The rest of the day passed quickly. Ellen and Gerald Holmes arrived back from Hawaii late that afternoon, and I agreed to see them at six p.m. They didn't look happy. They sat on the sofa, as far away from each other as possible.

"I'm sorry your trip was a disappointment," I said, even though I'd suspected all along that the idea of a so-called second honeymoon had been a bad one, since Ellen still wore her anger like a medal. At the same time, I had hoped they would be able to put their differences aside and simply enjoy spending time in one of the most beautiful locations in the world.

Neither of them responded. They didn't even look at each other.

"So, where do we go from here?" I asked.

"I don't know that I'm going to be able to forgive Gerald," Ellen said. "Ever," she added. "And to be honest, I don't think this was his first time to cheat."

"That's a lie!" Gerald said. He bolted to his feet and put his finger in his wife's face. "You know what your problem is, Ellen? You think I'm your father and, frankly, I'm tired of being compared to him."

She shot him a dark look. "This has *nothing* to do with my father," she said. "This is about *us!*"

I looked from one to the other. "What about Ellen's father?" I asked.

Gerald backed away from his wife. "He cheated on Ellen's mother for most of their marriage," he said. "He eventually walked out."

"You have no right to discuss what happened between my mother and father," Ellen snapped.

"I have *every* right," he said, "because I've been paying for his sins our entire marriage." He wiped his hands down his face and looked at me. "I thought it was cute that Ellen was jealous of other women when we started dating exclusively. But after we married, it got worse."

"Worse how?" I asked.

"She went through my wallet, my closet, and my drawers. She checked my cell phone records and credit card receipts. I stopped going to the gym after work because she was always checking up on me. It was embarrassing. It's like she *wanted* me to cheat so she could say, 'Aha!' I can't take it anymore."

Ellen didn't respond, but her eyes filled with tears. Before long she was sobbing. "You have no idea what it was like," she told her husband. "I adored him. My whole world came crashing down on me. I blamed myself."

"Most children blame themselves, Ellen," I said, "but it wasn't your fault. You're going to have to let go of it."

"It's so hard," she said.

Gerald looked sad for her. "Dr. Holly is right, Ellen. Don't do it for me. Do it for yourself," he added.

She stood on shaky legs. "I'm so sorry, Gerald," she said. "I want to change."

He reached for her, and she stepped closer. He closed his arms around her, and they simply held on to each other, tears streaming down their faces.

I got up from my chair and slipped quietly from my office, giving them the time they needed together. They still had a long way to go, but I felt they'd made progress.

At the end of the day I looked up to find Mona standing in my doorway, dressed head to toe in black, including a hat with a veil attached that hid her face. Her hands were stuffed into black, elbow-length gloves.

She struck a pose. "What do you think? I bought this outfit when Mr. Moneybags died. I decided to save it in case I married another old man with money."

"I know you have a perfectly logical reason for wearing mourning attire," I said, "but it's going to take me some time to figure it out."

"I'm trying to hide my rash," she said. "Saks just got in their new spring line today. The manager called and said I could take a peek before they put anything on the floor."

"Like I can afford Saks," I muttered. "How come Kmart never calls me when Jaclyn Smith's frocks arrive?"

"So, do you want to go?" she asked. "Jimbo is outside with the limo. We can have dinner afterward at this place I know where the lights are dim and the booths tall so people can't see us. I'll be able to remove this stupid veil.

Besides, we need the diversion. It'll take our minds off Crazy Abigail."

"Have the police discovered anything?"

"The address she gave the temp agency turned out to be an abandoned building. The police are still looking into it, but like you said, there is no proof that she did any of the things we suspect."

I couldn't hide my disappointment, but I did not want to spend the evening dwelling on Abigail. "I'd love to go with you," I said. I grabbed my purse and locked the office. Jimbo, dressed in his chauffeur's outfit, held the limo door open, and we climbed in.

"How are your mom and Tiara?" I asked once we were on our way to Phipp's Plaza, where all the "best" stores were located.

"They're practicing birthing techniques in my bathtub."

"Huh?"

"Tiara is going to have a water birth."

"I thought only fish did that sort of thing."

"My mama's patients were birthing babies in water long before it became popular with those earth-mother types, as I call them. You know, those women who wear Birkenstocks, don't shave their legs and armpits, and wouldn't take an aspirin if they were having their gallbladder removed with a handsaw. I don't believe people should suffer pain when there are good drugs available. Not that I'm ever going to have children, mind you. I saw too many births growing up."

"You don't want *any* children?" I asked, surprised that Mona seemed so dead set against it.

"Nope."

"I would like to have at least one," I said. "Preferably

two," I added. "And I wouldn't mind having them at home with a midwife. I mean, your mom is so attentive."

"Maybe so, but attentiveness can't compare to a morphine drip."

We continued to debate the issue. "I don't know why we're talking about it," I said. "It doesn't look like I'm going to get pregnant anytime soon, and I wouldn't want to unless I knew for certain that Jay and I could work out our problems."

"You will," Mona said. "I'm sure of it."

Jimbo pulled behind Saks where the manager, a forty-something-year-old man with graying hair at his temples and exemplary taste in clothes waited for us. He took Mona's gloved hand in his.

"I'm so sorry for the loss of your brother," he said. "I would certainly have understood had you not felt like coming this afternoon."

Even through the dark veil I could see Mona's impatience to be inside where the racks of clothes waited. "I'm fine," she said, waving the comment aside. "Besides, he and I weren't close."

The man led us inside. The room resembled a warehouse, with the exception of a Persian rug, two overstuffed chairs, and a bottle of fine chardonnay chilling in a wine bucket. Mona and I each took a chair, and the manager filled two glasses and handed them to us. Several women began presenting one outfit after another.

An hour later, Mona had made her selections. I had learned that rich people didn't need as much time to shop as the average person, because they didn't have to look at the price tags.

"As always, you have excellent taste, Mrs. Epps," the

manager said. "I will see that the clothes are delivered to your home tomorrow."

Mona was still riding a wave of shopping euphoria as Jimbo drove us to a popular restaurant where she had made reservations. The maître d' led us to a high-backed leather booth at the very rear and offered Mona the wine list. The cost of the bottle she ordered would have paid my entire utility bill.

"How is the rash?" I asked once we were alone.

"It's getting worse despite all that Mama has done. It has spread to other parts of my body." Mona removed her veil.

"You were right about the dim lighting," I said. "It's barely noticeable."

"I've got an appointment next week with a specialist at Emory University Hospital," she said. "In the meantime, I'm trying not to let it get me down and maybe make it worse. Easier said than done," she added.

Our wine was served, and we were handed menus. "I highly recommend the chicken breast stuffed with spinach and feta cheese," Mona said.

"Sounds good," I said. Once we'd placed our order, I noticed Mona was studying me closely.

"Is something wrong?" I asked.

"You look tired."

I shrugged. "I haven't been sleeping well. Every little noise jars me awake."

"What kinds of noises?" Mona asked.

"It's an old house," I said. "It creaks and groans. It never bothered me before, so I know I'm just anxious. I searched my office this morning to make sure nothing was out of place."

Mona looked concerned. "If you're afraid of staying alone, you should come back to my place."

"I can't live in fear of Abigail," I said. "I still have to carry on my life and my work."

"Have you heard from Thad?"

"Not since he left for West Palm Beach. I don't blame him for not calling. I wasn't very friendly the last time I saw him."

"I should probably tell you he called me," Mona said.

"For what reason?"

"He's worried about you."

"See what I mean? Abigail is creating problems for everyone. I'm so angry."

"Let's not talk about it," Mona said as our salads arrived. "Tonight we're just going to enjoy ourselves, even if we have to fake it."

I arrived at my office the next morning and was looking over my appointments for the day when I heard the door to my reception room open. Obviously, my first appointment had arrived early. I stood but didn't make it far before Abigail Davis walked into my private office. I felt a surge of adrenaline.

"I didn't get the bank job," she said.

"I want you to leave. Now," I said.

"You said bad things about me, didn't you?"

I walked into my office without answering her and picked up the phone.

She followed. "Who are you calling?"

"Security," I said. "If you won't leave on your own, I'll have them escort you out."

"You're going to pay for this, Kate," she said.

I noted the fury in her eyes and felt a chill. "Are you threatening me?"

She was silent. A moment later, she stormed out without a word, but I knew I hadn't seen the last of her.

When my first patient arrived, I tried to concentrate on what she was saying, but my thoughts kept returning to Abigail. Was I going to jump every time I heard the door open in my reception room? Was I going to spend the rest of my life holding my breath, wondering what she would do next? The thought angered me. I was not going to give in to fear, I told myself. I was not going to give her that much control.

I decided to go downstairs for a sandwich, if for no other reason than to get out of my office for a while. I locked up and rode the elevator down to the lobby.

I spotted Abigail immediately, sitting on a chair in the corner of the sandwich shop, reading a newspaper and sipping coffee. I assumed she was going through the classifieds, because she had a pen in her hand and was making marks on the page. She glanced up and caught me staring, and I turned away quickly. Ignoring her seemed to be the best way to handle it.

It struck me then, as I was standing in line waiting to order. What the hell was wrong with my brain? The police were looking for her. I needed to call them and let them know where she was. I stepped out of line and started for the door. I glanced in her direction once more. But she was gone.

I visited Alice Smithers again after work. She was still depressed and afraid of losing her job. I felt bad for her after all she'd been through. Although I had told her in the beginning that patients with multiple personality disorder weren't cured overnight, I hadn't wanted to tell her it sometimes took years—and even then, the myriad personalities might not be fully integrated. Instead, I saw her twice a week, pro bono. In the meantime, all I could do was try to comfort her and offer hope.

I was leaving the hospital when Jay called my cell phone. I almost did a happy dance. "Can you hear me?" he asked.

"Perfectly. How are you?"

"I'm rested. I'm on my way back to the site, so I thought I'd touch base with you while I'm able to communicate."

"I'm glad you called," I said. "How's it looking?"

"We're still dealing with high winds. The best we can hope for right now is trying to contain the fire. Oh, get this. Last night, dozens of Native Americans arrived by bus. They're going to perform various ceremonies. Rain dances, I suppose." He paused. "The main reason I'm calling is to find out what the police had to say about the woman who has been giving you trouble. You *did* call them, right?"

"The police have been notified," I said, "and they're looking into it." It wasn't a lie, I told myself, since Mona *had* actually contacted them.

"Has she bothered you any more?" he asked.

I hesitated. "She would be foolish to try," I replied, "since she knows law enforcement is now involved."

"Maybe you should hang out at Mona's for a few days," he said. "I don't like the thought of you being alone."

"If I feel like I'm in danger, I'll do that," I said, "but I don't think she is going to risk jail time just so she can harass me."

"Hold on," Jay said, and I heard him speaking to someone. "I need to go, Katie. We're loading up."

"I love you, Jay," I said.

He hesitated, and I knew he would feel uncomfortable telling me in front of his crew. "Me, too," he said before hanging up.

My day suddenly seemed brighter.

As I left my office at the end of the day, I decided I needed to do something nice for myself. I stopped by the video store and chose a newly released movie, then picked up a medium-sized pepperoni and cheese pizza, which I planned to share with Mike.

I pulled into my driveway ten minutes later, and as I walked toward the house, the fresh air felt good on my face. I could not remember the last time I had been out. I unlocked my door and carried the pizza inside. Instead of diving into it first thing, I snapped Mike's leash to her collar and took her for a walk, thankful for the streetlamps that lit our way.

I was surprised to find that several For Sale signs had sprung up in the neighborhood since the last time Mike and I had ventured out, which proved what a lazy slug I was for not exercising on a regular basis. Jay had enabled my laziness by installing the doggie door leading to the fenced backyard, meaning I didn't have to walk her.

"We're going to start walking again," I promised Mike. "Maybe it will help alleviate stress." Of course, I couldn't imagine why my *pet* would have stress, but *my* anxiety level was at an all-time high. I was sort of embarrassed that I constantly advised my patients to eat well and get plenty of sleep and exercise when I did neither.

Mike and I returned home and ate the pizza in front of the TV. I was glad I'd chosen an upbeat movie, because it took my mind off my troubles. Afterward, I ran a bath, praying that Mad Ethel would cooperate. She must've felt sorry for me, because I was able to fill the tub with plenty of nice hot water. I sprinkled in my favorite bath salts and soaked for an hour. I put on my pajamas and climbed into bed, thankful to have the day behind me. I slept soundly through the night and awoke the next morning feeling better than I had in days.

I spent more time on my makeup and hair than usual and chose my favorite outfit. I said good-bye to Mike as I headed out the front door, only to discover that my mums had been yanked from the front flowerbed, the flowers and stems flattened and ground into the dirt.

I simply stood there, stunned at the destruction that had obviously occurred during the night while I slept. Who would do such a thing?

Dumb question, I thought. I already knew.

chapter 12

•••••••••••••••••••••••••••••

It pained me to look at the dead flowers, especially since my mother and aunt had bought and helped me plant them. My fingers shook as I unlocked my front door and went back inside. Mike looked overjoyed to see me. I'd been told animals have no concept of time, so she obviously figured I'd just returned home after a long day.

I made my way straight to the laundry room and pulled a black lawn-and-garden bag from a box. Outside, I picked up the now-destroyed mums and dropped them inside. Tears filled my eyes. I could not remember feeling so angry. I put the tie on the bag and dragged it behind the house in case I needed the dead flowers as evidence.

Still, I had no proof of who did this. Just my own instincts.

I saw three patients before lunchtime rolled around, when I headed downstairs to the vending machine, only to discover it was out of order. So I decided to grab a sandwich.

I was shocked to find Abigail behind the counter taking orders.

"What are you doing here?" I blurted when my turn came.

"I work here," she said coolly. "It's only temporary, of course, until I find something better. What would you like?" she asked, her pen poised above her order pad.

I lowered my voice. "I'd like to know why you destroyed my flowers last night."

She didn't so much as bat an eye. "Why would I do something like that?"

"For the same reason you slashed Mona's tires," I said.

"Did anyone actually *see* me do it? Were there witnesses?" she asked.

"I don't need witnesses. You're the only one I know who is crazy and vindictive enough to do such a thing."

She leaned closer. "You've already cost me one job. If you don't leave me alone, I'm going to call the cops and report you for harassment."

I couldn't believe my ears. "You're sick, Abigail."

"Are you going to order or not?" she asked.

"I've lost my appetite." I stepped out of line and left the sandwich shop.

I was trembling by the time I climbed the four flights of stairs to my office. I unlocked the door and entered my reception room. I sat in my office quietly. Finally, I called Mona.

"The woman is dangerous, Kate. You need to file a police report."

"I've already told you," I said. "I have no proof that Abigail is responsible."

* * *

At five p.m. I was sitting in my car in the parking lot of my office building, visor down, sunglasses on, watching the front door. There were several white sedans in the parking lot. I wanted to see if Abigail was driving one.

At five fifteen, a steady stream of people began exiting the double glass doors leading from the building. I watched closely, my eyes peeled for Abigail. By six o'clock, she still had not come out. It occurred to me that maybe she only worked part-time at the sandwich shop.

Still, I waited. At six thirty, I gave up.

I checked my messages as soon as I returned home. I had several hang-ups, and Ruth Melvin had left a message for me to call her as soon as possible. I dialed her number.

"Kate, I only arrived back in town last night, and I was so sorry to hear what happened at the anger management group. I understand you were quite the hero."

I didn't want to make Ruth feel bad by telling her how it had pretty much screwed up my life. "I'm just glad nobody was hurt," I said.

"I knew old lady Bea was mean," Ruth said, "but I never suspected she would actually try to shoot her daughter-in-law."

"They need to lock her up and throw away the key."

"Are you kidding? Her son bailed her out right away. She's back in the house, living with him and the daughter-in-law. And you're not going to believe this." She paused. "The judge ordered her to take an anger management course."

I don't know who burst into laughter first, but before I knew it, Ruth and I were howling. "You're making that up," I said.

"As God is my witness," Ruth said.

We finally managed to pull ourselves together.

"The other reason I'm calling," she began, "is because several of the members want to keep meeting a couple of times a week, and guess who they want to run it?" She didn't wait for a reply. "You," she said.

"Me? Why would they ask for me? I didn't think anyone there even liked me."

"Well, Sarah-Margaret thinks you're a Satanist for shooting the picture of Jesus, but she's always been, um—"

"A raving lunatic?" I suggested.

Ruth laughed. "You're much too kind. Actually, she has been hospitalized several times. She does fairly well as long as she takes her medication, but when she gets off, watch out! So, what do you think? Are you interested in running the group?"

"Sorry, but you're going to have to find someone else," I said. I'd had it with anger management.

Once we hung up, I went upstairs to change clothes. Mike followed me, and I told her about my day. There were times when she cocked her head a certain way and I felt she understood me.

When my doorbell rang, I headed downstairs, dressed in my jeans, a lightweight sweater, and my sneakers. I groaned when I spied Brother Love through the peephole. I knew if I didn't answer he would continue to ring the bell. I pulled the chain off, unlocked the dead bolt, and opened the door.

"Ah, Sister Kate, it's so nice to see you. I might add that you're looking well."

"What do you want?" I asked.

"Well, ah, I didn't come here to bother you. I'm getting ready to travel to Tallahassee and join in a prayer vigil in hopes the Lord will be merciful and end the drought. But I could not leave without seeing you. I'd like to discuss a personal matter." He glanced past me. "May I come in?"

"It's not a good time," I said.

"Sister Kate, I don't know how else to say this, but I have developed strong feelings for you. I can't get you off of my mind, even though I've prayed hard about it. The last thing I need is to become involved with a divorced woman who has fallen away from the flock, but I can't help myself."

I just looked at him.

"I have these urges," he said. "I may be a man of God, but I am still a human being, and when I think of you—"

"Perhaps you shouldn't share this information with me," I interrupted. The last thing I wanted to think about was Brother Love's urges.

"I was hoping, once I return from the prayer vigil, I could help you find your way back to the Lord so that we could start seeing one another," he said.

"Hmm. Let me see if I have this straight," I said. "You want to save my soul so you can date me?"

He nodded.

I could have gotten upset had I not been used to dealing with so many weirdos in my life and work. "I'm afraid I could never aspire to be good enough for you, Brother Love," I said, "for inside of me beats a sinful heart."

"Oh, but you can repent!"

"Plus, I've decided to become a Jehovah's Witness."

He looked stricken. "Surely you jest!"

"Nope. I've decided to make it my life's purpose to knock on people's doors during the dinner hour and hand out pamphlets. So you see, we could never be together."

My telephone rang. "Oops, I have to go," I said.

"But Sister Kate—"

"Also, I'm involved with someone."

"Is he the reason you became a Jehovah's Witness?"

"Have a nice life," I said and closed the door. The phone rang again, but when I answered, the caller hung up. I looked at Mike and shook my head. "I don't know why you want to live in this crazy house," I said. "I would run away if I were you."

The doorbell rang again, and I muttered a four-letter word. I yanked the door open, ready to give Brother Love a piece of my mind, only to find Thad standing beside the preacher, wearing a confused expression.

"Oh, darling, I thought you'd never get here," I said, taking his hand and yanking him inside.

He looked from me to Brother Love and back to me. "I came as quickly as I could, sweetheart," he said.

Brother Love frowned.

"Was there something else you wanted?" I asked him.

He took a step back. "Um, no, I—"

I closed the door and turned to Thad. "I thought you were in West Palm Beach."

"I decided to return earlier than I'd planned."

The phone rang. I ignored it.

"Aren't you going to answer that?" Thad asked.

"It's probably a crank call. I've been getting a lot of them."

The answering machine picked up. Abigail spoke from the other side. "I hope you're happy, Kate," she said, "that I had to take that crummy job in the sandwich shop. I will never forgive you for screwing me out of the position at the bank. Never," she added and hung up.

"A friend of yours?" Thad asked.

"Remember the receptionist who refused to put you through to me when Alice ended up in the ER? I fired her.

She's trying to get back at me. The best thing to do is ignore her. Do you want a beer?"

"Do you have any good scotch on hand?"

"No, but I have some mediocre scotch."

"That'll work," he said and followed me into the kitchen. I pulled the bottle out and grabbed a glass. "Just add a little water and a couple of ice cubes," he said.

I prepared the drink, handed it to him, and grabbed a diet soft drink from the refrigerator for me. "So, why did you leave West Palm?" I asked.

"I was worried about you."

"That's very sweet," I said, "but I hate that you cut your trip short."

The phone rang again. Thad and I looked at each other. "Do you want me to answer it?" he asked.

"No."

I was not surprised to hear Abigail's voice again. "I'm trying really hard to deal with my anger, Kate," she said, "but the more I think about how you did me wrong, the madder I feel."

"I should put a stop to this," Thad said.

"She is just looking for attention," I said. "Don't give her the satisfaction."

"How long has this been going on?"

"The calls just started."

"Have you reported her to the police?"

"And tell them what? You didn't hear her actually threaten me. She's too smart for that."

"I hope she doesn't show up at your door."

"She already has." He listened as I told him about the clock and my flowerbed. "I immediately drove to the office and gathered all my keys."

"Damn, Kate!"

"I don't know why I'm telling you all this. I keep hoping she'll get bored with her little games and go away." I felt myself getting anxious. "Could we just not talk about it? I'm sick to death of thinking about her. Let's go in the living room."

Thad sat on my sofa, and I took the chair next to him. "So tell me about your trip," I said.

"I wasted my time going. It was just a diversion."

"What do you mean?"

He hesitated. "I feel bad for bringing this up when you've got all this other stuff going on, but my dad is seriously ill."

"Oh, no! What's wrong with him?"

"I don't want to get into specifics, but it doesn't look good."

"I can't believe you didn't tell me at dinner the other night. How long have you known?"

"A couple of weeks. I just haven't felt like talking about it." He shrugged. "Anyway, it got me to thinking about my own life, you know? I'm thirty-six years old, and I'm still acting like I'm in my twenties, sipping margaritas in my hot tub with naked women. I have nothing to show for the time I've spent on earth."

"That's not true. You have a wonderful practice. You help people."

"I'm talking about my personal life. I should have a family by now, Kate. A wife and kids," he added. "I have nothing substantive or meaningful in my life."

"You know what I think?" I said. "I think you're doing exactly what everyone does when they suffer bad news; you're going through the various stages of grief. And when we're grieving, we need the support of family and friends."

"I don't have many friends," he said.

"You have tons of friends!"

"Most of them are on the shallow side. You're about the only person I know who has any depth."

"That's very kind, Thad, but I'm not as deep as you might think. Still, I want you to know I'm here for you. If you need to talk to someone, you can always call me."

"Thanks, Kate." He took a sip of his drink. "By the way, I stopped by the hospital to check on Alice Smithers. Liz Jones didn't come out to play."

"I thought you took yourself off the case."

"I decided to stay on for Alice's sake. I know she feels safe with me. Besides, I don't want Liz to think she got the upper hand. If she wants to show up for her session minus her underwear, I'll refuse to see her."

My phone rang. Thad and I both looked at it. Thankfully, it was Mona's voice that we heard, not Abigail's. "I should be going," Thad said, standing.

"I can call her back."

Thad finished his drink and handed me his empty glass before walking to the door. He hesitated. "I'm really concerned about you, Kate. Please promise me that you'll lock your dead bolts and put the chains in place."

"Of course," I said.

"And that you'll call me if things get out of hand with Wacko Woman."

"Absolutely."

I watched him walk to his car and climb in. He pulled from the drive, waved, and drove away.

I realized he had changed.

Abigail called twice more before I climbed into bed. Again, she chose her words carefully. I checked the locks on my windows and turned on the floodlights before I went to bed, only to lie there staring at the ceiling for the next hour or so. What the hell did Abigail want from me?

It felt as if I'd barely drifted off when I was wakened by Mike's growling.

"What is it, girl?" I asked, my heart beating rapidly. I glanced at the alarm clock. Two thirty a.m. I lay very still and listened. Nothing. But I knew Mike's hearing was much better than mine. Finally, I got up and peered out my bedroom window. The floodlights created a golden path around my house, but I didn't see anything. No shadows or movement.

I grabbed my flashlight from the night table and headed downstairs, shining the light on the steps so I wouldn't stumble and fall. Mike followed. I could tell she was anxious. I turned off the flashlight and looked out several windows. Again, I saw nothing, but I noticed the wind had picked up. I wondered if that's what Mike had heard.

I sat on the living room sofa, remaining as still as I could. It was so quiet I could hear the wall clock ticking in the kitchen. Finally, Mike curled at my feet and went to sleep. I grabbed a throw from the back of the sofa, covered up, and tried to relax.

I woke up at five thirty and couldn't go back to sleep. I knew the sandwich shop in my office building opened at seven a.m., so Abigail would have to get there early. I planned to be sitting in the parking lot when she arrived, either by bus or car.

I showered and dressed quickly and walked out the door at six fifteen, only to discover the tires on my car had been slashed. "Dammit!" I yelled at the tires as though they had done it to themselves. Obviously, Abigail had paid me a visit during the night, which explained why Mike had acted so strangely.

I went inside my house, locked the doors, and called the police. I was passed through to an officer. I explained what had happened and gave him my name and address. He promised to come right away.

I checked my appointment book and saw that I had an early patient. I called and rescheduled. I barely had time to hang up before the doorbell rang. I checked my peephole. Two police officers stood on the other side. I wondered if there would ever come a time when the police department didn't play a major role in my life.

I opened the door.

"Kate Holly?"

"Yes."

"I'm Officer Jenkins, and this is my partner, Officer Waters. We took pictures of your tires," he said. "We need to get some information from you."

I invited them in. "Please sit down," I said. They each took a chair, and I sat on the sofa.

"Do you have any idea who slashed your tires?" Jenkins asked.

"Yes, but I can't prove it."

I gave them Abigail's full name and how I came to hire her and why I fired her after only a few days. I told them everything. "She slashed my best friend's tires, too, the night before last. If you check, you'll find that my friend filed a police report; but, again, there's no proof, and nobody knows where Abigail lives. I'm sure she has been in my house," I said and told them about my wall clock.

Jenkins took notes. "What kind of car does she drive?"

"The car that has been following me is a white sedan. I

don't know the make and model, and I can't swear she's the one driving it. She claims she takes the bus to work. That's why I haven't filed a police report sooner."

"You say she has been calling you?" Officer Waters asked.

"Yes." I got up and hit the Play button on my answering machine. They listened.

"Make sure you keep those messages," Jenkins said.

I nodded. "She also barges into my office whenever she feels like it. Most of the time she's angry," I added. "I worry that she'll lose it in front of one of my patients."

"You're a doctor?" Jenkins asked.

"Clinical psychologist," I said and waited until he wrote it down.

"Do you have any idea where can we find Miss Davis?" Waters asked.

"I don't know where she lives, but I can tell you where she works." I gave them the name and location of the sandwich shop. "It's on the first floor of the building where I have an office," I said.

"That certainly makes it convenient for her to harass you," Jenkins said, making note of it. "Can you give us a description?"

"She looks a lot like me," I said. "At times the resemblance is almost eerie." Both men looked confused until I told them about Abigail's so-called makeover.

"We'll need your office address and the best way to reach you."

I gave them the information, including my cell phone number.

"We'll check it out," Jenkins said. "In the meantime, you need to document every encounter you've had with this woman, and try to include the dates and times. I strongly suggest that you change your locks."

"I should get a restraining order," I said.

"In the case of stalkers, it usually doesn't do any good. More often than not, a restraining order just makes them angrier."

"Stalkers?" I said, feeling as though I'd just been punched in my stomach. "You think she's a stalker?"

Jenkins and Waters exchanged looks. "Well, you've heard the old saying," Jenkins said. " 'If it walks like a duck . . .' "

"Stalkers are big on slashing tires," Waters said.

I could barely make out his words for the roaring in my ears. My face felt numb, my lips rubbery. In a matter of seconds my whole world had turned upside down and inside out.

For the first time, I was really afraid.

chapter 13

••••••••••••••••••••••••••••

The officers continued to advise me. "You're going to have to call your family and friends and tell them what's going on, because stalkers will stop at nothing to get your attention," Jenkins said.

I wondered how I would break the news to my mother without her going off the deep end.

"You need to change your routine," he continued. "For example, you might find another way to work. Don't make it easy for her. Once you start listing the times she harassed you, you'll probably notice a pattern."

Waters nodded. "The most important thing is to stay away from her. Don't put yourself in a precarious position. Don't answer her calls or agree to meet with her. If she shows up at your front door or your office, call the police immediately."

I tried to make sense of what they were saying. I should have recognized the signs. I had counseled a number of patients who'd been stalking victims. Why had I not realized it was happening to me?

"I'd like to send someone from the crime lab to dust Miss Davis's work area for fingerprints," Jenkins said.

"Of course."

I watched them walk to their patrol car, and a moment later they pulled away. I had never felt so alone. More than anything, I wished Jay was with me. I considered calling him, but I hated to worry him when he had his hands full with the wildfire.

The longer I sat there, the angrier I became. How dare Abigail Davis come into my life and make me feel helpless and scared. How dare she!

I searched my phone book for a tire company. Even though it wasn't quite seven o'clock in the morning, I got an answer. After telling the employee my situation and giving him the make and model of my car, he promised to come within the hour. Next, I called a locksmith in my area and left a message.

I tried to quell the anxiety that had taken root in my gut the minute I realized what I was up against. I took a deep breath and tried to remember from counseling other stalking victims what to do and what not to do. It echoed what Officers Jenkins and Waters had told me. I would have to start paying closer attention to my surroundings. I'd have to watch my back.

I grabbed a notebook and pen and began making a list of the interactions I'd had with Abigail. Just as I'd been told, I could see a pattern emerging. Why me? I asked myself. What did Abigail want from me?

The locksmith returned my call. The soonest he could meet me was at noon.

My doorbell rang, and I jumped. I closed my eyes and sucked in air. I had to get a grip on the situation, or I would go nuts. I tiptoed to the door and looked through the peephole. I was surprised to find Mona on the other side, dressed in her black widow's wear. Jimbo stood behind her. I unlocked the door and let them in.

"I see the bitch slashed your tires," Mona said. "I hope you reported it."

I nodded. "The police just left." I told her what they'd said.

"They actually believe she's a stalker?" Mona said.

"Yes. And when I think about it, she fits the description. By the way, what are you doing here so early?"

"Thad called me this morning," she said. "He's very concerned about your safety, just as I am. Have you told Jay what's going on?"

"Not all of it," I said. "He has enough on his plate."

"You're going to have to come home with me until they catch her," Mona said.

"No. I'm not going to let her run me out of my own home. I refuse to give her that much power."

"Are you crazy?" Mona said. "You need to do whatever it takes to stay safe."

The phone rang. When I didn't make a move toward it, Mona gave me a funny look.

"Let the answering machine pick up," I said. We waited. I was not surprised to hear Abigail's voice. She sounded as though she'd been crying. "Kate, I'm sorry I was rude yesterday," she said, "and I'm sorry I accused you of being responsible when I didn't get the bank job. I now realize that Mr. Cox would naturally hire the candidate with the most experience." She sniffed. "I'll try to reach you later." She hung up.

Mona looked at me. "Do you think she's really trying to make amends?"

I shook my head. "Nope. The next time she calls she'll be furious."

"Now I know how the term 'sick puppy' came into being," Mona said. "What's your diagnosis?"

"If she's not a psychopath, she's pretty close to it."

"Well, that settles it. Jimbo and I are going to the office with you."

"But—"

"It's not open for debate, Kate," she said.

When Mona used that tone, I knew it was useless to try to reason with her. "I have to come back at noon to meet a locksmith."

She nodded. "We can do that."

"What are you going to tell people when they ask why you're dressed in mourning clothes?"

She shrugged. "I'll tell them my parakeet died."

"Remember, don't touch anything on the desk," I said as I unlocked the door to my reception room.

"I don't like that Abigail took the Rolodex," Mona said. "That means she has access to your patients."

I pressed my fingers against my temples. "Yes."

Mona yanked a tissue from the box on the desk and used it to pull open the middle desk drawer. "The keys—"

"I have them," I said quickly. "I took them after I discovered the battery missing from my kitchen clock."

"All of them?" she asked pointedly.

I knew which keys she was talking about. "I didn't see the need, since they're hidden."

Mona immediately sat in the chair at her desk and

began running her fingers along the underside of the middle desk drawer where the key to my private office had been affixed with duct tape. She looked at me. "It's not there."

"It has to be."

Mona scrambled to her knees and stuck her head beneath the desk so she could get a better look. "It's gone, Kate."

I felt a sense of dread as I crossed the room and checked the door to my office. It was unlocked. I wasn't sure I wanted to go in, even as I stepped inside and flipped on the light switch. My file drawers, which were locked in my absence, were now open, and dozens of files had been yanked out and strewn about the floor. I heard a gasp and turned. The look on Mona's face mirrored my own feelings.

I pulled Officer Jenkins's card from my purse and handed it to Mona. "Please call him for me."

She took the card and nodded.

I quickly made my way around my desk, where a set of spare keys had been taped beneath the middle drawer—the keys to my filing cabinets. I was not surprised to find them missing as well.

Trying not to disturb anything in case the police insisted on taking photos, I knelt on the floor and, using an ink pen, I lifted files and glanced at the ones beneath. It was several minutes before I realized a number of them were missing; in particular, one belonging to a senator whose wife had insisted he get help for his sexual addiction. Thad had referred him to me because the man was a close family friend. I immediately went into panic mode. I called Thad's cell and left a message, then spent ten minutes in the bathroom washing my hands.

* * *

When Officers Jenkins and Waters arrived, a crime scene technician was right on their heels, taking photos and dusting for prints. If any of them thought it strange that Mona was dressed head to toe in black, they didn't say.

Jenkins went first. "We've spoken to the person in charge of the temp agency," he said. "We're running Abigail Davis's social security number as well as her driver's license. Turns out she not only didn't show up for work this morning, she didn't bother to call her employer."

"Also," Waters said, "one of the employees at the sandwich shop said she got a look at Abigail's cell phone and was pretty sure she was using a disposable one, because the employee had purchased one just like it for her son. Same shape and color," he added. "So that's a dead end."

"That's why we need to get a decent fingerprint," Jenkins said. "We'll run it through the system right away and, hopefully, get a hit."

"If she is even in the system," I said.

Jenkins looked at me. "I think she's smarter than we're giving her credit for. I think she's done this sort of thing in the past."

"I'm done here," the crime scene tech said. He looked from me to Mona. "I'll need to get both of your prints so we can rule them out."

I was still badly shaken as the technician took my prints, using an ink pad and fingerprint card. It was over in five minutes, and Mona took her turn. He thanked us and left.

Jenkins and his partner hung around a few minutes longer, then left, promising to be in touch and reminding me to follow through with their earlier suggestions.

They hadn't been gone fifteen minutes before Thad came through the door. He arched one brow at the sight of the oversized Jimbo sitting in the reception room reading a magazine.

"My chauffeur and bodyguard," Mona said, pulling her black, elbow-length gloves in place.

Thad nodded and regarded Mona. "Who died?" he said, motioning to her outfit.

Mona sniffed. "You obviously never met my goldfish, Huey," she said.

Thad looked amused. He turned to me, and the smile left his face. "I came as soon as I could. Did you find the missing file?"

"No."

He slumped into one of the chairs in the waiting room. "We're screwed," he said. "No, we're worse than screwed. We're finished, kaput. Dead in the water." He looked at Mona. "At least you're dressed for the occasion."

"Thad, I go to great lengths to protect my files," I said.

"Yeah? Well, the crazy bitch got to them anyway." He wiped his hands down his face. "This isn't just about us, Kate," he added.

"Do you really think you have to remind me?" I said. "There are other files missing as well, and they are just as important to me as the one you're so concerned about."

"Do you know how many she took?"

"I haven't had time to take a close look. The police just left."

"You didn't say anything to them?"

"Jeez, guys," Mona said. "What are you trying to cover up?"

"Don't ask," Thad said. He looked at me. "May we speak privately?"

I looked from Mona to Jimbo. "Would you please excuse us?" I said. Thad and I went into my office, and I closed the door.

He looked at the files scattered across the floor. "Did you check through these to see if—"

"The senator's file is not here, Thad."

"This is bad."

"Yes, it is."

"Do you know how to get in touch with this Abigail person?"

"The police warned me against having any contact with her."

"Why the hell didn't you get rid of the file?" he asked. "It has been three years."

"I still see him from time to time, Thad," I told him and was rewarded with a look of disbelief.

"I didn't know."

"Now you do."

He sat down. "Well, it's all going to come out now," he said, "and my dad will never forgive me for not protecting his friend. The timing really sucks."

"Listen, Thad. Abigail is from California. Who's to say she would even recognize the name of a senator from Georgia?"

"I want the file back, Kate," he said, "and I don't much care how we go about getting it."

Mona insisted that Jimbo drive me home to meet the locksmith while she rescheduled my appointments and Thad picked up files and tried to bring about some kind of order to my office. Jimbo and I arrived at my house only minutes before a truck bearing the name Block's Locks pulled up. A bald man, weighing about sixty pounds more than he should, emerged and met us at the door.

"Kate Holly?" he said.

"Yes."

"Let me guess," he said. "You kicked your old man out. That's the bulk of my business these days. If it weren't for the high divorce rate, I wouldn't have a job."

I didn't bother to correct him. "Do you have other appointments scheduled for this afternoon?" I asked. "I'd like to have the locks changed at my office as well."

"Holy cow, he must be on some personal vendetta to think of breaking into your office. Maybe you should get one of those protective orders or whatever they're called."

"I would appreciate it if you could fit me in sometime today," I said.

He scratched his head. "Well, I was planning to get some lunch after this."

"It's really important," I said.

"Where is your office?"

I told him, then added, "There's a sandwich shop downstairs."

He took a long time answering. "Well, I have this favorite place I go for lunch because they serve curlicue fries with their sandwiches."

"I appreciate the sacrifice you're making in order to help me," I said. Still, he looked disappointed.

When the three of us returned to my office more than an hour later, I found that Thad had managed to clear the floor of files, and Mona was returning them to the filing cabinet in alphabetical order. I was surprised to find them deep in conversation, since they had never gotten along well.

"Abigail called while you were out," Thad said. "You may want to listen to the message."

I asked Mr. Block to change the lock on the reception room door first so I could listen to Abigail's message in my office. Thad, Mona, and Jimbo joined me. I pressed the button.

"You screwed up big-time, Kate," Abigail said, "by getting the cops involved. I don't know what lies you're spreading about me, but I saw them waiting for me at the sandwich shop. You cost me another job. When you do bad things to people, it always comes back to you, so don't be surprised if something really bad happens to you." She hung up.

"That sounds like a threat to me," Thad said.

I shook my head in disbelief. "She acts like *she's* the one being victimized."

"Because she's insane!" Mona said. "That's why I think you should stay with me until the police have enough to throw her behind bars."

"I'm not going to hide from her," I said, sounding braver than I felt.

Finally, Thad spoke up. "If you're determined to go home tonight, I can spend the night. In case there's trouble," he added.

Mona, who would normally have made a snide comment, merely nodded. "Jimbo and I will stay with Kate during the day," she said.

"I hate this!" I almost shouted.

"You can hate it all you like," Mona said, "but no way am I going to leave you here by yourself."

I was thankful I had a busy afternoon ahead of me; even so, I could barely concentrate during the sessions. I was relieved when five p.m. arrived.

My cell phone rang, and I snatched it up, hoping it was Jay. My heart did a triple beat at the sound of Abigail's voice. I wondered how she'd gotten the number, then remembered she had Mona's Rolodex.

"Kate, I'm sorry for everything," she said tearfully. "I've been sobbing my guts out over this. I don't know what has gotten into me, but I want to return your files and everything else I took."

My hopes soared, but I was still distrustful. "That would be nice, Abigail."

"Where should I bring them?"

"You can drop by my office."

"No, I don't want to run into anyone from the bank or the sandwich shop. I'm embarrassed, you know? I'll meet you some other place."

I remembered what Jenkins had said about not meeting with Abigail. Hell, I wasn't even supposed to be talking to her, but getting my files back was paramount to everything else. I gave her directions to the park near my house.

"You have to come alone," she said. "I'm feeling very afraid, and if I see a police car, I will leave."

"I understand." It was difficult to hear someone in so much pain. The woman was sick and needed help, but I had to take things one step at a time.

"I'll see you at six thirty p.m.," she said. "Like I said, I expect you to be alone."

We disconnected. I noted how badly my hands shook. Mona picked that time to knock on my door. She came in without waiting for me to answer. "Well, that's it for the day," she said. "I need to go home and get out of this drab outfit. What's wrong? You look like you've seen a three-headed ghost."

I tried to keep my voice steady. "I'm just tired."

"Mama is making her famous meat loaf and real mashed potatoes tonight," she said. "I don't normally eat meat loaf, but hers is to die for. You could bring Thad. He just called and said he was on his way."

"I can't make it for dinner tonight, Mona," I said. "I need to, um, visit a patient at the hospital." I hated lying to her, but I knew it was for the best.

"Do you want Jimbo to drive you?"

"Thad can drive me, since he's the psychiatrist on the case."

"Are you okay with him staying at your place tonight?" she asked.

"I suppose." I grinned. "You seem to be taking it in stride. If I didn't know any better, I would say that you and he are almost able to tolerate each other these days."

"Desperate times call for desperate measures. Does Thad carry a gun?"

"I hope not."

"We're talking about a crazy lady who is trying to hurt you any way she can," Mona said. "You need protection."

"I don't trust myself *or* Thad to carry a gun," I said. "One of us would only end up shooting ourselves in the foot."

Thad arrived some fifteen minutes later. Mona and Jimbo said goodnight. I looked at my wristwatch.

"I'm meeting Abigail at six thirty," I told Thad. "She plans to return the files."

"I'll drive you."

"I'm supposed to be alone."

"Then we'll make it look that way, but I'm not letting you go by yourself."

I pulled into the park ten minutes early. It was already dark; the only light came from the old-fashioned street-lamps that surrounded the perimeter and lit up the side-walks but did not reach into the shadows. It was cold. I wished I had stopped by my house for my coat, which I seldom wore, since I was inside an office most of the time.

I spied a couple walking a collie, two women in sweats power-walking, and a man wearing an old coat and knit cap, rifling through trash cans for recyclable items.

I sat on a bench and tried to steady my nerves. I didn't hear Abigail come up from behind, and I jumped when I saw her.

"You're a little on edge, Kate," she said and sat beside me. She was empty-handed.

"Where are the files?" I asked.

"They're safe," she said.

"You promised to bring them!"

"First, we talk."

"That wasn't part of our agreement." I tried to keep my anger and frustration at bay.

"I need answers, Kate. I need to know why you're be-ing so cruel to me when you led me to believe we were so close."

The woman was clearly disturbed. I just looked at her.

"You won't find anyone as devoted to you as I am," she

said. "Not even Mona. She doesn't love you like I do."

I felt myself frown.

"You and I are so much alike." She laughed softly. "Honestly, it's hard to know where one of us ends and the other begins." She paused. "If you would just give me a chance, I would prove my loyalty to you. We could be happy together." She covered one of my hands with hers.

I kept my hand still. I did not want to risk making her angry. "What do you want from me, Abigail?" I asked.

"Surely you've figured it out," she said. "I want to be your best friend and lover."

I should have seen it coming. Maybe I had and didn't want to believe it. I had no choice but to play along. "You've hurt me deeply, Abigail."

Her expression became gentle. "I didn't want to, but it was the only way I knew to get your attention. You're too wrapped up in Mona and Thad."

"They're my friends, though," I said.

"With me in your life, you won't need other people."

"What about Jay?"

"Is it worth spending the rest of your life worrying that he could end up seriously injured or dead? Besides, he will never love you as much as I do."

Behind Abigail, I saw the overhead light flash on in my car, and I knew Thad was trying to slip out. What the hell was he planning? I wondered, wishing there was some way I could motion for him to stay put. It was difficult to keep up with what Abigail was saying, even more so to keep my gaze fixed on her when I had no clue what Thad was up to.

Some sixth sense must've alerted Abigail, because she

turned and saw the light in my car. She bolted to her feet. "You brought someone with you! I told you to come alone." She reared back and slapped me hard across the face. "You'll never see those files again," she said, then ran into the shadows and disappeared.

chapter 14

....

I didn't try to follow her. I was too numb to move.

"I saw the whole thing," Thad said, hurrying my way. "Are you okay?"

Tears stung my eyes. I stood. "You were supposed to stay in the damn car!" I shouted. "Why didn't you stay in the car?"

"I was afraid for you," he said. "I was just trying to get closer in case she tried anything. I saw her hit you. Are you hurt?"

"I'm too damn angry to be hurt."

"Where are the files?"

"She didn't bring them. And now that you've screwed up everything, she'll probably *never* hand them over." I heard a car and saw the white sedan heading toward the main road. "Can you tell the make and model of that car?" I asked quickly.

Thad followed my gaze. "It's a Ford Focus," he said. He put his hands on his hips. "What the hell excuse did she give for not bringing the files?" he asked.

"What does it matter *now*?" I said loudly. "You frightened her away. Things were going fine until she realized I'd brought someone with me."

"What did you expect me to do, Kate? Hide in the backseat while you met with a psychopath?"

"That was the plan."

"I didn't like that plan to begin with."

I swiped at the hot tears on my cheek. I wanted to punch him. "I don't feel like talking to you right now, Thad."

"You're shivering," he said, shrugging out of his jacket and draping it across my shoulders.

"She probably had no intention of bringing the files to begin with," I said, more to myself than Thad. "As long as she has them, she has me in her clutches. She has control." I felt hot tears on my cheek.

"Come on," Thad said gently. "I'll drive you home."

"We have to go by the office for your car."

"I don't think you're in any condition to—"

"I'll be okay. I just need a minute."

We walked to my car in silence. Thad opened the door on the passenger's side, and I got in and strapped on my seat belt. He climbed in on the other side. Once he started the engine, he turned the heat on high and aimed the vents at me. Only then did it occur to me that my teeth were chattering. I leaned back against the headrest and closed my eyes. Thad remained quiet.

We arrived at the office building twenty minutes later. I got out and walked around to the driver's side. I handed Thad his jacket.

"Wait for me," he said. "I want to follow you."

We met back at my place. Mike growled at Thad when

he stepped inside the door. "It's okay, girl," I said, reaching down to pet her. Nevertheless, she did not take her eyes off him.

"She obviously doesn't like me," he said.

"Normally she's very friendly, but I think she senses something is wrong."

Thad grabbed a throw from the sofa and wrapped it around me. I couldn't seem to get warm. "Here, sit down," he said, leading me to a chair. I sat. "You need to drink something hot." He hurried into my kitchen. I heard him opening and closing cabinet doors, heard the hum of my microwave.

He returned a few minutes later with a mug. "It's hot chocolate," he said, offering it to me. "It should take the chill off."

"Thank you." I gave it time to cool off. Thad paced the floor as I took tentative sips.

The phone rang. I froze. Thad's gaze met mine as we waited, but the caller hung up. I knew it was Abigail.

Thad sat down on my sofa. "What does she want from you?" he asked.

"She wants us to be lovers. More than that, actually. As weird as it sounds, I think she wants to *be* me. That's why she went to so much trouble to look like me." Thad was quiet as I finished my hot chocolate. The phone rang again. I tensed. After three rings, the caller hung up. I wondered how long it would go on.

"Are you hungry?" Thad asked.

My stomach felt hollow. I realized I hadn't eaten all day. "I could make us a grilled cheese sandwich," I said.

He laughed. "Now, there's an offer I haven't had in a

long time. You still don't know how to cook, do you?"

I knew he was trying to lighten the mood. "I can cook," I said defensively. "It's just easier to make grilled cheese sandwiches. Besides, you used to like them."

"I'd love to have one, if you're up to it," he said.

I'd finally stopped shivering. I went into the kitchen and gathered the ingredients I needed and pulled out a skillet. The phone rang again, and I felt my shoulders sag. I was relieved when Mona spoke.

"Kate, if you're there, pick up."

I heard the urgency in her voice. I grabbed the phone. "Hi," I said.

"Abigail Davis just called me," she said. "Why would you ignore Officer Jenkins's advice and meet with her when you know she's dangerous?"

"She promised to give me the files," I said.

"And?"

"She lied." I gave a huge sigh. "Why did she call you?" I asked.

"She wants me out of your life. She said the two of you were in love, but that I was getting in the way. Those were her exact words."

"I'm sorry," I said, feeling weary. "I never meant to get so many people involved." My voice cracked.

"Is Thad with you?"

"Yes."

"Let me speak to him," she said.

I handed Thad the phone. I went about making the sandwiches as he gave Mona a summary of the evening's events. "Kate's a little shaken over it, but who wouldn't be?" he said. "Don't worry, I'm not going anywhere."

He and Mona chatted for a few minutes before he hung

up. We ate our sandwiches in the living room so I could watch CNN and get the latest on the fire. The good news was they had it about fifty percent contained. The camera panned out and captured at least a dozen Native Americans dancing. They were painted and feathered; some wore ornate headdresses. Not far away, a prayer group held candles.

"How long do you think Jay will be gone?" Thad asked.

"He won't leave until the fire is out."

"Maybe you should drive down and visit him."

"He hasn't invited me," I replied glumly.

"You need a break from all this," he said. "If you can get out of town without Abigail following you, you'll be able to relax for a couple of days."

"Are you and Mona afraid I'll go off the deep end?" I asked, giving a rueful smile.

"We're all on the same side here, Kate," he said.

"I know."

"The problem is, we have no idea how long this is going to go on."

Once we'd eaten our sandwiches, Thad turned to the sports channel, and I curled up on the sofa beneath the throw, pretending to be interested. I thought about what he said about me getting out of town, and the thought of seeing Jay made it even more tempting. Of course, I would have to tell Jay what was going on.

I yawned and closed my eyes.

"Kate?"

"Huh?"

"You should go to bed."

"That would make me a pretty crappy hostess."

"I'm a big boy; I can entertain myself."

Finally, I sat up and stretched. "Okay, I'll get sheets and blankets for the sofa," I said, standing.

"I'm really sleeping on the couch?"

"Yup."

"Well, there goes the *other* reason I offered to stay tonight."

I heard the amusement in his voice as I started down the hall for the linen closet. Actually, I felt bad that I had never set up a guest room. The two spare bedrooms contained all my worldly possessions. Without them I would have had to rent a storage facility, which didn't come cheap.

"Hey, did I tell you Mona flirted with me today?" he asked.

I turned. "No way!"

"She's got it bad for me, Kate. I should probably ask her out. Only I think I'll wait until that rash clears up, if you know what I mean."

"What about your cute receptionist, Bunny?"

"There's nothing going on between us. She's just eye candy."

"Sexist," I said, frowning.

"I'm teasing, okay?"

I grabbed pillows and bedding from the closet and returned to the living room. "If you hurt Mona, you'll have to answer to me."

"I keep telling you I've changed." His cell phone rang. He pulled it from his pocket and checked. "It's my answering service. I hope none of my patients got into the arsenic."

"That is so *not* professional."

"Lighten up, Kate."

Thad spent ten minutes on the phone talking to a distraught patient while I made up the sofa and saw that there were fresh towels in the downstairs bath. He hung up his cell and stuffed it back in his pocket.

"Everything okay?" I asked.

He gave a grunt. "You know how it is. Patients wait until you close shop to get depressed."

He pointed to the rolled-up newspaper in the chair. "Is that today's paper?"

"Yeah." I turned the TV back to CNN, where a reporter was interviewing a woman who had traveled to Tallahassee with her church to pray for the end of the fire. I suddenly recognized her. "Well, I'll be damned if it's not Sarah-Margaret!" I said.

"Should I recognize the name?" Thad asked.

"She's the one who convinced everyone in Atlanta that I'm an atheist!" I turned up the volume. The reporter was asking her a question.

"Ma'am, are you saying that this fire is God's way of punishing sinners?" he asked.

"Absolutely," she said. "It's a wake-up call for all who have sinned and fallen short of the Glory of God." She surprised the reporter by taking his microphone. She looked right into the camera. "I just want everyone to know it's never too late to repent. Now I would like to sing a song that I hope will inspire the whole world to get down on their knees and pray."

She started singing a hymn, proving to the listening audience that she couldn't hold a tune in a Mason jar. The reporter tried to get his microphone back, but she held on tight, eyes closed, singing her heart out. He was trying to wrestle it from her as they went to a commercial.

I shook my head sadly. "I should introduce her to Bitsy Stout," I muttered.

Thad folded the newspaper.

"Nothing interesting?" I asked.

"It's all about the fire."

The phone rang. Thad and I looked at each other. After several rings, the caller hung up. "This could go on all night," I said. "I'm going to unplug the phones so we can get some sleep."

"Give a shout if you need me."

"Thanks for staying tonight," I said. "I'm really sorry I yelled at you earlier."

"I enjoyed it," he said. "It reminded me of old times."

I smiled. "You should find everything you need in the bathroom, including a toothbrush. If you get hungry, there is Ben & Jerry's in the freezer. Or you can make yourself a peanut butter and jelly sandwich."

He patted his stomach. "I'm still stuffed from the grilled cheese."

I went about the house locking up and sliding the chains in place. I set up the coffeepot, unplugged the downstairs phone, grabbed my cell phone, and headed upstairs. Mike followed.

I unplugged the phone in my bedroom as well. Then, remembering that Abigail had my cell number, I made certain it was off as I plugged it into the charger. I pulled off my clothes and left them on the floor, then took a shower and washed my hair, at the same time trying to rid myself of all the yuck I'd been through that day. As I dried off, I could not remember when I had felt so tired. I grabbed my Big Bird sleep shirt, pulled it over my head, brushed my teeth, and climbed into bed. Mike jumped to the foot and curled at my feet.

I lay there for a moment, thinking I had forgotten something important, but I clearly recalled locking up and setting up the coffeepot. I shoved the worries from my mind and welcomed sleep.

I was awakened by a knock on my bedroom door the next morning. It was almost seven a.m. I'd slept for nine hours.

"Come in," I said.

Thad pushed the door open. He held two steaming mugs. "I poured you a cup of coffee."

I yawned widely. "My hero," I said.

He carried the cup to the bed and offered it to me. As I took it, I noticed the odd look on his face. "Damn, Kate, you've done it now. You've gone and turned me on with your sleepwear."

"Don't hate me because I'm sexy," I said.

He sat on the edge of the bed as though it was an everyday thing for him to be in my bedroom. We sipped our coffee in silence.

"You want to take a shower first, or should I?" he asked. "Or would you rather we shower together, which is more economical when you think about it."

"You go ahead," I said. I thought it only fitting that, as a guest, he should have a shot at the hot water.

He started from the room. "You don't happen to have a good razor on hand, do you?" he called out.

"Left side of the medicine cabinet."

"Thanks."

I finished my coffee, plugged in the phone, and started downstairs, pausing in the living room to turn on the TV and CNN. I turned up the volume and hurried into the kitchen for a second cup of coffee, pausing to plug in that phone as well.

The doorbell rang. I froze. I tiptoed toward it and looked through the peephole. I groaned at the sight of my mother and aunt. How had I missed the sound of their monster truck? I opened the door.

"Why aren't you answering your phone?" my mother demanded. "I've called three times. I even called your cell phone."

"It's complicated, Mom."

"So, what else is new?" She suddenly became tearful. "Kate, why didn't you tell me you were a lesbian?"

I blinked several times, figuring the caffeine had not hit my brain yet. "Excuse me?"

"Bad enough everybody thinks you're an atheist, but you should have come to me and discussed your sexual preferences. Trixie and I would never turn our backs on you. I mean, we've got a half man, half woman living with us."

"Mom, what are you talking about?"

"I got a call this morning from a young woman named Abigail who claimed the two of you were lovers. I told Trixie it was no wonder you and Jay were having problems." She looked at Trixie. "Isn't that what I said?"

Trixie nodded. "Those were your very words."

"But this poor Abigail person said you broke her heart. It was the saddest thing I've ever heard. It brings tears to my eyes just thinking about it. You could have at least let her down gently."

I heard whistling from the bathroom. The door opened, and Thad came down the hall wearing only a towel. "Uh-oh," he said the minute he saw my mother.

My mother slapped her hand over her mouth in horror.

"I think you just rendered her speechless," Trixie said.

I could feel a stress headache coming on. "Mom, I know it looks bad," I said, "but—"

"I think I understand now," she said. "You swing both ways."

I was in no mood for a lengthy explanation, but I knew she would gnaw on it like a bone unless I said something. "Mom, please, I don't have the time or energy to explain everything right now, but this Abigail person is crazy."

"I can vouch for that," Thad said, still standing there wearing his towel. "I only stayed the night to protect your daughter. See? My covers are still on the sofa."

"It could be a ruse," my mother said, "to throw me off."

"See what I keep telling you, Dixie?" my aunt said. "You always assume the worst. You should at least give Kate the benefit of the doubt."

"On second thought, I don't really need shaving cream," Thad said. "I'll just use soap." He turned and strode down the hall.

My phone rang, but I was still trying to calm my mother so I didn't think. Abigail's voice came on. "Kate, I'm willing to forgive you for last night and give you what you want, but I refuse to take a backseat to Mona. I know of a cheap motel where we can meet. Call me." She gave me her phone number.

My mother gasped. "Is Mona a lesbian, too?" she whispered. She looked at Trixie. "That would certainly explain why she has never remarried."

I didn't bother with a response. The doorbell rang. I gave a sigh that felt like it had come up from my toes. I could already tell it was going to be a bad day. I checked the peephole. Mona stood on the other side in her black outfit. I opened the door. She spoke to my mother and aunt, who took a double take at her attire but said nothing.

"I didn't sleep all night," she said. She lifted her veil. "Just look at the circles under my eyes."

"I'm sorry," I said.

"Sorry doesn't cut it, Kate. I am still angry with you for meeting Abigail behind my back. If you do that again, I'm never going to speak to you."

"Mona, please try to understand," I said.

"Furthermore, you're sleeping at my place tonight. I don't trust you not to go running to her the minute she calls."

My mother gaped.

"We should go," Aunt Trixie said.

My mother stood and headed for the door. She turned and looked at me. "I suppose you're too busy to come to dinner tonight," she said. "I promised Mr. Smith a home-cooked meal. It's the least I can do for a big war hero like him. Plus, Trixie and I have a surprise for him."

"I'd love to come to dinner," I said.

"Fine, but I would appreciate it if you wouldn't tell Arnell what you're up to these days. He's already confused enough."

Aunt Trixie kissed me on the cheek. "Everything is going to be okay," she said. She looked at Mona. "I'm sorry for your loss. I hope whoever died is at peace now." They hurried out.

"Did I miss something?" Mona asked.

"I'll try to explain it when I have more time."

"Well, you need to get ready for work. Jimbo is waiting in the car. Where is Thad?"

"In the shower." I heard a shout from the bathroom.

"Uh-oh, he just ran out of hot water. Good thing I grabbed a shower last night. Tell Jimbo to come in and have a cup of coffee. It won't take me long to get ready."

Once I'd dressed, I hurried downstairs. Mona and Thad were chatting face-to-face on my sofa, and Jimbo was trying to put the previous day's newspaper in order.

"Why are you reading yesterday's paper?" I asked him.

He glanced up. "Today's hasn't arrived yet."

"I think we have a new carrier," I said, "because the paper has been late several times over the past week. I noticed it wasn't here when we left for the office yesterday."

I barely got the words out of my mouth before I realized the significance of what I'd just said. "Oh, no." I covered my mouth.

"What's wrong?" Thad said, coming to his feet.

I moved my hand. "Did you bring the newspaper in last night?"

"No. I grabbed it from that chair." He pointed to where Jimbo was sitting. "Why?"

I clearly remembered him reaching for it, but I'd thought nothing of it at the time. Only later did I have the niggling feeling that something wasn't right, but I was too tired to figure it out. Now I knew.

I walked into the kitchen and searched for the pad of paper on which I had recorded my encounters with Abigail. It was gone.

"What is it, Kate?" Mona asked, standing in the doorway.

"The newspaper hadn't been delivered when we left for

my office yesterday," I said. I went into the living room. "Jimbo, did you bring the newspaper in when we met with the locksmith at noon?"

He shook his head. "I don't even recall seeing it, but I wasn't looking for it."

"Somebody else brought it into the house," I announced. "That same person also took the diary Officer Jenkins told me to keep, listing all my interactions with Abigail." I took a deep breath. "The bitch has been in my house again."

chapter 15

●●●●●●●●●●●●●●●●●●●●●●●●●●●

I sat on the sofa between Thad and Mona. I couldn't stop shaking. It was as if I'd caught a chill and was unable to get warm. It was not fear-based. I was angry enough to chew my way through a chain-link fence.

"Okay," Thad said, "before you start getting paranoid, remember, you already suspected Abigail of coming into the house while you were away. That's why you had the locks changed to begin with. She probably came by after you left for work and carried the newspaper inside, knowing you would figure it out and get scared. She *wants* you to be afraid."

"But she can't play her little games anymore," Mona said, "because the key she has no longer fits. Think how PO'd she's going to be when she discovers she can't get inside."

"I'm not afraid of her," I said. "I just can't get the upper hand as long as she has those files. I do *not* like feeling powerless. I do *not* like feeling victimized."

"You're not a victim," Mona said.

I looked at her. "What do you call it when your friends have to go to work with you or sleep at your house because there's a damn psychopath on your ass? And it's not enough that she is out to get *me*; she has to involve my friends and family." I realized I was ranting.

"How damaging are the files?" Mona asked.

Thad looked at her. "The one we're most concerned about would make great tabloid fodder and devastate everyone involved, including a public figure."

"See what I mean?" I said. "It's not an even playing field. If it were just me, I could handle it, but there are too many others involved."

"That means you can add blackmail to her list of bads," Jimbo said. "Which means more jail time for her when she's caught."

"*If* she's caught," I added.

Officer Jenkins called shortly after Mona, Jimbo, and I arrived at my office. "I just got off the phone with Abigail Davis," he said. "She said she met with you last night in hopes of calling a truce, but you and another person tried to start trouble. She said she fears for her life."

"Oh, great," I said. "You know, this would be laughable if it weren't so sick," I said. "Looks like I can add pathological lying to psychosis."

"Did you actually meet with her?" he asked.

"Yes. I know you're against it, but she promised to return the files she stole from my office." I explained the importance of one of the files without giving the senator's name.

"How do you suppose she knew to contact me?" he asked.

"She was in my house again. Obviously, she went in

before I had my locks changed. She took the diary you suggested I keep. I stapled your business card to the first page so I wouldn't lose it."

"That makes sense."

"What about the fingerprints?" I asked.

"I'd planned to call you this morning. The crime lab was only able to get a partial. My guess is she wiped everything clean when she broke into your office."

"Meaning we aren't any closer to locating her or proving she is guilty."

"I'm sorry. All we can do is keep trying."

Arnell was my first patient of the day. He wore a dove gray skirt and jacket with a pale blue blouse, and a scarf that pulled it all together. "I have bad news," he said. "John Smith is a phony."

"What do you mean?"

"There were two John Smiths at Magnolia Place for almost a year, which is a coincidence, but not so unusual, since the name is so common."

"Okay, I'm confused."

"There was John Smith, the war hero, and our John Smith, who never served in the armed forces."

"How did you find that out?"

"Well, John is always complaining about the food at Magnolia Place, so, unbeknownst to him, I went to see the director yesterday and asked if I might serve a special dish for the residents once a month. Told the guy I would even cover the costs."

"That's awfully nice of you," I said.

Arnell shrugged. "Anyway, we got to talking about John, and that's how I found out."

"How did John know so many details about Lenore Brown, not to mention Pearl Harbor and the rest of it?"

"The late John Smith, who I understand was quite an extrovert, shared many of his stories over meals in the dining room. He was real popular. When he died, some of his personal belongings came up missing, but nobody ever suspected our friend. Also, since their names were the same, the mail often got mixed up."

"So what do we know about *our* John Smith?"

"It's kind of sad," Arnell said. "He has no family, and most of his friends passed away long ago. The director said he spent most of the time sitting in his room alone."

"That *is* sad. My mom and aunt will be disappointed."

"That's what I wanted to talk to you about," Arnell said. "The guy is ninety years old, and his health isn't as good as he pretends. Dixie and Trixie enjoy him as much as he does them." Arnell looked thoughtful. "I don't like lying to people, but I don't think we should say anything."

I debated it. "Okay, we'll keep Mr. Smith's true identity a secret for now. As long as nobody gets hurt," I added.

It was after six o'clock when I arrived at my mom and my aunt's apartment, which was over their studio in Little Five Points. I could smell mom's cooking—chicken-fried steak with all the fixings—as I took the back stairs to the second floor. John Smith, wearing a white dress shirt and bow tie, greeted me heartily.

"You're late," my mother said.

"Now, Dixie, you promised to be nice," my aunt Trixie said. She smiled at me. "You're just in time."

"Only because I held off serving dinner," my mother replied.

"I'm sorry I kept everybody waiting," I said, knowing an apology was the only way to win my mother's forgiveness. That, and guilt, I reminded myself. "I just feel awful," I added.

Arnell winked at me. He'd changed into a silk lounging outfit and ballerina slippers.

My mother sniffed. "Well, go ahead and wash up while Trixie and I put dinner on the table."

In the bathroom, I washed my hands three times. I returned to the kitchen to find everyone seated. Arnell sat next to Mr. Smith and was admiring his bow tie.

"Arnell, would you please say grace?" my mother asked. "And you might add a little prayer for Kate, since she is in such dire need of help."

I gave an inward sigh and wondered if I should have stayed home and eaten a frozen dinner.

We bowed our heads while Arnell prayed. Once we raised our heads, my mother began passing the food. She served Mr. Smith, filling his plate so high that I couldn't help but wonder how such a slightly built man could hold so much food.

"Mr. Smith," I began.

"Now, now, I told you to call me John," he reminded me with a kindly smile.

"I was wondering. Do they offer many activities at Magnolia Place?"

He nodded. "We have an activities director. First thing in the morning, we gather in the sunroom and do stretching exercises while she plays the piano. Dixie, these are the best biscuits I've ever tasted," he said.

She glowed.

"What else do they offer?" I asked.

"Why are you asking so many questions?" my mother said. "Are you shopping for a nursing home for me? If you are, you're wasting your time, because you're going to cause me to have a fatal heart attack long before I have to go into assisted living."

"Dixie, for Pete's sake!" Aunt Trixie said. "What is wrong with you today?"

"I have a lot on my mind," she said, pursing her lips and looking directly at me.

I decided to ignore her.

Mr. Smith wiped his mouth on a napkin. "We also have arts and crafts," he went on, as though our conversation hadn't even been interrupted. "We're painting birdhouses right now. We play cards and work puzzles, and one of the caretakers reads a chapter or two from a book each night. The residents get to choose the book. Plus, the staff goes all out on holidays, and families are invited to come." He shrugged. "It's not so bad. I just wish the food was better and the caretakers prettier." He smiled and winked.

Arnell tapped his iced tea glass with a spoon. "I have an announcement to make," he said and looked at John. "I visited Magnolia Place today and offered to prepare a gourmet meal once a month."

"That's so thoughtful of you!" Aunt Trixie said.

"Very thoughtful," my mother agreed, nodding, and I nodded as well.

But John looked troubled. "Did you meet with the director?" he asked.

"Yes, and he was thrilled with my idea."

John's smiled looked forced. "That's just splendid!" he said, although his tone didn't match his words.

I wondered if he feared being found out. "Arnell is an artist in the kitchen," I said, then hoped my mother wouldn't take offense, "but nobody can top my mom's chicken-fried steak and biscuits."

"Amen to that," Arnell said. "I've got the extra pounds to prove it."

She waved off the remark, but I could tell she was pleased. "Well, then," she began, "since we're making announcements, Trixie and I have one of our own." She turned to John. "We cleaned up the old trunk containing the letters you sent Lenore, and we are giving it to you as a gift to celebrate our friendship."

"Oh, my," John said, his face coloring. "I don't know what to say."

"You don't have to say anything," Aunt Trixie said. "Dixie and I will deliver it right to your room at Magnolia Place. Along with the letters you wrote."

Arnell and I exchanged looks.

"I'm deeply touched," John said, and I noted a sudden glistening in his eyes. "Every time I look at it I will think of my new friends."

Once dinner was finished and we all had dessert—key lime pie—I offered to clean the kitchen.

"We'll do it together," my mother said. "It will give us time to talk."

Trixie shot me a look of sympathy as she invited Arnell and John into the living room for coffee so my mother and I could be alone.

"Abigail Davis called again," my mother said as soon as everyone was out of hearing range. "She asked me to talk to you about your, um, relationship."

I stepped closer to her. "Mom, I didn't want to bring you into this, but Abigail has serious emotional problems.

She desperately needs help. If she calls you again, hang up; otherwise, you're going to be inundated with phone calls from her. She is just looking for attention."

"I wish Jay were here. He would know what to do."

"It's up to me to solve my problems, Mom," I insisted.

She looked surprised. "You sound angry."

"The only person I'm angry with is Abigail. As for Jay—" I shrugged and swallowed back the lump in my throat that felt the size of a goose egg. "I'm just hurt, I guess. I always try to be there for him when he needs me, but he's never around when I need him. He didn't have to go to Tallahassee; there were plenty of volunteers. I will always play second fiddle to his career."

"Firefighting is in his blood," she said. "Just like it was in your father's. He was off duty the night he died, but that didn't stop him from going to that fire once he saw how bad it was. I was as angry as you were when he didn't make it out of that building."

I looked at her. "I don't remember being angry. Just sad," I said.

"Oh, honey, you were mad enough to eat barbed wire. You didn't even want to attend his funeral. I'm surprised you don't remember. Why do you think I put you in counseling?"

"I guess I forgot."

"I don't think you've completely gotten over it," she said. "Maybe that's why you take it out on Jay. There's a term for that, I'm sure."

"It's called displaced anger. Why did you wait until now to tell me?"

"You're the psychologist," she said. "I figured you knew."

I didn't know what to say. I didn't remember a lot of what occurred after my father's death except thinking my world had come to an end. My eyes burned. Had I un-knowingly been punishing Jay because my father, who'd been my best friend, had died? It suddenly occurred to me that my hand washing had begun after Jay was injured. Even worse, he'd seemed to enjoy spending time with his buddies more than he did me. Had he sensed my hostility?

"I know you think I butt into your business more than I should," my mother confessed. "I promise to try to do better if you'll promise not to blow up your office again."

She was never going to let me forget that little incident. "Okay, Mom," I said. "It's a deal."

I arrived at Mona's with a change of clothes and my faith-ful dog and rang the doorbell. Mona answered. She was not dressed in her mourning clothes, so the first thing I noticed was that her rash had worsened. The second thing I noticed was an expression of stark fear.

"What's wrong?" I asked.

She grabbed my wrist and yanked me inside. "Tiara is in labor," she cried. "She's in my bathtub as we speak."

"But I thought she wasn't due—"

"The idiot went through Mama's medical bag this morning and found a bottle of castor oil! She drank every drop. She went into labor an hour ago, and everything is happening so fast. Mama is furious with her."

I heard Willie-Mae call out from the second floor, "Mona, come quick. I need a spare hand!"

"I can't do it!" Mona whispered to me. "This is why I left home in the first place. You have to go up there and help."

"Me? I don't know anything about birthing babies!"

A loud yowl from the second floor made me jump.

"Monaaa!" Willie-Mae shouted. "We need you!"

Mona pressed her hands against her ears. "I can't stand it!"

"Dammit!" I said, dropping my purse and outfit on the sofa. I raced upstairs. "I don't know why this sort of stuff always happens to me," I muttered to myself.

"I'm dyyyiiing," Tiara cried.

I ran toward the bathroom and skidded to a stop just inside. Tiara was in the oversized tub, water barely covering her massive stomach, naked as the day she was born. Willie-Mae sat on the edge of the tub behind her, legs fully immersed, prodding Tiara on. "Quick short breaths, Tiara," she said.

"What do you need me to do?" I asked, dreading what the answer might be.

"The baby is coming," Willie-Mae said. "I'm going to need you to catch it when it comes out."

My world stopped turning. "Did you say—?"

"Roll up your sleeves and get ready."

I began rolling up my sleeves. "But what if I miss it?" I cried. "I've never been a really good catcher."

"Yeeoww!" Tiara wailed.

Willie-Mae looked at me. "Front and center, Kate."

I knelt at the tub.

"Okay, listen to me, Tiara," Willie-Mae said. "On the next contraction, I want you to push."

"I'm too tired," she said tearfully.

"You can do it, hon," Willie-Mae said. "It's almost over. Get ready, Kate."

I nodded, but I wished I had stayed home.

Tiara tensed, her eyes shot open, and her mouth formed a big O. She let out a squeal.

"Push!" Willie-Mae ordered.

As I placed my hands between her thighs, I felt something slip right into them. I thought my heart would stop beating. I gently but firmly grasped it and pulled it from the water, a tiny little thing coated with some kind of white and greenish stuff. A cord was attached to its navel.

"Oh, it's a baby!" I cried.

Willie-Mae looked amused. "What did you think we were delivering? A goat?"

"What am I supposed to do with it?"

"Is it a boy or a girl?" Tiara asked, tears streaming down her cheeks.

I checked. "It's a girl!"

"Lay her gently on Tiara's stomach," Willie-Mae said. "Be careful with the cord."

I did so. Willie-Mae suddenly became very busy, suctioning the baby's mouth and nostrils. The infant let out a howl.

I was awestruck. "What's her name?" I asked Tiara, whose face glowed with happiness.

"Lucy, after my mother," she said. "Quick, grab the camera. I want pictures for her daddy."

I got up and hurried to the vanity, pausing to wash and dry my hands and arms. I grabbed the digital camera and snapped pictures as fast as I could. Only then did I realize tears were streaming down my cheeks.

An hour later I was still dazed as Mona and I pulled leftovers from the refrigerator, per Willie-Mae's instructions. Willie-Mae joined us in the kitchen; she looked tired but pleased.

"How is Tiara?" I asked.

She smiled. "She and the baby are doing very well. I'll take something up to her later. You did a great job. Have you ever thought of becoming a midwife?"

Mona slid an amused look in my direction.

"I'm really happy I was able to take part in the birth," I said, "but I think I'll keep my day job."

We dined on cold meat loaf sandwiches. Willie-Mae carried a tray upstairs to Tiara, while Mona and I straightened the kitchen. When Willie-Mae returned, she was frowning. "Tiara spilled an entire glass of juice on the comforter. It will need to go to the dry cleaners."

"I'll get Jimbo to take it in the morning," Mona said.

Willie-Mae reached into the refrigerator for a container of bottled water. "I need to run this up to Tiara."

"I'll do it for you," I said. "You should rest."

"Thank you, hon," she said. "I think I'll kick back on the sofa for a few minutes, maybe catch my second wind. I'll probably be up and down most of the night."

I carried the water upstairs. Tiara and the baby looked different than when I'd last seen them. They were clean and dry and dressed in crisp gowns. Little Lucy was nursing at Tiara's breast.

"She's beautiful," I said.

Tiara smiled. "Thank you," she said. "And thank you for being there for me."

"I was glad I could help," I said.

"My husband will be so proud." She yawned. "Would you mind putting Lucy in the bassinet for me?" she asked.

"Um . . ."

"It's okay, she won't break," Tiara said. She held the baby out to me. "Just make sure you support her head."

I very gently took the sleeping infant from her, taking great care to hold her correctly. "I've never held a newborn," I said.

"You can practice holding Lucy all you want," Tiara said. "That way you'll know how to do it when you have your own baby."

"I don't know if I would be very good at taking care of a baby," I said, placing Lucy in her bassinet. "I'm having trouble raising a dog."

I saw that Tiara was having trouble holding her eyes open. I quietly slipped from the room.

Downstairs I found Mona on the phone. When she hung up, she turned and faced me. "That was Thad," she said. "He just wanted to make sure you were okay. I told him you were helping Mama deliver a baby, but I don't think he believed me." She paused. "I should probably tell you something."

"What?" I asked.

"Well, Thad came on to me in your office when you and Jimbo drove to your house to meet the locksmith."

"Really?" I had no intention of telling her Thad had given me a different story.

"He sort of hinted over the phone that the two of us should get together."

"Maybe you should."

"I don't know. I would sort of feel funny going out with your old boyfriend. Especially knowing that he cheated on you. And he has been known to be somewhat shallow."

"That was a long time ago, Mona."

"Would it bother you if I went out with him?"

I smiled at her. "Frankly, I think it would be cool if my two closest friends got together."

"I'll think about it," she said. "It would be nice to date someone close to my age. I wouldn't have to take so many Botox treatments. By the way, he wants you to call him back."

I grabbed my cell phone from my purse and checked my messages. I was not surprised to find that Abigail had called several times. I dialed Thad's number.

"Abigail called me," he said.

"I'm not surprised. She called me, too, although she didn't leave any messages. What did she want?"

"She saw my car at your house last night. I won't repeat all that she accused me of, but if words could kill, I would be on a slab wearing a toe tag right now."

"Did she threaten you?"

"You could say that."

"Maybe you should call Officer Jenkins," I said, feeling weary, "but to be honest, I don't know what to do anymore."

"You're going to have to be very careful, Kate," he said. "If she's driving by your house in the middle of the night, she's almost certainly following you. I'm thinking I should call the senator and give him the heads-up."

"I don't know, Thad. Don't you think it's odd that Abigail hasn't mentioned him? She still may not know what's in the file."

He was quiet for a moment. "I guess I could hold off for a little while longer," he said. "By the way, has Mona said anything about me?"

"Um."

"Is she within hearing distance?"

"Yep."

"You think I should ask her out?"

"I think I'd like to stay out of it."

"By the way, I plan to go by the hospital first thing in the morning to check on Alice and Friends if you want to meet me there."

"I can be there about seven thirty."

"That'll work." We hung up.

"Did he say anything about me?" Mona asked.

I debated answering. "I so don't want to be in the middle of this," I said, "but, yes, I think he's interested." I glanced at my wristwatch. It was still early, but I was emotionally spent after helping to deliver a baby. "I think I'll take Mike out to do her business then turn in early," I said. "All this excitement has worn me out."

chapter 16

....

I got up earlier than usual the next morning. Although I didn't normally work on Saturdays, I'd promised to meet with a patient who'd been out of town all week and wasn't doing so well. Since I planned to be in the office anyway, I agreed to touch base with Bill Rogers as well.

After taking Mike out, I poured a cup of coffee and sat down at the kitchen table. A tired-looking Willie-Mae joined me.

"You don't look like you slept much last night," I said.

"The first twenty-four hours are crucial where newborns are concerned. I'm proud to say all is well. I wish I could say the same for Mona."

"I noticed the rash is getting worse."

"Yes, and I've used everything in my bag of tricks. I'm glad she made an appointment with the specialist at Emory University." Willie-Mae smiled. "I'm proud of her, though. She has been a real trouper the last few days. Something like this would have torn her out of her frame a few years ago."

As though acting on cue, Mona stumbled into the kitchen in cream-colored satin pajamas with black piping. She mumbled a good morning, poured a cup of coffee, and joined Willie-Mae and me at the kitchen table. She looked up and caught us staring. "You don't have to pretend I'm getting better," she said. "I know I look bad. And the thing is, I've pretty much accepted that I'm being taught some kind of universal lesson." She took a sip of her coffee.

"What does that mean, exactly?" I asked.

"It means, in order to grow, we all have to come face-to-face with our biggest fears."

Willie-Mae patted her hand. "Oh, honey, that sounds so—" She looked at me for the word.

"Profound," I said.

Mona nodded. "I have to confess that I've spent my entire life not feeling quite good enough or bright enough, so it was important that I maintain my looks." She looked at me. "I'm not like you, Kate. You don't have to try so hard, because you're smart and have a great career."

"You've got a lot going for you, Mona," I said. "What about all the fund-raising you're doing to build youth centers and curtail gangs?"

She nodded. "From now on, that's what I plan to concentrate on," she said, "and not worry so much about my looks."

There was a knock at the back door. Mona got up, punched numbers on the alarm keypad, and opened the door. Jimbo stepped inside. "You have errands for me?" he asked Mona.

"Mama does," she said.

"I've made a list," Willie-Mae said. "I'll be right back." She hurried from the room and went upstairs.

"How is the new baby?" Jimbo asked.

I smiled at him. "She's beautiful. You'll probably get a chance to see her later."

"I'm not good with babies or kids," he said.

"That makes two of us," Mona said.

Willie-Mae returned a few minutes later with the comforter and her list. "Do you know what a breast pump is?" she asked Jimbo.

Mona and I exchanged amused looks.

He looked thoughtful. "No, but I have a bicycle tire pump that you're welcome to use."

"Never mind," Willie-Mae said. "I'll try to get out later and pick one up. The silly girl forgot to bring hers." She handed him the folded comforter. "This needs to go to the dry cleaners. Take this envelope of cash. It should be more than enough to pay for everything on my list. I'd better check on my patient," she said and hurried from the room.

"What's on the agenda today?" Jimbo asked.

"I have to visit a patient in the hospital this morning, then go into the office for a little while," I said. "My first appointment isn't until ten a.m."

"Should I drive you?"

"I'm going with her," Mona said. "We'll be fine."

"I'll meet you at the office at ten," Jimbo said. He headed out, and Mona and I went upstairs to get dressed. I was relieved that she had forgone her mourning outfit. Instead, she had used something on her face to conceal the rash.

"It doesn't look so bad, does it?" she said, trying to sound brave.

"It's barely noticeable."

We said good-bye to Willie-Mae, climbed into Mona's Jag, and took off.

Thad was standing at the nurse's station looking through Alice Smithers's file when I arrived, leaving Mona to wait in the reception area with a magazine.

"I have a patient who is sort of in crisis," I told Thad. "I'm seeing him this morning."

"What's the problem?"

"Fear of public speaking. Unfortunately, it comes with the promotion he received some weeks back. I've been using relaxation and visualization techniques, but he is literally paralyzed with fear and afraid of losing his job."

"I can write him a script for something to reduce his anxiety," Thad offered.

"That would be a huge help," I said. "I don't think he's going to be able to continue therapy until he settles down. I can fax the information to your office for your records," I added, as Thad wrote out the prescription and handed it to me. I thanked him and put it in my purse.

"So, how is Alice this morning?" I asked.

"Her depression has lifted," he said. "Do you want us to go in together?"

"Of course."

We found Alice sitting on the edge of her bed, writing in a notebook. She had showered and put on makeup.

"I'm glad you're up," I said. "You look like you're feeling better."

She nodded. "I've been writing in my journal."

"May I take a quick look?" I asked. She offered it to

me, and I scanned a couple of pages. I wasn't as interested in reading the words as I was in studying the handwriting, since each personality wrote differently, both in style and tone. While one personality might be right-handed, another could very well write with the opposite hand. Liz Jones wrote in big, black, bold letters and used foul language.

I held it out for Thad to see. "No recent entries from Liz," I said.

He smiled. "That's good news."

"When can I go home?" Alice asked.

I looked at Thad. "It shouldn't be too terribly long," I said without committing to an actual date. I felt she needed to be there longer. "Would you mind if we had a word with Sue?"

Alice shrugged. Not only did I see the internal change that produced her alter personality, I also noticed that Sue took off the clunky eyeglasses that Alice still insisted on wearing. The weird thing was, Alice needed glasses, but Sue did not.

"Hi," Sue said, giving us a bright smile.

"Have you seen Liz lately?" I asked.

Sue shook her head. "I think she's on vacation. I hope it's a long one. I should tell you, Emily and I have been trying to take more control."

"Excellent!"

We chatted with her for a few minutes before asking to speak to Emily, who was the gregarious personality of the group. "Did Sue tell you we're trying to edge Liz out since she took the overdose?"

I nodded. "That's great news."

"She feels stupid, not only for swallowing the bottle of

pills but for having us committed. I guess you could say she's laying low."

"Keep up the good work," I said. Thad and I chatted with Emily for a few minutes before saying good-bye.

We were discussing Alice's case when we stepped outside and found Mona still reading a magazine. "You ready to roll?" I asked. I may as well have been talking to the moon, because she and Thad had their gazes locked on each other in such a way that I knew the world had ceased to exist for them at that very moment. And I was stunned. When had this happened? Why hadn't I seen it coming? Had I been so caught up in *my* stuff that it had passed me by?

I gave them a few more minutes before I walked to the elevator and punched the button. The metal doors slid open. "Are you guys coming with me?" I asked as I stepped inside and held the door for them.

Mona drove me to my office. "I feel really weird," she said.

"Weird in what way?" I asked.

"I can't explain it."

"How long have you and Thad been carrying on?"

"We've talked on the phone a few times because we've been so worried about you. One night, we talked for three hours."

"Wow. I would have had to take a bathroom break."

"I don't know what to do about it," she said. "Maybe I'm making a huge mistake."

"Or not," I said. "I think his father's illness really shook him up."

"Thad and I both agree you should visit Jay," she said. "You need to get out of town for a while. It'll give you a break from Abigail's crap."

"I'll think about it," I said.

Theo Pearson was waiting outside my door when the three of us stepped off the elevator on the fourth floor. One look at him, and I could tell he was indeed in crisis.

"I have a big presentation next week," he said once we were alone in my office. "I've listened to the tape we made over and over, but I'm still terrified."

It amazed me how many people feared public speaking. It was right up there with plane crashes and snakes.

"I have a prescription for a medication that will help you with your anxiety," I said.

"Really?"

I stood and walked to my desk, and reached for the scrip that Thad had written.

"This will lessen my fears?" Theo asked, looking hopeful.

"Yes," I said, "but it's not your 'get out of jail free' card. You need to continue listening to your relaxation and visualization tape and join Toastmasters so you can practice speaking in front of a group. The medication will make it less frightening, but the members of Toastmasters will offer you the support and skills that will help you as well. You just might end up being one of the best public speakers in all of Atlanta," I added with a smile.

He looked relieved.

"And Theo?"

"Yeah?"

"One way to help with your anxiety is to try not to

focus on yourself while you're speaking. Instead, think about how you can help those listening to you."

"I never thought of that," he said.

I escorted him out and was surprised to see a dozen red roses sitting on Mona's desk. "They're for you," she said. "I'll bet Jay sent them." She handed me the small card that had come with them. I opened it and froze at the words.

> *Just a little something to let you know I've been think-ing of you. Let's get together soon.*
>
> *Love, Abigail*

I blinked several times as a feeling of unreality swept over me. I dropped the card on the desk and stepped back. Would it ever end?

"What's wrong?" Mona said, reaching for the card. She read it and frowned. "I don't know what the hell kind of game she's playing, but she has taken 'sick bitch' to a whole new level." Mona dumped the roses into the trash. "That's why Thad and I think you need to take a breather," she said.

I barely had time to go into the restroom and wash my hands before Bill Rogers, my patient who feared germs, arrived. Fortunately, he wasn't drenched in cologne this time.

"How's it going?" I asked.

"I've been listening to the tape we made," he said. "I listen to it after dinner and right before I go to bed."

"Has it helped?"

"I think so. I decided not to have my carpet and drapes cleaned after my, er, accident. I still worry from time to time, but it's not as bad as it was. I still can't help washing my hands."

Join the club, I thought. "You need to give it time, Bill," I said. "It's not going to happen overnight. I want you to focus on your successes, not your setbacks."

He nodded. "Thanks for putting a fire under my butt, Dr. Holly."

"Hey, it's my job." I walked him out and headed for the bathroom, where I washed my hands several times.

Jay called my cell phone shortly after I'd seen Bill out. "I just arrived at the motel," he said. "I wanted to call while I have good reception."

"How are you?"

"Pretty tired right now," he said, "but new crews have been arriving, so those of us who've been putting in the most hours were told to take some time off. I've got the next forty-eight hours to myself."

"That's great," I said. "Maybe I could visit." I held my breath.

"Actually, that's not a bad idea, if you don't mind spending four hours on the road."

I would have driven any distance to see him. "I don't mind at all," I said.

"I'll grab a nap in the meantime. Once I crash for a few hours, I'll be fine."

"Is it okay if I bring Mike?"

He laughed. "Sure. It's not like we're staying at the Hilton, but it has hot running water, and the beds are comfortable."

I laughed. "You know what a sucker I am for hot water."

He gave me directions. "I'm in room twelve," he said. "I'll give you time to rest. See you soon."

We hung up. "Yes!" I shouted. I jumped up and did a little happy dance.

Mona stood in the doorway, wearing a grin.

Mona and Jimbo followed me home after lunch and waited until I'd packed a bag, as well as Mike's belongings.

"Take my Jag," Mona said, offering me her car keys. "Abigail is going to be looking for your car, not mine."

"You still need to check your rearview mirror," Jimbo said, "and make sure you're not being followed."

I hit the road shortly afterward. I took my time, stopping once to grab a hot dog from a convenience store and another time to walk Mike. The news came on, and experts were questioned about the fire. They gave a rundown on all that was being done to contain it, but the bad news was that fifty homes had burned, and more people were being evacuated from various locations because of smoke density.

The town where Jay was staying was not far from Tallahassee. It was easy to find, and the motel he'd described was right off the interstate. Even though it wasn't quite four p.m., the sky looked dark. A gray cloud hung over the town like a pall, which was why I wasn't surprised when the smell of smoke hit me as soon as I opened my door. I suspected it wouldn't be long before officials cleared the area.

Mike followed me to room number twelve. Jay opened the door, wearing only his jeans. I fell into his arms, seeking the heat of his bare chest. He smelled of soap, aftershave, and smoke. "I'm so glad you're okay," I said.

He held me for a long moment and kissed me tenderly,

then laughed when he caught sight of Mike doing a little jig. He released me and stroked her ear. "It's great to see you two," he said and closed the door. "Welcome to my humble abode."

The room had two double beds with ugly floral spreads, a dresser on which a TV had been bolted, and a small round table with chairs on either side. "It looks comfortable enough," I said.

"Have you eaten?"

"I grabbed a quick lunch, but I could eat again."

"Let me slip on a shirt and shoes, and we can try to find a place where there aren't twenty-five firefighters in line. This place has a restaurant attached, but the food stinks."

While Jay finished dressing, I unloaded the remaining items from my car, including Mike's things. I found myself scanning the parking lot for a white sedan, then realized I was being paranoid.

Inside the motel room, I filled Mike's bowls with food and water and turned on the TV so she wouldn't feel lonely. Jay locked up, and we climbed into his SUV.

We drove a distance before we came upon Moe's Diner. Although there was a line of firefighters, we didn't have to wait long. I noticed the bone-weary looks on their faces and the smell of smoke that clung to them despite their clean clothes.

Jay and I were finally shown to a table. He ordered coffee, but I declined and had water. I noted the deepening lines on either side of his mouth. His eyes were bloodshot. "How are you holding up?" I asked. "Tell me the truth."

"My ribs are still a little sore from the injuries, but it's not so bad."

I gave a deep sigh of frustration. "How long can this fire go on?"

He rubbed his eyes. "We're doing everything we can."

"This town is filled with smoke," I said.

"Yeah. I expect we'll be moving to another motel soon."

Our food arrived: fat burgers with extra onions, and a pile of fries. I reached for the bottle of ketchup.

"Katie?"

I looked up and met his gaze.

"I'm sorry I came down on you so hard before I left. The thought of something happening to you scares the hell out of me."

My heart softened. "I know." I knew because I experienced the same fears where he was concerned.

He smiled. "So what have you been up to since I left?"

I told Jay about Mona's rash and the anniversary party, including the part where Jeff drank moonshine. I told him about Hoss, who tried to pick up Arnell. "I even helped deliver a baby," I said proudly.

"No kidding?"

"It was awesome, Jay, even though I was terrified at the time."

He looked amused. I was glad I could give him a reason to smile. I decided not to ruin the moment by mentioning Crazy Abigail. "I'll be glad when you come home."

He nodded. "That makes two of us."

Once we'd finished our burgers, Jay drove us around the small town. "There's not much to do here," he said. "Not that it matters. Once we leave the fire site, we're more interested in cleaning up and hitting the sack."

Back at the motel, I walked Mike. When I returned to the room, Jay was lounging on the bed with the TV turned on low. In almost no time, he drifted off to sleep. I curled up beside him and closed my eyes. He pulled me closer. I dozed.

It was well into the evening when we awoke. In the quiet of the motel room we made love, and as Jay filled me I clung to him. Afterward, we shared long, lingering kisses and snuggled. I felt as though my soul had been renewed.

"I need to talk to you about something," I said after a while.

"I'm listening."

"It concerns the woman from the temp agency, the one who called you."

"Is she still harassing you?"

"Yeah. The police are looking for her."

"Do you think you're in physical danger?" He didn't give me a chance to respond. "Maybe you should cancel your appointments and hang out here for a while," he said. "Or move into the loft."

"I'm going to stay at Mona's. She has a state-of-the-art security system. During the day, she and Jimbo accompany me to the office."

He was quiet for a moment, and I prayed he wouldn't accuse me of constantly putting myself in life-and-death situations as before.

"Would you tell me if you thought you were in danger?"

I plucked at the bedspread. "Of course."

We spent Sunday lazing around the room, but I could tell Jay had a lot on his mind. He'd questioned me several more times about Abigail. I did my best to play it down.

"Do you want me to come back to Atlanta with you?" he asked. "Because I will if you need me."

I was touched by his offer. "Abigail would love nothing

more than to create more upheaval in my life," I said. "I don't want her to have that much power. I think we should let the police handle it," I said.

We made love again, and Jay napped while I read an old magazine someone had left behind. When he awoke, I noticed the lines around his eyes and face weren't as prominent. It was almost five p.m. when I began stuffing clothes into my overnight bag for the return trip home. I could tell Jay was concerned about my leaving. He helped me carry my belongings to the car. Mike hopped in the front passenger's seat. "You'll be at Mona's?" he asked.

"Yes." I wrote down her home and cell phone number and gave it to him.

"And you'll call me if you feel you're in any danger?"

I nodded. He kissed me tenderly. "I love you, Katie. Please be careful. Don't take any risks."

The drive home didn't seem to take as long as the trip down. I stopped by my place long enough to trade out my clothes. Mona and Thad were watching a DVD in the media room when I arrived at Mona's house.

"How'd it go?" Mona asked.

"Really well," I said.

"Did you tell him what was going on?" Thad asked.

"Most of it. I figured I'd slip it to him in bits and pieces."

"Well, I have fantastic news!" Mona said. "We discovered the cause of my rash."

"No kidding?"

"Remember I had all the bedrooms redecorated?"

It was hard to keep up, because Mona was always having at least one room in her house done. "Yeah."

"I purchased high-quality bedding and linens from a reputable company; the comforters were supposed to be one hundred percent goose feathers. Well, you remember that Mama sent the comforter Tiara was using to the dry cleaners?"

"Yes," I said.

"Guess what? Not only did the stitching come apart, we discovered it was stuffed with chicken feathers. I am extremely allergic to chicken feathers. Needless to say, we've stripped all the bedrooms and put the old comforters back on the beds. In the meantime, I've already contacted my attorney."

"So it wasn't stress-related after all?" I asked hopefully.

"Nope."

"Jeez, Mona. Do you know how guilty I've felt thinking I was to blame?"

I went into the kitchen and grabbed a diet soft drink and several cheese cubes from the refrigerator. Mona and Thad joined me.

"There's a box of fried chicken in there," Mona said.

"I'm not all that hungry."

"I'd like to talk to you about Alice Smithers," Thad said. "I have an idea."

"I think I'll look in on Tiara and Mama while you guys talk shop," Mona said, slipping from the room.

"What's your idea?" I asked Thad.

"First, I've never done anything like this, so I have no idea what the outcome will be, but what would you think of recording our conversations with Alice's alter personalities and playing them back for her to hear?"

"I hadn't thought of that," I said, "but it sounds like a good idea. At least she would know the others are watching her back. When would you want to do it?"

"I'm still on vacation, so I'll work with your schedule."

I didn't have my appointment book with me, but I was almost certain I had no late-afternoon appointments the following day. "Why don't we meet with Alice around four p.m.?" I said. "That will give us plenty of time before she goes to dinner. I have a voice-activated tape recorder, so I'll bring it."

He nodded. "I'll pick you up at your office and take you to Mona's afterward."

I nodded, but my thoughts were centered on Alice. She had been through so much. I only hoped Thad's idea helped her.

chapter 17

....

The next morning, I came inside after letting Mike out and found Willie-Mae sitting at the kitchen table, sipping her special tea and thumbing through a thick binder. The pages were brittle and had long since yellowed.

I poured a cup of coffee and joined her. "What are you reading?" I asked.

"It's a collection of folk remedies passed down from my great-grandmother."

"Was she a healer?"

Willie-Mae nodded. "The gift runs in families."

"How do you know if you have it? The gift?" I added.

She smiled. "You just do. I knew when I was eight years old."

"If it runs in families, why doesn't Mona have it?"

"It sometimes skips one generation and shows up in another," Willie-Mae said, "but even if Mona were blessed with the gift, she would close herself off to it. She wanted nothing to do with healing or birthing babies, but I'm sure you already know that. I think my work embarrassed her. She never invited her school friends over." She sighed.

I knew the feeling. Although I was genuinely proud that my mother and aunt had turned their junk business into a gold mine, I'd been demoralized growing up in a house surrounded by it. But I had never stopped loving them. "Mona may not understand why you chose to become a midwife and healer," I said, "but she still loves you. I know that for a fact."

"I was touched that she turned to me in her time of need," Willie-Mae said. "That means more to me than she'll ever know. But I'm going to have to head home in a couple of days. I have other patients."

"Will it be okay for Tiara and the baby to travel?" I asked.

"I'll prepare a bed for them in the back of the van. In the meantime, I'm going to make up this salve for Mona's rash. To keep the itching down. She should heal quickly now that we've got those dang chicken feathers out of the house."

Mona, Jimbo, and I arrived at my office at eight thirty, a half hour before Bonnie and Len Freemont were due in. I was curious to see how they had gotten through the anniversary of their son's death.

"Why don't you put on the coffee," Mona suggested, "and I'll check the phone messages."

"Sure." I knew she was trying to protect me. I'd checked my messages at home, and Abigail had left several not-so-nice ones. I decided to touch base with Officer Jenkins later. I made coffee, opened the door to my private office, and pulled out the Freemonts' folder. They arrived shortly after. It was difficult to read their expressions.

"So, how did the weekend go?" I asked.

Bonnie smiled. "It went very well," she said. "Despite the short notice, we had about fifty guests, including Jason's high school and college friends, and, of course, family and church friends. Our two children invited their friends as well. Everyone had something nice to say about Jason." Her eyes misted. "I felt he was right there with us. I felt he had his arms around me saying, 'Everything is okay, Mom.'"

"I'm so glad," I said. I'd had a number of patients who'd claimed their loved ones had appeared or made themselves known somehow after their deaths, but, even though I tried to keep an open mind, I was skeptical. If anyone deserved a visit from a loved one who'd passed, I would have been at the top of that list; but my father had never tried to contact me from the other side.

I looked at Len. "How was it for you?"

He shifted in his seat. "Well, as you suggested, I took some photos and had them made into posters, and I hung them everywhere, so that part was nice. And since it was a celebration, nobody tried to make us feel better by saying stupid things." He swiped at a tear. "So many people said they were glad they had the chance to know Jason." He paused and swallowed hard. "It helped me, because it was the first time I really opened up."

Bonnie reached for his hand, and they held on tight to each other, even as tears streamed down their faces. I was quiet. Nothing else needed to be said.

* * *

It was a slow day for me, but I was glad to have time to think. Abigail had kept my thoughts skewed for so long that I'd had little time to ponder the relationship between Jay and me. Spending time with him had given me a reason to hope we might one day work things out.

Thad and I arrived at the hospital at four p.m. and found Alice in the sunroom working a jigsaw puzzle with another patient. She looked surprised to see us. "Am I going home?" she asked.

"Soon," Thad said.

I smiled at her. "Alice, would you mind stepping into the conference room with us?" I asked. "Dr. Glazer and I would like to chat with you for a few minutes."

She nodded, and the three of us started down the hall. I asked one of the nurses if we could borrow the conference room for an hour. The woman was young and didn't take her eyes off Thad as she told us to use it as long as we liked.

Inside the conference room, the three of us sat at one end of the long table. I made certain my chair was close to Alice's in case she became anxious. "Are you feeling okay?" I asked before taking out the recorder.

"I'm bored and ready to go back to work."

"I know," I said. "But you've been afraid for a long time, Alice, of the other personalities that come out from time to time."

"Yes. Liz Jones."

Thad clasped his hands together on the table. "That's understandable," he said, "but Liz is not the only one who comes out. You have alter personalities that are actually very helpful."

"Yes, I've been told."

I smiled and touched her hand. "How would you like to meet some of them?" I asked.

She looked surprised. "How is that possible?"

I pulled out my voice recorder. "We can record the conversations and play them back for you."

Her eyes darted back and forth between Thad and me. "That sounds a little scary."

"Wouldn't you feel less afraid knowing you had personalities who cared deeply for you and only wanted to help?" I asked. "Remember, there is strength in numbers," I added, hoping a little humor might lessen her anxiety.

"I think it's a good idea," Thad said, "and I think we should continue to do this sort of therapy from time to time so all of you are on the same page, so to speak. There are no guarantees," he said, "but my feeling is, the stronger you and your alters are, the less inclined Liz will be to come out."

She looked relieved. "I'll do anything if it will keep Liz away," she said.

"I'd like to start with Sue," I said.

After about twenty minutes of chatting with the others, I asked to speak to Alice. I played what I had recorded. Afterward, she looked calmer.

"I appreciate your recording them," she said to Thad and me. "It's one thing to be told I have different personalities, but I loved hearing from those who want to help me. I feel stronger knowing they have my back."

Thad and I left the hospital. "I think that went well," he said.

I nodded. "It's going to take time," I said. "Hopefully, Alice will begin taking more control. We both know she is going to have to master her own anger if she hopes to get rid of Liz."

"True," he said. "Hey, are you hungry?" he asked.

"I would really enjoy a good steak."

"Your wish is my command."

Thad drove to a popular steakhouse. We grabbed a booth and ordered. Our salads arrived at the same time Abigail walked through the door. Thad must've noticed the look on my face. "What is it?"

"Abigail."

He turned. "I'll be damned," he said.

The hostess led Abigail to a booth not far from ours. She pretended not to see us.

My heart was pounding so hard I could barely hear over it. "I didn't think to check if we were being followed," I said. "We need to cancel our order. Just pay for the salads."

"Why?"

"Because I plan to beat her at her own game."

"Whatever that means," he said, motioning for our waitress. He dropped a twenty-dollar bill on the table to cover the salads and tip.

"Grab your salad, drink, and silverware, and follow me," I said.

"I hope you know what you're doing."

Thad and I walked the short distance to Abigail's booth and slid in. She was clearly shocked.

"What do you think you're doing?" she demanded.

"It's obvious you followed us here, so I have to assume you want to talk to us. You don't mind if we join you?" I added.

"Actually, I mind very much."

I pretended to look crushed. "Now, Abigail, you know you don't mean that."

"Would you please pass me the salt and pepper?" Thad asked me as though he hadn't a care in the world.

I handed them to him, and he thanked me. He looked at Abigail. "I don't mind splitting this salad with you if you like."

She fumbled with her silverware, looking from me to Thad and back at me. "I don't know what you think you're doing," she said, "but I want you to leave my table right now."

"Sorry, Abigail, but we can't do that. In fact, you can count on seeing a lot of us from here on out."

"What's that supposed to mean?"

"You won't have to follow us anymore, because we're going to be right behind you."

"You're both crazy!" she said.

The waitress brought Abigail a glass of iced tea. "Are you ready to order?" she asked.

"I'm not staying." She slid from the booth and hurried from the restaurant. Thad and I followed.

She had already reached her car. Thad and I wasted no time jumping into his, and as Abigail squealed from the parking lot, we were right behind her. She drove fast, changing lanes, turning corners at the last minute, but we stayed on her tail. I wrote down her license tag and wished I had Officer Jenkins's phone number with me.

Abigail took another turn so quickly that her car fish-tailed.

"I don't think this is in the stalker's handbook," I said.

"What do you mean?" Thad asked, keeping his eyes on the road.

"I don't think we're supposed to stalk a stalker."

"Sometimes you've got to break the rules."

"Let's just hope she doesn't have an accident or cause someone else to have one."

"I think the crazy bitch should have a taste of her own medicine," he said.

"Yeah, but she's ill, and we're not."

He looked at me.

"Okay, so we have a few issues," I said. "I've never claimed to be the poster child for wellness."

After half an hour, Abigail pulled into the parking lot of a Harris Teeter grocery store and slammed out of her car. She waited until Thad and I had come to a complete stop before she began screaming and yelling and pounding her fists on the hood of his Mercedes.

"Oh, hell," he said. "She's going to put a dent in my car."

We climbed out. "Why are you doing this?" she screamed at me.

I stepped up to her. "You want to know why, Abigail? Because I am drawing the line in the sand. You are not allowed to skulk about my yard or break into my house or office anymore, because I'm going to be on you like white on rice. I'll temporarily close my office until this is over, because when you look in your rearview mirror, you're going to see me."

Thad had pulled his cell phone from his pocket and was dialing.

"Who are you calling?" she asked him, fear replacing the anger in her eyes.

"The police, of course."

Abigail turned for her car. Thad and I followed on

foot, even as he spouted information into the phone. Abigail unlocked her door and started to climb in, but Thad held it open so she couldn't close it and be on her way.

By sheer luck I spotted the files in the backseat of her car, along with what seemed to be all her worldly possessions. With her front door open, I hit the master lock, yanked open the back door, and scooped up the files. Abigail fought Thad as he tried to wrestle her car keys from her. People in the parking lot turned and stared.

I did not see the steak knife until it was too late, until Abigail had already thrust it into Thad's stomach. I screamed. Thad staggered, staring in disbelief at the knife protruding from his stomach. He fell back against the car that was parked beside Abigail's, and I screamed again when he yanked out the knife and the front of his shirt turned a bright red. He was going down. I dropped the files and wrapped my arms around his waist to try to prevent him from hitting his head when he landed on the pavement. I went down first, and he sank on top of me. I heard Abigail squeal away in her car.

I spied a couple climbing from their car not far away, watching us with horrified expressions.

"Call nine-one-one!" I shouted. "We need an ambulance." Cradling Thad's head in my lap, I searched for the wound and pressed my fingers against it to try and stop the flow of blood.

Thad looked up, incredulous. "The bitch stabbed me," he said. "Do you believe that?"

"Try to be very still," I told him. "Help is on the way."

"Do me a favor?" he asked.

"As long as it doesn't involve getting naked with you in your hot tub," I said, trying to make light of the situation and keep us both calm.

"If I don't make it, tell my father I love him. And hang on to those damn files."

chapter 18

•••••••••••••••••••••••••••••

Sirens lit up the parking lot, and a crowd had gathered as Thad was loaded into the ambulance. I suddenly recognized Officer Jenkins.

"I heard the call come in," he said. "I'm sorry about your friend. Are you okay?"

I saw that I had blood on my hands and clothes, but I was uninjured. "This is all my fault," I said, tears streaming down my face. "I confronted Abigail Davis. I was so angry, but I never thought she would go this far." I suddenly remembered her toying with her silverware, but I hadn't seen her grab the knife.

"There was no way you could have known," he said.

"I was able to get her tag number." I hurried to Thad's car and grabbed my purse. "I handed Jenkins the slip of paper I'd written it on. "The car is a 1999 white Ford Focus."

"Excellent. We also have the knife. But you know the routine. We'll have to take prints of those who may have handled it so we can rule them out."

I gave him the name of the restaurant where Abigail had pilfered the knife. "I have to go with my friend to the hospital."

"I'll drive you in my patrol car," Jenkins said.

We were on our way in minutes, following the squealing ambulance. I couldn't stop shaking. I remained quiet as Jenkins fed information to dispatch.

"Why didn't you tell me you were married to Captain Jay Rush?" he asked after a few minutes.

I gave him a blank look. I wondered how he'd found out, but I was more concerned about Thad. "I didn't think it was important."

I reached inside my purse for my cell and realized I had not turned it back on after visiting Alice in the psych ward. I saw that I had messages. It rang as soon as I turned it on.

"Why haven't you been answering your damn phone!" Mona demanded as soon as I answered. She was crying. "Please tell me Thad isn't dead."

"Of course he's not dead," I said. "Who told you that?"

"Abigail called Jay and me. She said she stabbed him to death with a steak knife."

"She did stab him, Mona, but I don't think the wound is life-threatening. Officer Jenkins and I are on our way to the hospital."

"Which hospital?" she asked.

I asked Jenkins and relayed the information to Mona.

"I'm on my way," she said.

"Could you bring me a change of clothes?" I asked. "I'm covered with blood." I realized how ridiculous my request was. Mona's size three would never fit me, and her mother was no larger.

"I'll see what I can do."

"I'm getting beeped, Mona. I have to go." I answered the call and found Jay on the other end. "Katie! Thank God you're okay. Where are you? You're not alone, right?"

"A policeman is taking me to the hospital," I said quickly. I gave him the name.

"I got a call from that bitch, Abigail. She said—"

"Thad isn't dead," I interrupted. "There was a lot of blood, but I think he's going to be okay."

"I'm on my way, sweetheart. A cop is driving me. He plans to use his flashing light, so it won't take me as long to get there. In the meantime, I do not want you alone for one minute while that woman is still on the street. Do you understand? Stay with the police officer until I get there. Why don't you just wait for me at the hospital. It's probably the safest place for you right now."

"Okay," I said, although I didn't relish the thought of spending several hours in the waiting room.

Jenkins and I arrived at the hospital and entered the ER. I noticed the stares from those waiting to be seen; no surprise, since I was covered with blood and being escorted by a member of the police department. I looked at Jenkins. "Could you ask them to apprise me of my friend's condition as soon as they know?"

"Sure." He went to the desk and spoke to the receptionist.

Mona and Jimbo showed up minutes later, as Jenkins was trying to take my report. Mona carried a Saks bag. I didn't realize how much blood I had on me until I saw the look on her face. My hands and arms were sticky with it.

"Do you know Thad's condition?" she asked.

I could tell she had been crying. "He's not critical," I said.

My cell phone rang, and I realized I wasn't supposed

to have it turned on inside the hospital. I grabbed it and answered. On the other end, my mom sounded frantic.

"Abigail called me," she said.

"I'm fine, Mom," I said, wanting to shake Abigail's teeth out for scaring everyone. "Thad is going to be okay."

"My heart stopped beating for a good two minutes when that crazy lady called me. You can ask Trixie; she'll tell you." She put Trixie on the phone.

"I thought I was going to have to perform CPR on your mother," my aunt said. "Give me the name of the hospital."

I reluctantly gave it to her. I knew my mother would cause a scene. I hung up and turned off my phone. I suddenly felt dizzy and nauseous as the reality of what I had just experienced set in. And to think, Abigail was still out there somewhere. I was thankful my stomach was empty.

"Are you going to be sick?" Mona asked. "Do you need to go to the restroom?"

I nodded. Jenkins followed us and checked out the bathroom before we entered. "I'll be right out here," he said.

I immediately went into one of the stalls, where I suffered a bout of dry heaves. What if Thad *wasn't* going to be okay? I thought.

I gasped at my reflection in the bathroom mirror. Blood was smeared on my face and neck, and it had already dried on my blouse. My slacks were torn at the knees and stained as well. I stripped down to my underwear and bathed at the sink. Mona pulled jeans and a bright red T-shirt from the Saks bag.

"What happened to your knees?" she asked.

I saw they were badly scraped. "I must've done it when I went down in the parking lot. I was trying to keep Thad from hitting his head on the pavement."

"You're a really good friend, Kate," she said.

"No, Mona. A really good friend wouldn't have gotten her friends and family involved in all this drama."

"There was no way you could have known how sick Abigail was," she said. "You didn't ask for this."

"Thank you for understanding," I said. I cleaned up as much as I could in the situation. Mona held out the jeans, and I stepped into them. The elastic waist was stretched and too large. "Are these maternity slacks?" I asked.

"Yeah. You and Tiara wear the same size when she's not pregnant. It was the best I could do on such short notice." Mona fished a safety pin from her purse and fixed the problem. She helped me into the shirt and reached into her purse for a brush. I checked my reflection in the mirror and tried to repair my hair. I noticed the shirt had the word "Baby" blazoned across the front, with an arrow pointing downward.

Mona stuffed my bloody clothes into the Saks bag.

If Officer Jenkins thought it odd that I was wearing maternity clothes when I exited the bathroom, he didn't say. We returned to the waiting room, and he pulled out a small notepad and began questioning me again. I hadn't answered more than a few of his questions when my mother and aunt rushed through the double glass doors, wearing matching pink overalls with the words Junk Sisters stitched over their left breasts. Arnell was right behind them, wearing a classic A-line dress and matching cardigan.

The look on my mother's face was borderline hysteria. I felt bad for always causing her so much worry. She threw her arms around me. "I was so afraid for you," she said, tears gathering in her eyes.

"I'm fine, Mom," I said.

"Cute shirt," Arnell said, giving me a hearty wink.

My mother finally released me and stepped back as though to make certain I wasn't bleeding or missing body parts. She arched one brow when she spied the maternity shirt. "I'm sure there's an explanation," she said, "and I'm sure it's complicated."

"Well, yeah," I replied.

She turned to Jenkins. "I demand to know who is in charge. I do *not* want my daughter to be alone as long as Abigail Davis is out there."

"We're doing everything we can, ma'am," Jenkins said. "I'll see that your daughter has police protection until we've arrested Miss Davis."

"How is Thad?" Aunt Trixie asked.

"I'm still waiting to hear," I said, "but there's no threat of him dying."

"I'm so sorry you had to go through such an ordeal," Aunt Trixie said, taking my hand in hers and patting it. "You must've been scared out of your wits."

Jenkins looked at me. "I really need to get more information from you."

"Maybe you and Aunt Trixie should go home," I told my mother, not wanting her to hear the lurid details of the stabbing.

"I'm not leaving you," she said.

I had no choice but to answer the rest of Jenkins's questions. Finally, he closed his notebook. "That should do it for now," he said. "I may think of something later." He glanced toward the entrance as another policeman entered. "Would you excuse me for just a minute?"

"Where are you going?" my mother demanded. "You're not supposed to leave my daughter."

"I need to speak to the officer," Jenkins said. "I'll only be a few feet away."

"I wish Jay would hurry up and get here," she said.

I took her hand. "Mom, I don't know how long this is going to take. You should go home."

"I want to make sure Thad is going to be okay," she said. She must've noticed my surprised look. "He might not be my favorite person in the whole world, but I don't want him to die."

"He's not going to die, Mom," I said.

Mona sniffed. "He can't die. I think I'm falling in love with him."

My mother looked at her. "Oh, you poor dear."

We waited. Finally, I was summoned by the receptionist and told I could see Thad. Mona insisted on going with me. We were buzzed through the metal doors that led to the treatment rooms. A doctor was waiting.

"How is he?" Mona said.

"The knife didn't penetrate any organs. We stitched him up. You can see him now, but he's probably going to be groggy, since we gave him something for pain. We're going to keep him overnight for observation."

Mona and I hurried inside the room, where we found Thad hooked to an IV, his stomach bandaged. His eyes were closed. I started to touch him, then thought better of it and stepped back so Mona could get closer. She stroked his forehead, and he opened his eyes.

"It's bad," he said, his voice thick from the drugs.

"No, no, you're going to be fine," she assured him.

"You don't understand," he said. "I'm going to have a scar." He closed his eyes again and nodded off.

Mona and I returned to the waiting room.

"How is he?" my mother asked.

I repeated what the doctor had told us.

"We should take John home," Aunt Trixie said. She

looked at me. "We were at the pizza place when Jay called, so we drove straight here. John insisted on waiting in the car so he wouldn't be in the way. He's such a nice man," she added.

"Even if he *is* a crummy liar," my mother added.

"What do you mean?" I asked.

"He's not who he claims to be."

"How do you know?" I asked, glancing at Arnell, who shook his head, letting me know the information hadn't come from him.

"Honey, we've known from the beginning," my mother said, "but he doesn't have any family or friends, so we decided to go along with it. He doesn't know we're on to him, of course."

"We've grown attached to him," Trixie said.

My mother looked at Jenkins. "I'm going to say this one more time," she said. "I don't want my daughter left alone for one second. If something happens to her, you're going to have to answer to me."

He nodded.

She and I hugged. "Call me when Jay arrives," she said. "I won't rest until I know he's with you."

I watched her go. I turned to Mona. "I'm a terrible daughter," I said.

Mona waved off the remark. "You're a great daughter. You just have terrible luck."

I was dozing in the chair when I felt someone nudge me. I opened my eyes and found Jay kneeling in front of me. "Hi, babe," he said. "Are you okay?"

I didn't trust myself to speak, so I just nodded.

"How is Glazer?"

"He's going to be fine, except for the scar," I said.

He shook hands with Jenkins, who filled him in. "We've got an APB out on Miss Davis, but so far, nothing. We're hoping to get prints off the knife handle, but it's going to take time."

"I want to go home," I told Jay, suddenly overcome with a feeling of weariness. "I need to check on Mike."

Jenkins arched one brow.

"Mike is her dog," Jay said. "Is it okay if I take Kate home now?"

"Sure." Jenkins handed Jay his card. "We'll be in touch the minute we know something. Also, I'll have someone watching the house tonight."

"Jimbo and I are going to hang around for a while," Mona said. "At least until they get Thad settled in a room."

Jay and I left the ER, and he helped me into his SUV. He got in on the other side. "I like your shirt," he said. "Is there something you want to tell me?"

"Not until I'm sure who the father is," I said.

He leaned over and kissed me tenderly. He raised his head slightly and stroked my cheek. "Katie, I was so damn scared when I got that call."

"I'm sorry for dragging you into this," I said.

He put his arms around me. "I'm the one who owes you an apology, babe," he said, his voice thick with emotion. "I never should have let you come back alone. I don't know what I was thinking. I should have taken the whole thing more seriously."

"You had no way of knowing," I said, "because I kept playing it down."

He looked confused. "Why?"

"I didn't want to burden you, what with the fire and all."

"Burden me?" he asked in disbelief. "How could you ever think I found you burdensome? You're my wife. Sort of," he added. "But I'm a lousy ex-husband. I wouldn't blame you if you never remarried me." He patted my stomach. "You and the baby would be better off without me."

I smiled. "I'm not letting you off that easily."

"Are you hungry?" he asked. "Have you eaten?"

"I'm too tired to eat. I just want to lie down. I want you to hold me."

His gaze softened. "Gladly." We arrived at my place, and Jay hurried around to help me out. I pulled my keys from my purse and unlocked the front door. Jay and I were both surprised when Mike didn't greet us.

"She's probably out back doing her business," I said. I went to the refrigerator and grabbed a slice of cheese, just something to fill the hunger in my stomach. Jay opened the back door and called for Mike. I joined him.

I saw the note taped to the door first. I motioned to it, and Jay pulled it off and read it out loud.

"You're never going to see your ugly mutt again."

That was when I knew I was going to be sick.

By the time the police arrived, Jay had searched the house and the backyard. I sat at the kitchen table, with a wet washcloth pressed to my face after another bout of dry heaves. I could not stop trembling. I could not stop thinking the worst.

Jenkins arrived. He looked as tired and frustrated as I felt. "How long has your pet been missing?" he asked.

"I've been away all day. Abigail could have taken her at any time."

"Maybe your neighbors saw something," he said.

"I don't know. Most of them work." I thought of Bitsy, who would have been the most likely person to notice anything, but she had left for Tallahassee with the prayer group.

"We'll still canvass the neighborhood," he said. "But I don't think you have anything to worry about as far as your dog. It's just one more way Miss Davis can get your attention. Stalkers know their victims won't meet with them unless there's a very good reason."

Jay looked stunned. "Stalker?" he said and looked at me. "This woman has actually been stalking you?"

I hesitated.

Jenkins nodded. "Afraid so," he said.

Jay muttered a string of obscenities and slammed his hand against the kitchen counter so hard I was surprised he didn't break something.

"That's *exactly* why I didn't tell you," I said.

He sat down at the kitchen table and wiped his hands down his face. I could tell he was trying to get his anger under control.

"Why the hell is the woman stalking Kate?" he finally asked Jenkins.

"She's obviously obsessed with your wife," the man said. "Stalking is more prevalent than people think." He looked at me. "Like I said, I'm going to put an unmarked car outside your house tonight. You look like you need to catch up on your sleep." He stood. "I'll be in touch if I learn anything."

Jay checked to make sure the place was locked up, then followed me upstairs. I pulled off the oversized T-shirt, kicked off my shoes, and stepped out of the maternity jeans. I sat on the edge of the bed in my bra and under-wear.

Jay knelt before me. "It's going to be okay, babe. It would take a pretty heartless soul to harm Mike."

"Abigail is psychotic, Jay."

He frowned at the sight of my knees. "You're all banged up."

"I fell in the parking lot trying to help Thad."

Jay leaned over and kissed my knees gently. "It's going to be okay, Katie. I promise."

I couldn't stop worrying about Mike. "I need to make a phone call." I called Jeff and explained the situation. As a vet, he would probably have some advice how I might find Mike.

"Oh, Kate, I'm so sorry," he said. "I'll call the shelters and rescue volunteers right away and ask them to keep an eye out. Let me know if there's anything else I can do."

I slept very little during the night. When I awoke the next morning, my eyelids felt thick from having cried so much. Jay held me against him.

"Are you hungry?" he asked. "We could go for waf-fles."

I couldn't remember when I had last eaten a decent meal. "I'm starving," I said, "but I don't want to go out with my eyes so swollen. I should probably put ice on them. And I really want a hot shower."

Jay looked out the window. "The unmarked car is still out front," he said. "I'll run to Waffle House and place a to-go order. Unless you'd feel anxious with me gone," he added.

"No, I'm fine. I would love a waffle." I led the way downstairs and grabbed the new house key from the rack near the kitchen door. "You'll need this," I said.

He took it and dropped it into his shirt pocket. "I want you to put the chains in place while I'm gone," he said.

I locked up and hurried upstairs to take a quick hot shower. I had just stepped beneath the hot spray of water when I heard a noise. I called out to Jay—maybe he'd forgotten his wallet or his car keys—but then I remembered that he would not be able to get back into the house with the chains on the door. I cut off the shower, and pulled the curtain aside.

A smiling Abigail was standing in the doorway holding a fluffy towel. "Hello, Kate."

I could almost swear that my heart stopped beating. It was followed by an adrenaline rush that left me feeling dizzy and weak-kneed. "How did you get into this house?" I demanded.

"Please don't be angry," she said.

"I want to know how the hell you got in here! I had the locks changed."

"I was already inside the day they were changed. The day you hung your new keys on the little rack by the kitchen door," she added.

I shook my head. "That's impossible. I would have known."

"Did you think of checking your attic?" she asked. "If you had, you would have found my sleeping bag and clothes. I've been bathing in your tub while you're at work. By the way, I love your bath salts," she added.

I couldn't believe what I was hearing, but it would have been easy for her to hide in the attic. It would have been as simple as pulling down the stairs that led up. I had to assume she'd found a way to pull them back up once she reached the attic, so I wouldn't notice. It would explain why I'd heard more creaking and groaning in the old house than usual.

I noticed Abigail was staring at my wet body. I yanked the towel from her and covered myself. "What have you done with my dog?" I demanded.

"Your little pet is fine," she said, "although it's obvious she misses you."

My throat tightened. "I want her back, Abigail. I want you to take me to her. And she damn sure better be okay, because if she's not, I swear to God—"

"Why would I hurt your dog, Kate?" she asked.

"Why?" I gave a harsh laugh. "I saw you put a knife in my friend's stomach yesterday. I don't know what you're capable of."

"Thad forced my hand."

I shook my head. "You took that knife from the steak-house. You'd already planned to hurt someone."

"He was coming between us," she said. "I've already lost at love once. I'm not going to lose you."

"That's no excuse," I snapped. "Do you think your ex-husband is the first man who ever cheated on his wife?"

She made a sound of disgust. "He could have slept with an entire harem for all I cared. Unfortunately, he wooed my best friend, who also happened to be my lover."

"So now you're looking for a replacement?" I asked. "Never mind that I'm in love with my husband, right?"

"How do you know you won't find more happiness with me if you refuse to even try?" she said. "No one loves you the way I do." She held her hands out, palms open. "All I'm asking is that you give us a chance," she said.

"Or what?" I demanded. "You hurt my dog? You put a knife through Jay?"

"I would rather avoid more problems between us."

"Great. Then you need to get out of my life and stay out." I sounded a lot tougher than I felt, but I was determined to maintain some of the control she had tried to take from me. Inside, my gut was churning. I grabbed my robe from the hook on the bathroom door and slipped it on. "Just so you know, Abigail," I said, "you're going to have to hurt me before you get to Jay."

Sudden tears filled her eyes. "Why are you making this so hard?" she asked. "Why can't you just love me as I love you?"

Her pain was so real, so heartrending, that I found it difficult to look at her. Despite everything, it was impossible not to pity her. "Listen to me, Abigail," I said. "You're not well. Let me help you." I could barely believe the words had come from my mouth after all we'd been through.

"Help me?" she said and gave a rueful laugh. "Last time someone offered to help me, I ended up behind bars."

"You spent time in prison?"

"A couple of months in jail."

"On stalking charges?"

She suddenly looked angry. "I wasn't stalking. I was trying to convince my lover she'd made a mistake by getting involved with my ex."

"My job is helping people, Abigail," I said. "And I can help you, if you'll let me."

"They'll lock me up."

"At first, yes," I said. "But I'm going to strongly recommend hospitalization for you. Incarceration didn't help you before, and it won't help you now."

"I will kill myself before I go to prison."

I jumped when the doorbell rang. I had not heard Jay's SUV pull into the driveway. He would not be able to get in with the chains in place. My gaze locked with Abigail's. "What's it going to be?" I asked. "We can do this the hard way or the easy way."

"How do I know you're telling me the truth?" she asked. "How do I know you will really help me?"

"Because I said I would. That should be enough."

The doorbell rang a second time. She just stood there, blocking my way.

"Face it, Abigail," I said. "I'm your last hope. And I'm more interested in seeing that you get the help you need instead of being punished."

Finally, she backed away so I could exit the bathroom. "Just follow me and do as I say," I told her. She looked reluctant, but she did as she was told. We headed downstairs. In the kitchen, I pulled out a chair for her, and she sank onto it.

"I'm going to let Jay in now, okay?" I said.

She nodded. I went into the living room and unlocked the front door. Jay stepped inside holding two take-out containers and a small white sack. "What took you so long?"

"Abigail is here," I said.

He gave me a funny look but followed me into the kitchen and set the containers and sack on the table.

I introduced them. They acknowledged each other with a nod.

When Abigail spoke, her voice trembled. "There is a white house with dark green trim, for sale at the end of the street," she told him. "You can sort of tell it has just been sitting there unattended, because the grass hasn't been cut in a while. My car is in the garage. Mike is in my car." She looked at me. "I've taken good care of her."

"Thank you, Abigail," I said. I looked at Jay. "Would you mind getting Mike for me?"

He looked from me to Abigail, then back to me. "Now?" he asked.

"It will be okay. I'll call Officer Jenkins."

He hesitated before finally turning for the living room. I heard him exit the front door. I dialed Jenkins's number, and he answered after the second ring.

"I was about to call you," he said, sounding excited. "We've learned a lot about the woman who calls herself Abigail Davis. She was thrown in jail in California on stalking charges. She must've met the right people while she was there, because she was able to get a new identity."

"Abigail is sitting at my kitchen table as we speak," I said.

"Huh? Are you serious?"

"I'm going to give her something to eat. Then she is going to turn herself in. She intends to cooperate fully."

"Um, Dr. Holly, you need to be very careful," he said.

"I know." I hung up the phone and opened one of the food containers. My hands trembled. I knew the woman sitting there could turn on me if I weren't careful. I placed the food before her and grabbed clean silverware. She just sat there staring at the waffle and bacon. I sat down beside her and reached into the paper sack for a container of syrup. I handed it to her. She fumbled with it, trying to peel away the seal with no luck.

"Let me help you," I said, taking it from her. I opened it and poured syrup on her waffle. She just sat there.

"You have to eat something, Abigail," I said, cutting the waffle into small pieces. "You've got a long day ahead of you."

She nodded. "I know the routine." She took a bite. Tears streamed down her cheeks. She looked weary.

"You're doing the responsible thing. Nobody can hurt you. I won't let them."

She surprised me by smiling. "See, that's the thing about us. We have this special bond. I felt it the first time we met. I'll bet you felt it, too. Like I said, I don't know where one of us ends and the other begins."

I smiled but did not reply.

I was lying in Jay's arms the following morning, riding my afterglow, having just made glorious love. Mike, who'd been curled at the foot of the bed trying to sleep, had obviously become annoyed with the sound and movement and had left the room. I suspected she had sought out the silence and stillness of her pillow in the laundry room.

Jay pulled me closer, enveloping me in his heat. He felt strong and solid and very male; his nearness through the night had allowed me to feel safe and cherished. His lovemaking had been a balm for my weary soul. I felt transformed.

"How do you feel this morning?" he asked.

With my head on his chest, I could feel the vibration of his deep voice against my ear. "Like a real girl-girl," I said on a contented sigh.

"That's my favorite thing about you," he said with a chuckle. "I was just thinking," he said. "If you moved back into the loft with me, you would never again have to worry about not having enough hot water."

"That's true."

"Of course, there are other reasons you might want to

move back," he added. "The fifty-two-inch flat screen with Blu-ray."

"I love that flat screen."

"Plus, all the appliances work, and you can plug in the toaster without blowing all the fuses."

"It's very tempting."

He kissed me tenderly.

The phone rang. I groaned but picked it up. Thad spoke from the other end.

"I'm waiting to be released from the hospital," he said. "You're certain Crazy Abigail has been locked up, and it's safe for me to be on the streets again?"

"Yes, Thad. I was there when she was led away in handcuffs." I didn't think it was a good time to tell him I planned to do all I could to help her get the treatment she needed.

"What do you think Mona would say if I asked her to bring me chicken noodle soup?"

"I'm sure she has a can of it in her pantry, but she's probably going to be grossed out over your scar."

"Very funny, Kate. Hey, have you seen the news?"

"No. Am I missing anything?"

"It's raining down south."

"Where?" I asked.

"Apalachicola National Forest."

"No way!"

Jay gave me a questioning look.

"It started at midnight," Thad said. "A real gully washer. They don't expect it to let up anytime soon. All those rain dances and prayer vigils must've worked."

"I have to tell Jay," I said. "I'll call you back later."

"What is it?" Jay asked as soon as I hung up.

"I have good news and bad," I said. "The good news is

Jesus came through for us, and it's raining buckets on that fire."

"That's great!" He looked delighted. "What's the bad news?"

I gave an enormous sigh. "The bad news is I'm probably going to have to start being nice to Bitsy Stout and to a preacher by the name of Brother Love."

"Aw, Kate, you're such a trouper." He suddenly grinned. "This calls for a celebration!"

Without warning, Jay ducked beneath the covers, and I felt his warm mouth on my inner thigh.

I didn't stand a chance.

Readers will love this
entertaining Kate Holly novel from
Charlotte Hughes

NUTCASE

Psychologist Kate Holly is about to get evicted
from her office, and her best option may be to
share space with her hot-tub-loving ex-boyfriend,
Dr. Thad Glazer. That's not going to help her patch
things up with her firefighter ex-husband. With
her oddball patients, her meddling mother, and
her eccentric secretary thrown into the mix—
not to mention a spate of suspicious fires—will
Kate put her life back together before she winds
up in a padded cell?

M542T1009

NEW YORK TIMES BESTSELLING AUTHOR

Charlotte Hughes

What Looks Like Crazy

**The life of a psychologist is enough
to drive anyone nuts…**

Psychologist Kate Holly's life has become the stuff of intensive therapy. She's divorcing her gorgeous firefighter husband, her mother is always meddling, and her psychiatrist ex-boyfriend won't stop calling to find out what color panties she's wearing. Now, Kate's being bombarded with mysterious threats, and the only person who can help her is the one man who always makes her lose her mind—and her heart.

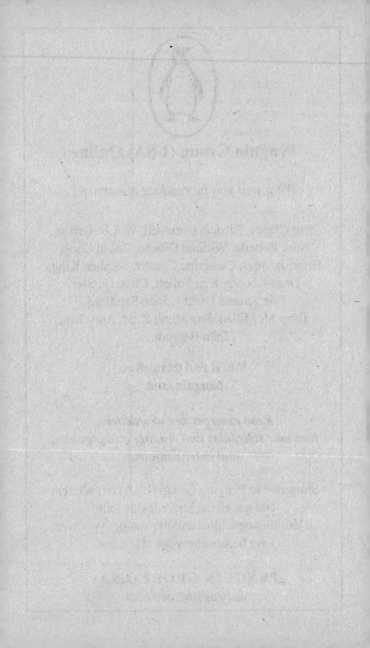